WORK OF HEART

THE FIRST REALITY-BASED ROMANCE™

Cindi Myers
WORK OF HEART

Health Communications, Inc.
Deerfield Beach, Florida

www.hcibooks.com

All haikus by Nina Barry and Danny de Zayas
ourstereo.com/haikuforyou

Library of Congress Cataloging-in-Publication Data

Myers, Cindi.
  Work of heart / by Cindi Myers.
      p. cm.
    ISBN-13: 978-0-7573-1558-9
    ISBN-10: 0-7573-1558-5
      1. Women artists—Fiction.   2. Disc jockeys—Fiction.   I. Title.
    PS3613.Y467W67 2011
    813'.6—dc22

                                                                    2010046512

Publisher: Health Communications, Inc.
        3201 S.W. 15th Street
        Deerfield Beach, FL 33442–8190

TRUE VOWS Series Developer: Olivia Rupprecht
Cover photo ©iStockphoto, ©Getty Images
Cover design by Larissa Hise Henoch
Interior design and formatting by Lawna Patterson Oldfield

For Jim,
who made my own true-life
romance possible.

Special thanks to
Michele, Olivia, Julie,
Barbara, Mica, and of course,
Nina and Danny.

Dear Reader

MY FAVORITE ICEBREAKER when I meet new couples is "So, how did you two get together?" There's always a great story there. I feel privileged to get to share Danny and Nina's story with you. I think whenever we hear or read someone else's true-love story we're either reminded of our own love story or we're encouraged about the possibility of true love in our lives. It's not just a concept put forth in romance novels—love is real.

I think Danny and Nina's struggles to find a common ground where they can be together will resonate with many people. As lovely as the fantasy of love is, real life so often gets in the way. It was wonderful to write about a couple who found a way to nourish the fantasy in the midst of all the real, everyday things we all have to deal with—making a living, dealing with relatives, even deciding where to live.

I hope you'll enjoy this story. You can find out about more real-life love stories at the TRUE VOWS website, www.vows.hci books.com, or visit my website at www.CindiMyers.com.

Cindi Myers

One

Where did you come from?
You traversed the whole world
Just to land on my plate.

"IT'S NOT REALLY A BLIND DATE IF YOU'VE already chatted with the guy online, right?" Nina Barry squeezed into the crowded Brooklyn nightclub behind her friend Erin. "Since You've Been Gone" blared over the hum of the crowd of college students and twentysomethings who packed the dance floor and filled the booths and tables.

"It's not a date at all." Erin grasped Nina's wrist and dragged her toward the back of the club and to the booth where the DJ oversaw this happy chaos. "You're just saying hi and seeing if anything clicks."

"Right." Nina swept her long bangs out of her eyes and tried to see into the dark interior of the DJ's booth. Being five-ten made it easier to see over the crowd, but the smoked-glass front of the booth screened the man inside from view. "Maybe this wasn't such a good idea," she said. "He's working and I shouldn't interrupt."

"What are you so nervous about?" Erin turned to face her. Short and curvy, with a fall of mahogany hair, Nina looked like a

1

titian Madonna. "You liked his Facebook profile, right? And the e-mail messages he sent?"

"I did." Nina sighed. "It's just never easy starting up the whole relationship thing." She'd been out a few times since she'd broken up with her last serious boyfriend two months before, but every new encounter left her feeling hollow inside. She was only twenty-three—too young to settle down, as her mother, who had married for the first time at eighteen, liked to remind her. But lately Nina found herself thinking about her future, longing for something *more*.

They reached the booth as "Dancing With Tears in My Eyes" began to play. Erin was right. There was no reason to be nervous. Randy was a nice guy. Someone she could have fun with. She knocked firmly on the door to the booth.

The door swung open and Nina caught her breath. The fuzzy snapshots on his Facebook page really hadn't done this man justice. Hair she'd thought was black was really the deep brown of dark sienna. Hazel eyes looked into hers from beneath perfectly groomed brows; and when he smiled at her, a little shyly, she noticed the dimple in his chin. "Hello ladies," he said. "What can I do for you?"

"I'm Nina," she said. "And this is my friend, Erin."

"Pleased to meet you. I'm . . ."

A blast of music drowned out the word, though Nina thought she caught the "y" on the end. "I didn't mean to interrupt your work." She looked past him into the booth where two turntables, a CD player, and stacks of CDs scattered like oversize coins littered the counter. "Maybe when you take a break, we could have a drink."

Did she imagine that half-second hesitation? Had he already decided they didn't "click"? But then the smile returned full force.

"Sure. I'm just filling in for a friend for a bit. He should be right back. Why don't you find a table and I'll join you in a minute?"

"So? What do you think?" Erin waited until they were a few feet from the booth before she leaned in and asked the question.

"He's very good-looking," Nina said. Maybe it was shallow to zero in on that first thing, but what could she say? Randy was much better looking than she'd expected. He really needed to update his Facebook profile.

"Maybe a little too good-looking," Erin said.

"What do you mean?"

"I never saw a guy with such great skin. And his clothes and hair were perfect. I hope he's not gay."

Nina had been so focused on Randy's face she hadn't noticed his clothes. She had a vague recollection of slim, dark jeans and a black T-shirt. "He is definitely not gay," she said. No gay man would ever make her pulse race the way Randy had. "He asked me out, remember?"

"Well, yeah. There is that."

They snagged a table near the dance floor as another couple was leaving, and ordered drinks from a passing waitress. Nina kept looking toward the booth, but the smoked glass made Randy invisible to her. She forced herself to look at the dance floor instead, at the writhing, swaying couples in slim jeans, short skirts, cocktail dresses, shimmery tops, plain T-shirts. If she let her vision blur, they formed a kaleidoscope of color and motion. She'd like to photograph them, perhaps a long exposure to blur the faces and bodies more, or a painting, almost impressionistic in its approach. . . .

"Earth to Nina. You need to pay for your drink." Erin's voice brought her back to the present. She paid the waitress, then jumped as someone touched her arm.

"I didn't mean to startle you." A young man with longish dark hair and thick dark brows held out his hand. "I'm Randy. Danny told me you were here. I'm so glad you could make it."

"Randy?" She stared at him, taking in the disheveled hair and doughy face that did, indeed, match the pictures on his Facebook profile.

"If you're Randy, then who is the guy in the DJ booth?" Erin asked.

"That's Danny. He works here, too. Sorry I wasn't here to meet you. I stepped out back for a smoke."

Nina nodded, fighting a sinking feeling.

"Let me grab a couple of chairs." Randy snagged two empties from nearby tables and fit them in alongside Nina and Erin. "Danny's going to join us in a minute." He turned to Nina. "Is this your first time at the Castle?"

"Yes." She looked again toward the crowded dance floor. "I'd like to bring my camera sometime, to photograph it."

"I thought you were a painter," Randy said.

"I paint, yes. And I take photographs, too."

"I'm envious of people with that kind of talent." Danny dropped into the chair beside her. He carried a clear drink with a slice of lime floating in it. "I appreciate art and movies and music, and I've done some writing, but no painting."

"Danny's the big businessman," Randy said. "He has his own online music store and a website."

"Then how can you say you don't have real talent?" Nina asked.

He shrugged, an elegant lift of the shoulders. "All my paintings would look like abstract art."

"Some people like abstract art," she said.

"Nina's from Russia," Randy said. Was he showing off his knowledge of her or merely making conversation? Nina could never be sure with men.

"I was born in Moscow," she said. "But I've lived in the United States since I was ten."

"I'm from Florida," Danny said. "But if you visited Hialeah, where I grew up, you'd think you were in Cuba—the language, the music, the food—it's like being in Havana."

"You're Cuban?" Nina asked. He didn't look Cuban, with his pale skin and light eyes.

"Half Cuban, half Swedish." He grinned. "I can make *ropa vieja* and Swedish meatballs."

"I could make you borscht, but you probably wouldn't eat it. Most Americans are suspicious of Russian food."

"You have to admit, Nina, that Russia isn't known for its cuisine," Randy said.

She bristled. Americans were so ignorant of Russia, yet they had no problem making pronouncements like that. "Russia has wonderful food," she said. "I bet you've never even eaten a Russian meal."

"No . . . but I've never heard anything good about it, either." He grinned. "They make good vodka, though."

Nina glared at him. No, there was definitely no chemistry between her and Randy. He was an oaf.

"I've never had Russian food," Danny said. "But I'd like to try it some time. Maybe we could go to a Russian restaurant here in New York and you could show me what was good."

Was he proposing a date? "I'd like that. Though the food here wouldn't taste as good as it does in Russia. Some of the ingredients are impossible to find in the States."

"Then maybe we'll go to Russia someday."

The easy way he said "we" sent a thrill through her. His attitude was all polite friendliness, but she could see something more developing. Or maybe that was wishful thinking. The capacity for fantasy that stood her so well in art sometimes led to disappointments in real life.

"I'd love to travel all over the world and sample the specialties of every country," Danny continued. "I'm an adventurous eater."

The description intrigued her. She had always seen life as an adventure to be explored through travel and art and music—and food.

"No borscht for me," Randy said. "I'm more of a burger and steaks guy. Maybe a little chicken or sausage now and then."

"I'm a vegetarian," Erin said. It wasn't true, but she enjoyed saying anything she thought would spark a debate.

"You look too healthy to be a vegetarian," Randy said.

"Healthy as in healthy, or healthy as in fat?" Erin challenged him.

"Definitely not fat." His gaze flickered to her chest. "I like a woman who looks like a woman."

"Meat has nothing to do with it."

As the two launched into a spirited debate, Danny leaned toward Nina. "I've never had much trouble telling women from men," he observed. He sipped his drink, studying her over the rim of the glass. She felt warmed by that gaze, her cheeks hot.

To cover her embarrassment at his scrutiny, she searched for some way to keep the conversation going. "What is this song that's playing?" she asked.

"'Little Girl with Blue Eyes,' by Pulp." He leaned closer. "Like you. You have amazing blue eyes."

She looked away from his scrutiny, though she was secretly pleased he'd noticed. She wasn't vain, but she thought her eyes were her best feature, and she played them up with dark liner and lots of mascara.

"I like the song," she said. The silence between them stretched, he seemed content to study her as he sipped his drink. Nina continued, "I like the music you were playing earlier, too."

"All British bands from the '80s and '90s and some newer stuff," he said. "Some pretty obscure stuff. I enjoy introducing people to it."

"How do you know all these songs?" she asked. "I mean, I like music, but I mostly know the bands I hear on the radio or the ones my friends turn me on to."

"I've just always been really interested in music. And movies and food and architecture and fashion." He laughed again, a low chuckle that made her feel quivery inside. "I'm trying to put the lie to that saying about 'jack of all trades and master of none.'"

"Randy said you run a website."

"Yeah. An online music magazine. I review CDs and bands, try to give some exposure to lesser-known talent. I can send you a link if you like."

"Thanks. I'd like to see it."

"Tell me about your art."

"Oh, well, what do you want to know?"

"What is it that made you want to be an artist?"

"My father is an artist and so is my grandmother. Her father was an artist, too." She remembered visiting her grandmother in her flat in Moscow, canvases lining the hallway, the smell of oil paint and solvents perfuming the air. It had been one of her favorite places in all the world, where she would sit for hours in her grandmother's studio, making miniature sculptures from scraps of clay, or designing elaborate wardrobes of Barbie clothes.

"So art is in your blood."

"Art is in my heart." She blushed, not having meant to say the words out loud, but his expression remained serious. Understanding.

"Danny, hate to interrupt, buddy, but if we're both down here, who's minding the music?" Randy asked.

"I put on a mix CD of my favorites," Danny said.

"You have good taste," Nina said.

"Of course." His mock seriousness made her laugh. Amazing how comfortable she felt with him when they'd known each other less than an hour. She couldn't stop looking at him, not just because he was good-looking, but because something drew her to continue to study his face. He had such interesting eyes—blue and green and gold depending on the angle of the light. One of them had a black dot in it. She imagined drawing his face, carefully placing the dot in his eye. It was the kind of small detail that made a portrait stand out.

"That CD isn't going to last forever," Randy said, with a pointed look at his friend.

"I'd better get back to work." Danny rose, with obvious reluctance.

"It was nice meeting you," Nina said.

"It was great meeting you, too. If you give me your e-mail, I'll send you that link to my website."

"Sure." Ignoring the way her heart leapt at this avenue for them to keep in touch, she dug in her purse until she found a pen and a gum wrapper. She scribbled her e-mail address onto the wrapper, then added her phone number too and handed it over.

"Thanks." He shoved it in his pocket without looking at it. She hoped he wouldn't toss it out later, thinking it was trash.

Then his eyes met hers again, and she felt once more a surge of warmth. "I hope we see each other again, Nina," he said.

"I hope so, too."

"I need a cigarette," Randy announced as soon as Danny had left them. "You want to come keep me company while I smoke?" he asked Nina.

She shook her head. "I really don't like smoke," she said.

"Ouch." He put a hand to his heart, as if wounded, but his smile didn't waiver. "I guess that's the way it goes sometimes. You can hit it off with someone online, but you never really know until you meet in person."

"Oh, I didn't mean . . ."

He waved away her protest as he stood. "It's okay. I'll still leave you on my friends list. Thanks for stopping by."

She watched until he was swallowed up by the crowd. She ought to feel disappointed that things hadn't worked out with him, but really, all she felt was relief.

"Talk about a postmodern kiss off," Erin said. "Instead of 'we can still be friends,' it's 'I won't unfriend you on Facebook.'"

Nina laughed. "He really wasn't my type."

"How would you know? You spent all your time talking to Mr. Metrosexual."

"Come on, Erin. Do you have something against a man with good grooming?"

"No. I'm just jealous. I wish a man would look at me the way he was looking at you."

"You're imagining things. He wasn't looking at me any particular way." But her heart beat faster at the thought.

"Uh-huh. And you weren't looking at him any particular way, either. You're a lousy liar, you know that?"

Nina gathered up her purse and stood. "I'm ready to go now."

"You don't want to stick around and see if Danny takes another break? You might even talk him into dancing with you."

She might. Or he'd dance with someone else and she'd have to watch. Or Randy might decide to give her a second chance. Better to leave now, while the evening was still perfect. "My mother always told me it was best to leave a man wanting more, especially when you first meet," she said.

"Your mother also said you should be eating a macrobiotic diet and that regular colonic cleansing would be good for your complexion."

Natasha Barry might have been born in Russia, but she was from Boulder now, a crunchy-granola girl into alternative health, alternative food—just about alternative anything.

"In this case, I think she's right." Nina wanted to go home now and replay the evening in her head, to think about everything Danny had said, and about his beautiful face. Maybe she'd draw that face, with those intriguing eyes and that beautiful, beautiful smile.

"She had a great smile, and the most amazing blue eyes."

"Who are you talking about?" John de Zayas looked up from his laptop computer at his younger cousin.

"This woman I met at the club last night." Danny leaned over John's shoulder to study the computer screen. "Haven't you been listening?"

"You're supposed to be helping me set up this inventory database, not mooning about some woman you met at the club."

"I'm not mooning. I was just telling you about this interesting woman. She's an artist, born in Russia, but she's been in the U.S. for years." Nina had such a fascinating background. Danny regretted he hadn't been able to spend more time talking with her; the little while they'd spent together had flown by too quickly. When he'd returned to the table during his next break he'd been disappointed to find her gone.

"Correct me if I'm wrong, but aren't you already involved with a woman? As in living with her?"

Danny frowned. Just because he was living with someone—his longtime girlfriend, Renee—didn't mean he couldn't have female friends. In fact, he preferred women friends, always had. Women had an emotional empathy he appreciated. "I never said I was interested in Nina romantically," he said. "I just think she's an interesting woman." He leaned over and clicked a few keys on the laptop. Time to change the subject, before John started lecturing him on the right way to conduct his personal life. "Looks like the business is doing pretty good." John ran a men's clothing company, Hombre, that sold upscale clothing and accessories.

"It would be doing even better if I had someone I could trust to help me with marketing." He gave Danny a significant look.

"And you think I'm that person?"

"You'll need a job when you graduate next month. I need someone to help me."

"My degree will be in independent studies, with an emphasis on film," Danny pointed out. "Not exactly a marketing background."

"I don't care what your diploma says. I've seen what you can do. How many businesses have you started successfully?"

Danny grinned. "Maybe half a dozen, if you count the band I had when I was twelve." He enjoyed exploring new ideas for making a living, combining his loves of music and art and culture into first a band, then later into several websites and his services as a DJ. Some ventures he abandoned when they bored him after a few months, while others continued for years, part time. He'd once characterized himself as a serial entrepreneur.

"You have an eye for fashion and business smarts," John said. "You'd be perfect for the position. Together we could make Hombre into a national concern."

It all sounded great. Danny believed John when he said they could do it. But he'd spent his whole life with his cousin telling him what to do. John was ten years older and had been Danny's chief babysitter when Danny was little.

But Danny wasn't little anymore, and he didn't need a baby-sitter, even one he was as close to as John. "I don't know what I want to do after graduation," he said. "I was hoping to take some time off this summer to travel."

"I need your help now. If you'll start right after graduation, I'll give you two weeks vacation this summer. You'll be making enough money you can go wherever you want."

The offer was tempting, but still Danny hesitated. "I always thought I'd do something more creative and exciting."

"You don't think growing a business like this is interesting? As for creative—be as creative as you like, as long as you find us the customers we need to grow. Of course, if you don't think you're up to the job . . ."

Danny recognized the challenge. John was a master of knowing what buttons to push to make his cousin pay attention. "If I do decide to come work for you, get ready," he said. "I'll have every store in the country begging for your merchandise."

"Say the word and I'll print the business cards." John's expression sobered. "Seriously, I want us to work together."

"I know." Danny rested a hand on his cousin's shoulder. "And I promise I'll think about it." It was a great plan, the two of them in business together. He'd go right from graduation to a good job with one of the people he loved most in the world. He'd be set for life.

But the idea didn't thrill him. Part of the fun of life was not knowing what was around the next bend. He liked being sponta-neous, always ready for the next adventure. Uncertainty was some-thing to be relished, not feared.

"You get a good job, settle down, maybe you'll think about marrying Renee. Starting a family."

John's words brought him out of his dream of adventure with

a jolt. "Who said anything about marrying Renee?"

John frowned at him. "You've been dating the woman for five years. You don't think she's expecting marriage?"

"Renee isn't like that." She never brought up the subject of marriage. Though when they'd shopped for a new apartment recently, he'd overheard her on the phone with a girlfriend, saying one place they'd considered had a spare bedroom they could use as a nursery. The memory made him light-headed. "You know I care about Renee," he said. "But I'm not sure she's the woman I want to spend the rest of my life with."

"What are you waiting for—a sign from above?"

More like a sign from within. "I just think when the time is right for me to settle down, I'll know." He liked Renee. He respected her and they had a comfortable relationship. But he didn't feel any sense of urgency about making their bond permanent.

"Fine. I don't care if you marry her or not, but say you'll come work for me after graduation."

"I told you, I'll think about it."

"Remember, I'm throwing in two weeks vacation after you've only been here a couple of months. You won't get a better offer from anyone else."

How did John know that? The world was full of options, and Danny liked to be open to all of them. Maybe that was the real reason he hadn't asked Renee to marry him; he wanted to be open to the option of someone even better coming along. Love—real love—was too important to risk making the wrong decision. And real love shouldn't be ordinary. Maybe he'd spent too many years listening to love songs, but when you found your soul mate, she ought to rock your world a little.

From: DDeZayas@newyorknet.com
To: NinaBarry@citytel.com
Subject: Rocking the Kasbah

Nina,

It was great meeting you the other night. Here is the link to the website. Let me know what you think. I'm DJing at the Castle Saturday night if you want to drop by. I have a bunch of cool new tunes to share and I want to hear more about your art.

Danny

Nina read the e-mail message again as she put on a pair of dangling silver-bead earrings. The earrings went well with the silver threads in her shimmery blue top and the silver buckles on her stiletto heels. Skinny black jeans and a silver charm bracelet completed the outfit. The tiny apartment didn't have a full-length mirror, but she guessed she looked pretty good. Maybe good enough to impress a guy like Danny.

She switched off the computer and was almost to the door when her cell phone rang. "Hello?"

"Nina, what's wrong?" Her mother's worried voice sounded far away over the phone line, as if she spoke from another dimension. Knowing Natasha, this wasn't far from the truth.

"Nothing's wrong, Mom."

"I had a premonition that disturbed me, and you sounded upset when you answered the phone just now."

"I'm just in a hurry. I'm getting ready to go out."

"On a date?" Natasha's voice sharpened with interest.

"I'm meeting friends at a club." Not a lie. Surely she and Danny were friends, and there would be other people there she might know.

"You're uneasy about this meeting, I can tell. I'm getting a very strong premonition you shouldn't go."

Nina rolled her eyes. Natasha had premonitions the way other people had indigestion—after every meal and six times on Sunday. She made so many predictions about things, some of her forecasts were bound to come true. "It'll be fine, Mom," she said.

"How is your art? Have you sold any more paintings?"

"I got a commission to do some illustrations for a website." She didn't bother mentioning the website was for a friend, who could only afford to pay minimum wage. But she hoped the work would lead to more.

"Your illustrations are charming, I'm sure, but your real talent is painting," Natasha said. "That is what you should be doing. If you were here in Boulder I could introduce you to a gallery owner I know. He would love to exhibit your work."

"I like it here in New York. This is a wonderful place to be an artist." Not that she didn't miss Colorado, but she'd needed to get away from her family for awhile, to prove she could make it on her own.

"Your soul is here in the mountains," Natasha said. "I know you'll come back here where you belong sooner or later."

"For now, I'm happy here," Nina said.

Natasha sighed dramatically. "Everything happens for a reason," she said. "There are no coincidences in life, so I can only surmise you are in New York now to learn a lesson, or perhaps to meet someone who will be a significant influence in your life."

A shiver raced up Nina's spine at these words. Though she discounted most of her mother's pronouncements, this last statement made her think of Danny. Of course, she hardly knew the man, but she couldn't remember being so strongly attracted to anyone before. If he returned her feelings . . . well, a man she loved who loved her would certainly qualify as a significant influence.

By the time Nina got off the phone with her mother, she'd missed the train that would take her closest to the club and had to wait another twenty minutes on the platform. Fortunately, the March night air was mild, with only a slight breeze. Maybe they were in for an early spring and an end to the damp cold that had made trudging through New York streets a trial.

Finally she reached the Castle and surveyed the crowd around the door in dismay. How would she ever get Danny's attention in that crush? She wasn't sure if she'd have the nerve to knock on the door of the DJ booth again.

She hadn't come all this way to get cold feet, she reminded herself. She made her way toward the back of the club, but before she reached the booth, Danny himself intercepted her. "Hey," he said, catching hold of her arm. "I'm glad you could make it."

His hand on her arm was warm and gentle, and his smile was so full of welcome she felt weak at the knees. So much for her mom saying she shouldn't be here tonight. She couldn't think of any place in the world she'd rather be.

"I've got a table over here with a bunch of people for you to meet." He led her to a group around two tables pushed together and began rattling off names: Randy was there with a magenta-haired woman named Deirdre, a couple named Patty and Mark, and a very tall young man whose name Nina didn't catch. Danny found a chair for Nina and squeezed it in next to his, then excused himself to return to the DJ booth.

"This next song goes out to a lovely young woman, Nina," he said, and she had to fight the urge to blush like a schoolgirl. The song she'd heard last week, "Little Girl With Blue Eyes," began to play.

"How do you know Danny?" Patty, who sat across from her, asked.

"We met last week, here at the club," Nina answered.

"You're the artist, from Russia," the tall man said.

Who was this man who was studying her so intently? "I'm sorry, I didn't catch your name," she said.

"I'm John de Zayas. Danny's cousin."

She could see the resemblance now, in the dark hair and dimpled chin, though John's eyes were brown and very solemn. Why did he look so serious?

"You're from Russia?" Patty asked. "I'll bet you were relieved to escape to the United States."

"We didn't escape from anything," Nina said. "We moved here because my mother married a British scientist who lived in Colorado."

"Still, from what I've seen on television, Russia's a pretty grim place." Patty made a face.

"Russia is a very beautiful country," Nina said. "And Moscow is a sophisticated city with amazing architecture and gorgeous parks and a rich history." She managed a tight smile. "We're not all a bunch of grim communists freezing to death in Siberia."

"Who says you're a communist in Siberia?" Danny slid into the chair next to her once more. A smile tugged at the corners of his mouth.

Nina flushed. "You're laughing at me," she accused.

"Not at all. I think it's charming that you're so passionate."

She flashed an apologetic look at Patty and Mark. "I'm sorry. I didn't mean to get so upset. Though I've lived in the United States a long time, I still feel the need to defend my home country."

"I can't say I've ever felt that way about Cuba," Danny said. "But that's probably because I've never been there. But I'd enjoy seeing Russia. I'd like to travel all over the world. I want to see Iceland and Ireland and Italy—everywhere."

"I love to travel," Nina said. "I want to visit all the world's great cities and paint them . . . and photograph them, too."

"You get a different view of the world through a camera lens," Danny said. "You see the objects in a scene as they relate to each other and as a whole. And you focus in on details you might not otherwise notice."

"Exactly!" Nina leaned toward him, thrilled that he understood this. "That is what art does. It makes you notice." The way she noticed the lushness of the dark lashes that framed his eyes, and the off-center arch of his eyebrows. Or the long fingers of his hands as he reached for his drink. . . .

"Sorry I'm late. The trains were running behind." A petite woman with a cloud of honey-colored hair stood by the table, her cheeks flushed, her words pouring out in a rush. "I was late getting off work and had to run home and change and I kept getting further and further behind. I thought about calling, but of course there's no signal on the subway and. . . ."

Danny put his hand on the woman's arm, silencing her. "It's all right," he said. "You're here now."

He turned to Nina, but his gaze didn't quite meet hers. She felt a chill that had nothing to do with the club's overenthusiastic air conditioning. Something about the way he rested his hand on this newcomer's arm, or the way the blonde looked at him . . . his words came to her like her mother's over the phone line, echoing and far away. "Nina, I'd like you to meet Renee. My girlfriend."

Two

I'm a daydreamer.
I may seem aloof, but I'm
Paying attention.

"AND YOU HAD NO IDEA he had a girlfriend?" Erin curled up on one end of the daybed that also served as the sofa in Nina's tiny apartment and helped herself to more popcorn from the bowl on the TV tray/side table. It was Sunday afternoon, and the friends had gotten together to review last night's disastrous "date" at the Castle.

"He never said he did . . . but he never said he didn't, either." She studied the illustration of Little Red Riding Hood she was working on for her friend's website. He wanted a series of scenes from popular fairy tales to advertise his catering services. Red was taking a picnic lunch to her grandmother—the link for her friend's picnic catering offerings. Nina added more cross-hatching to the picnic basket.

"Still, if he was giving you the vibe that he was interested . . ."

"I don't think he was trying to mislead me," Nina said. "I think I just misinterpreted." She began sketching in the wolf—tall and thin, with a pencil moustache. "He's a nice guy who was trying to be friendly and I read all his signals wrong."

"I don't know about that." Erin set aside the popcorn bowl. "I saw the way he looked at you that first night, and I thought he wanted to be more than friends. Maybe he wouldn't have told you about the girlfriend if she hadn't shown up at the club."

"No. I'm sure he'd invited her to be there last night. And he didn't look the least bit guilty when he introduced us." Though he hadn't looked her in the eye. But maybe that was only because he'd sensed the direction her feelings for him were headed and he wanted to let her down gently. She sketched in the wolf's eyes and added a black dot in one iris and brows arched slightly off center.

With a strangled noise, she ripped the drawing from the sketch pad and crumpled it into a ball. "What?" Erin asked. "Why are you tearing up your drawing?"

"It wasn't coming out right."

"So what are you going to do now?"

"I don't know." She turned to face her friend. "He e-mailed me last night to tell me the man who owns the café where he works is interested in exhibiting art from local artists and suggested I stop by. It would be a great opportunity, but it would mean I'd have to see Danny again."

"I wasn't talking about Danny." Erin looked amused. "I meant, what are you going to do about the drawing you just tore up?"

"Oh. I'll do another one." She glanced at the crumpled paper.

"As for what to do about Danny—getting a place to exhibit your work would be good. Maybe you'd sell some things."

She nodded. "I think he really wants to be friends."

"You have lots of guy friends. Is this one so different?"

Yes. Which was crazy, since they'd never had a real date, and certainly had never kissed or done anything more than talk. But

she felt as if she could have talked to him for hours, about anything. Surely she could get past this silly romantic infatuation for
a chance at those conversations. . . . "I'd be crazy to pass up the
opportunity to show my work."

"Maybe Danny has an unattached brother he can introduce
you to," Erin said.

"I did meet his cousin—John. He was at the club last night."

"Is he as good-looking as Danny?"

"Not really. And he's quite a bit older. He was so serious—
almost as if he didn't approve of me."

"You must be imagining things. How could he disapprove
when he doesn't even know you?"

John had spent the evening watching her. Every time she
looked his way she caught his studious gaze. He hadn't said anything, but she'd felt an undercurrent of disapproval. "Maybe it's
because I'm Russian. I don't think there's any love lost between
Cuban expats and Moscow."

"That's stupid," Erin said. "You all live here now."

Nina shrugged. "Loyalties to our heritage run deep in some of
us," she said. Why else would she feel so compelled to defend a
country she hadn't seen in years?

"So, are you going to go to the café where Danny works?"

"I think so." She turned back to the sketch pad and picked up
her pen once more. "My mother says everything happens for a
reason. Maybe I met Danny just so he could introduce me to
the café owner, who'll show my work at his business, and I'll be
discovered by a wealthy collector."

"And maybe the collector will be young and handsome and
will appreciate more than your art."

Nina laughed. "That part doesn't matter so much. I'm in no
hurry to settle down." Though her mother claimed to have had

two happy marriages and got along well with both her ex-husbands, Nina wanted to believe in the promise of the fairy tales she illustrated. She was willing to wait for her happily ever after.

"That's the last of the boxes." On the last Saturday in March, two weeks after meeting Nina, Danny set the carton down by the door and surveyed the apartment. Every flat surface was covered with cardboard boxes, each carefully labeled in Renee's neat handwriting. "How did two people ever acquire so much stuff?"

"Most of it's your stuff." Renee looked up from unpacking a carton of dishes. "I just have my clothes and kitchen stuff and a few books."

Danny studied the labels on the cartons again. *Danny's Books. Danny's CDs. Danny's Art. Danny's DVDs.* Three-fourths of the cartons bore his name. He looked back at Renee. She'd pulled her hair back into a short ponytail and wore one of his old soccer jerseys over a pair of cut-off jeans. "Why don't you have more stuff?" he asked.

She shrugged. "I guess you have enough for both of us."

He moved beside her and opened a box marked *Danny's Spices.* The carton was filled with bottles and jars of the seasonings he used to make Cuban and Indian and his favorite Thai food. "I'm serious," he said. "Don't you have hobbies or interests or something you like to do just for you? Music or books and movies of your own?"

She shook her head. "I like the music you listen to and the movies you watch. And I'm too busy with school and work to have hobbies."

Her answer sent a cold chill through him. He'd known Renee a good part of his life. They went to high school together and started dating their senior year. When he'd moved to New York to attend college she'd followed, and it had seemed only logical that they should move in together. But how was it possible he'd known her all this time and never realized she had no interests of her own? She was like a chameleon, adapting to whatever environment he wanted.

He'd even chosen this neighborhood for them to move to, because it was an easy commute to the café where he worked now, and to John's office where he'd be working soon. Renee worked at a steakhouse across town, but she'd never brought this up while they were looking at apartments. She was perfectly happy to live wherever he wanted to live. To do whatever he wanted to do.

"I meant to get shelf paper at the store yesterday and I forgot," she said, frowning into the cabinet. "I guess I'll just put everything away for now, then take it back out later to line the shelves."

"I'll run get it." He set aside the box of spices. He needed to get out of the apartment for a bit, to process this new revelation about their relationship.

She gave him a grateful smile. "That would be great. Get blue— the spongy kind that cushions everything. About six rolls should do."

He'd already grabbed his wallet and was headed out the door. He hurried down three flights of stairs, eager to be away from the suddenly stifling air in the apartment.

When he reached the sidewalk, he slowed his pace and breathed deeply of the warm spring air. The oppressive heat and humidity of summer hadn't yet arrived, and a soft breeze ruffled the leaves of the trees planted in octagonal-shaped sections of dirt beside the walk, and in pocket parks between the apartment buildings and shop fronts of this part of Brooklyn. As he walked, he felt some of the tension ease from his shoulders. He'd been silly to panic the way he had just now. Renee was still Renee—the woman he'd known and loved for years. She had her own interests and talents, even if she chose not to indulge them right now. She wasn't some clinging vine who made him responsible for her happiness. He could never be happy with a woman like that.

He'd make it a point to encourage her independence as much as he could. What had she been interested in before they met? And what did it say about him that he couldn't remember?

He spotted a sign for a dollar store up ahead and decided to try for the shelf paper there. What had Renee said—the spongy kind?

As he reached the door, it opened and a woman emerged, her hands full of plastic shopping bags. He reached up to hold the door and stared into a familiar pair of big blue eyes. "Nina?" he asked, even as he wondered if he was hallucinating.

"Danny!" Her smile and the look of pure joy on her face dazzled him. "What are you doing here?"

"I came to buy shelf paper." He turned and followed her out onto the sidewalk.

"Are they having a really spectacular sale?" She glanced back at the store, then gave him a puzzled look. "Is it a special kind of shelf paper?"

"The spongy kind, whatever that is."

She looked so adorable, eyes wide, nose wrinkled slightly as she tried to figure out this new puzzle. She probably thought he was nuts. "Renee and I just moved into a new apartment up the street." He nodded in the direction of their building. "She needed shelf paper."

Her expression cleared. "So you're living here now? That's wild."

"And you live here, too." *Wild.* "Let me help you with those bags." He relieved her of half her burden. "Where do you live?"

"Just two blocks up the street." She pointed in the direction opposite his apartment.

"I want to see," he said. "Let me help you carry these home."

She gave him a long look, then started walking, which he took for a yes. "I told my boss about your paintings and drawings," he said. "He's eager to see them."

"How do you know about my paintings and drawings?" she asked.

"I looked you up on the web."

Her cheeks flushed a darker pink, like a rose blooming in one of those time-lapse films that had fascinated him in school. Just as she fascinated him now.

"The fairy-tale drawings are my favorite," he said. "The children in the woods."

"Hansel and Gretel," she said. "Yes, that's one of my favorites, too."

They reached her apartment building and she led the way up four flights of stairs. He didn't complain about the climb, instead enjoying the view of her shapely legs and backside as she mounted the steps.

"Home sweet home," she said, unlocking a door and ushering him inside.

The first thing he noticed was that it was tiny, scarcely larger than the interior of a travel trailer one of his uncles owned, with a galley kitchen, a daybed and small table with two chairs, and a slanted draftsman's table by the window.

The second thing he noticed was the art. Every inch of the walls was filled with paintings, drawings, and collages. Delicate mobiles hung from the ceiling, and shelves in one corner were filled with sculptures, books, and CDs. A set of Russian nesting dolls filled a niche by the door, and a row of tiny blown-glass bottles caught the light in the kitchen window. It was a room full of color and texture and light.

He picked up a sculpture of a girl playing with a dog. It was no more than six inches tall. The girl had pigtails, and the dog looked at her with a winsome expression. "Did you make this?" he asked.

"Yes. When I was about eight." She took it from him, and handed him a more sophisticated piece—a woman in a long gown, hair flowing down her back. "This is my more recent work."

He smoothed his fingers down the statue, which she'd managed to imbue with such grace and movement. Carefully, he returned it to the shelf and studied the books—a primer on speaking Italian, a French dictionary, even a guide to American Sign Language. "Do you speak all these languages?" he asked.

She shrugged. "A little. I always want to be better." She reached up and touched the next shelf, which was filled with oversized books, some of them with titles written in the Cyrillic script he recognized as Russian. "My grandmother gave me these. She is a famous artist in Moscow."

She had a modest CD collection, eclectic but well chosen, he thought, as well as a stack of popular novels. He stopped before a watercolor of the sun setting over the Brooklyn Bridge. The colors bled into each other, giving the scene a fog-shrouded, dreamy feeling. "This is beautiful," he said.

"Thank you." She touched his arm, only the tips of her fingers brushing his skin, yet he felt it deep within. "And thank you for talking your boss into looking at my work," she said. "That was very kind of you, when you hardly know me."

"We're friends," he said, turning and breaking the contact with her fingers. "Now that we'll be living only a few blocks apart, we'll be seeing even more of each other."

"What will Renee think about that?"

"Why should she think anything? She'll be your friend, too." Though he had a hard time imagining what Renee and Nina might talk about. Not art or languages or even novels, since Renee was interested in none of these things. The thought made him sad, and he pushed back the heavy feeling.

"It's lucky I ran into you today," he said. "I might not have known you live so close."

"My mother would say luck had nothing to do with it." Her eyes met his and he felt again the magnetic pull of her. What was it about her that drew him so?

"Your mother doesn't believe in luck?"

"She believes everything happens for a reason." She shrugged. "You would have to know my mother. She's into all sorts of New Age things like yoga and astrology and all of that."

"It's an interesting way to look at things," he said. "Though I don't know if I like the idea of God or fate or whatever you want to call it moving us around like so many chess pieces. I think things happen and it's up to us to act on those happenings."

"Oh, I don't think she's discounting free will. It's only that we should be open to possibilities . . . think of all the things that could happen if we approached life as if every encounter was meaningful."

This moment, standing here in this color-filled apartment, so close to Nina he could see the rise and fall of her chest as she breathed, suddenly felt weighted with meaning. But he didn't want to think too much about what that meaning might be. He was glad Nina was his friend, but he didn't have room in his life for more. "I should go now," he said, as much to himself as to her.

"Yes." She took a step back. "You should get back to Renee. Don't forget the shelf paper."

"Right." He groped for the door handle, his eyes still locked to hers. "I'll see you around."

"Yeah. See you."

He left before he changed his mind, and took the stairs two at a time on the way down. He would tell Renee he'd had to go a long way to get the paper. To another country, inhabited by a fascinating, amazing, compelling woman.

Photos instead of paintings, Nina decided as she assembled a portfolio to take to the café a few days later. She had more of them to choose from, and she could price them less than paintings, making them more appealing to the café crowd. The dollar store sold cheap black frames that would do fine for showcasing the photographs, and she could cut her own mats.

She busied herself with all these details, determined *not* to think about Danny. Gorgeous, amazing Danny, who now lived only a few blocks away.

With his beautiful blonde girlfriend, Renee. Nina certainly couldn't forget *her*. What kind of cruel joke was it that the first man she'd found interesting in ages was attached to another woman? Her mother, who put a positive spin on almost everything, would no doubt tell her she was to learn some valuable lesson from this new relationship.

"Like I'm better off staying single," she muttered as she gathered up the portfolio and headed out the door.

The café, the Palette, sat on a busy corner amid a cluster of office buildings. Nina stepped into the crowded shop and inhaled the rich aromas of roasting coffee beans, baking bread, and Italian spices. Three people waited ahead of her to be seated, so she took her place in line behind them and studied the restaurant. Small tables covered in white cloths filled most of the space, which was flooded with light from large front windows. The walls displayed several small paintings as well as a few tacked up notices of local concerts and charity fundraisers.

Satisfied that there was plenty of room for her photographs, she turned toward the open kitchen at the back of the room and allowed herself the luxury of watching Danny while he worked. A red apron over his slim jeans and close-fitting T-shirt, his hair absolutely perfect, he might have been a handsome actor playing the part of a waiter, laughing and bantering with the patrons and with the older woman who worked the cash register, serving up their soups, salads, and quiches with the panache of an experienced performer.

Or maybe, she thought as she inched closer to him, Danny was merely a man who found something to enjoy in every aspect of his life, whether he was serving meals or playing music. He struck her as someone who did everything well; a man who never struggled with the doubts that sometimes plagued her.

The hostess showed the couple in front of her to their seats. Nina stepped up to the hostess's podium just as Danny looked her way. His face lit with a brilliant smile as he spotted her and he hurried over. "It's great to see you," he said. "What can I get for you?"

"Oh, nothing. I stopped by with my portfolio to show your boss." She indicated the photo album in her hand.

"Great. I'll let him know you're here. In the meantime, let me fix you the Danny special. On the house."

"What's a Danny special?"

"A surprise." He retreated once more to the kitchen, but returned shortly, motioning her to join him.

She followed him to a door in the back corner of the café where a young Asian man only a little older than Danny sat at a cluttered desk in a closet-size office. "Hello! Come in. Excuse the mess." He half stood and offered his hand. "I'm Rob Yuen."

"Nina Barry."

"Sit down, Nina. Danny said you have some photographs to show me."

"I'll be right back," Danny said, and left them.

Rob flipped through the photographs, pausing every now and then to study a picture more closely. Nina had chosen a mixture of New York scenes and photographs she'd taken on her last visit home to Boulder. "I like these." Rob handed the album back to her. "They'll look great here. We don't have any other photographers exhibiting right now."

Danny returned and handed her a steaming cup. "The Danny special?" she asked. She took a sip. The sweet, smooth flavors of caramel and vanilla mingled with the sharper bite of coffee, and another flavor she couldn't identify.

"Caramel, vanilla, and a dash of hazelnut," he said.

"It's very good."

"Thanks. May I see?" He reached for the portfolio.

"Sure." She handed over the book.

"Let's get out of Rob's way." He led her out of the office and around the counter. The lunch crowd was thinning and the other waitress, a middle-aged woman with a long braid of red hair, waited on a single customer, an older man. Danny indicated a small table tucked into an alcove at the back of the café. Several books were piled on top.

"Isn't someone sitting here?" Nina asked.

"The books are mine," he said, and held out a chair for her.

She sat, and he took the chair across from her and opened the portfolio.

She sipped her coffee, stomach shimmying nervously as he

studied the photographs. "These are amazing," he said at last. He angled the album toward her and pointed to a picture of a Ferris wheel. She'd shot it from below, looking up, and lengthened the exposure to blur the lights, lending the photograph a sense of movement. "I love this one."

"That was taken at Coney Island a few months ago."

"Really." He cradled the album once more and turned the page to more photos from that day at the popular vacation spot. "I've never been to Coney Island."

"How can you live in Brooklyn and not have been to Coney Island?"

"What can I say? I'm a beach snob. I grew up in Florida. I can't imagine a beach in New York."

"You should go. It's a lot of fun."

"Maybe we can go together some time," he said. "You can take some more photographs."

He said the words so casually, not looking at her. Was he serious or merely making conversation? "I'd like that," she said.

He continued to flip through the album, commenting on photos he liked, asking about the location. She tried not to stare at the wave of hair that fell across his forehead as he bent over the album, or the way the muscles of his shoulders bunched as he shifted the album in his arms.

She forced herself to look away, to the books in front of her. *The Economics of Politics* and *The New Film Revolution*. "Are you studying for school?" she asked.

He nodded. "Finals next week. Then graduation." He closed the album and handed it back to her. "I'm graduating early, but it can't happen soon enough."

"What will you do after you graduate?"

"My cousin's offered me a job. I'll probably take it."

"Doing what?"

"Marketing. He owns a clothing company and wants to expand nationally. I can help him do that."

He spoke with such confidence, as if being successful in business was as easy as making a coffee drink. "This is the cousin I met at the club?" she asked.

"That's right. John."

"He seems a lot older than you."

"Ten years." He grinned. "I'm the baby of the family. My sister is six years older, and all the cousins are older, though John and I were always closest. He always accused me of being spoiled."

She returned the smile. "I'm an only child. My cousins always said *I* was spoiled."

"In my case, it was probably true. My parents let me get away with a lot. But despite the age difference, I'm pretty close with my cousins. Especially John, now that we both live in New York. We'd do good working together."

"What about Renee? What will she do?" She hadn't meant to bring Renee up at all, but talking about her was another way to remind herself that Danny was off-limits as anything more than a friend.

"She has a job lined up with a firm on Wall Street. She'll be making the big bucks." A furrow formed in the center of his forehead. "She's already talking about saving for a house and a new car."

"A house—for the two of you?" Buying a house together sounded more permanent than merely renting an apartment. Though really, why should she care? The man couldn't be any more out of reach than he already was.

"Yeah. But I don't think I'm ready for that. I told her I thought we should wait."

"I'm sure it will all work out." She bit her lip, ashamed to have said something so utterly bland. What she wanted to say was *Don't do it. Don't buy a house with her.*

"What about you?" he asked. "Do you have any big plans for the future?"

She shook her head. "I want to be a successful artist, but art isn't like an ordinary business, where you earn your degree, then get a job in your field and do this and this and this and you're a success. It depends so much more on chance. I work and put my work out there and hope and dream and one day, if I am lucky . . ." She shrugged. "I may not ever be rich, but I love what I do."

"And how many people can say that? How many people have the courage to pursue their dreams instead of opting for the safe and conventional?"

He understood! She felt light with the knowledge. "My parents are very supportive, but then, art has always been very important in my family. But not everyone is so understanding." Her last boyfriend had pretended, at first, to care about her work, but later he'd pressured her to get a "real" job. He disparaged her small apartment and frugal ways—and dumped her for a woman who worked on Wall Street.

A woman who was probably a lot like Renee. She set the half-finished coffee drink on the table. "I should go and let you get back to work."

"Let me know when you're ready to hang your photographs, and I'll make sure I'm here to help," he said.

"All right. Thanks." She stood and he rose also, ever the gentleman. Could the man not have at least one flaw? He probably watched too much sports on TV or snored.

But really, would those things matter, if the man who did them was a man she loved? Women who spent their lives looking for perfection were foolish. The right man for her didn't have to be flawless. He only had to be kind and intelligent and creative and funny and a little good-looking.

She stopped in the doorway to take one last look at Danny, who was waiting tables once more, smiling at a woman and her little boy. Her heart squeezed tight and she sucked in a jagged breath. And single. The man she fell in love with had to be single, and ready to fall in love with her.

Three

My friends don't get it
But I can see the glamour
Where others cannot.

APRIL AND THE FIRST PART OF MAY raced by in the crush of work and studying for exams. Danny managed to see Nina regularly at the Castle and occasionally at the Palette, though she hadn't yet hung any of her photographs at the café. When he asked, she said she was busy choosing the right images and framing then, but she'd politely refused his offer to help. She seemed more amused by his impatience than anything else. Once he had an idea for making money, he acted on it quickly. Apparently, Nina liked to spend more time in contemplation—though some might view this as procrastination.

By the end of May, he was glad to get back into the routine of his life after the stress of exams and graduation. His parents and sister came for the ceremony, and his mother wept happy tears and embraced him, telling him how proud she was of him. John was there, too, staying in the background, carefully steering all conversation away from questions about his own life. Since his divorce earlier that year, he'd felt the weight of his family's disappointment.

35

"This weekend, they can be happy focusing on the perfect de Zayas offspring," he told Danny, with no trace of bitterness.

Danny might have protested that he wasn't perfect, but he knew in his mother's eyes, at least, he nearly was. All that kept him from ultimate perfection was marriage to the perfect woman and production of a handful of perfect children. His long-term relationship with Renee apparently gave his mother hope that those things would soon follow. And Renee did nothing to quell his mother's hopes. When all the de Zayas went out to dinner with Danny and Renee, she mortified Danny by talking about the house she wanted to buy soon, "with at least three bedrooms and big backyard."

"Perfect for grandchildren," his mother had exclaimed, causing Danny to almost choke on his Tom Kha Gai.

Now the folks were gone and things had quieted down, but Danny's unease hadn't subsided. He and Renee had argued only this morning. He wanted to do something special this weekend, his last free weekend before he started work with John. But Renee had signed up for an extra shift at the steakhouse. She started her new job Monday also, so she certainly didn't need to work this weekend. "But I couldn't pass up the tips," she said. "They're always better on weekends, and it'll be that much more money we can put in the house fund."

"I'm not ready to buy a house," he said. "We just moved into this apartment."

"I'm tired of renting," she said. "I want a house of my own. Something permanent."

That she wanted *them* to be permanent also went unsaid, and Danny got the message as clearly as if she'd said it. But he was less and less certain he could ever commit to spending the rest of his life with Renee. He still cared for her, but with the distant fondness he felt for anyone who had once been important in his life.

He felt like a heel for even thinking it, but there was no sense lying to himself. Or continuing to lie to Renee. Or rather, to allow her to think he felt things he didn't. But how did you break things off with a woman who'd been devoted to you for the past five years?

He carried this dark mood with him to work at the café one morning in the first week of June. He only had three more days there; Rob had offered to let him out of the shifts, but Danny didn't want to leave him shorthanded. And keeping busy, interacting with the customers, beat sitting at home and brooding.

He was surprised when he arrived at work to find some of the tables pushed away from the walls and all the handbills and posters pulled down. Then Nina stepped out of Rob's office, and Danny felt the black cloud that had hovered over him all morning vanish in the brightness of her smile. "Hello, Danny," she said.

"Are you here to hang your photos?" he asked. "Why didn't you call me?"

She flushed. "I knew you were busy with finals and getting ready for graduation."

"That's all over with now."

"Congratulations." Her smile broadened. "Even though I didn't call, I was hoping you'd be here."

He tied on his apron and checked that all the condiments were stocked and the silverware wrapped. "As long as we're not busy, I can help you," he said.

"There's not a lot to do," she said. "I brought hangers and a hammer."

"What pictures did you bring?" He joined her by a table where a box sat filled with framed photos. He picked up the top one—a shot of mountains in snow. "The customers are going to love these," he said.

"I hope so." She carefully measured down from the ceiling and made a tiny mark with a pencil, then measured across from this mark and made another.

Two women came in and Danny left to wait on them. As he waited for their orders to be ready, he watched Nina as she pounded nails and hung framed photographs. She was so tall—almost his height—that she didn't have to stand on tiptoe to work. She had long legs clad in slim jeans, a trim waist, and rounded hips. He liked women with real curves. What could be sexier?

"Your orders are getting cold."

Rob's voice jerked Danny from his reverie and he looked over to see two plates of food sitting under the heat lamp. Silently cursing, he rushed to grab the plates, and forced his attention back to the customers.

By the time the two women left, Rob was talking to Nina, who had completed hanging one wall of photographs. "We'll post a notice by the register, reminding people the photos are for sale," he was saying when Danny joined them.

"That would be great." Nina tucked a lock of hair behind one ear. She was a little bit taller than Rob, Danny noted.

"Maybe we could go out some time," Rob said. "I'd like to take you to dinner."

Nina's smile faded. Her eyes darted to Danny's, her expression confused. Danny wasn't confused at all; he was furious. He told himself it was because Rob had upset Nina. Of course that wasn't all there was to it.

He clapped Rob on the back. "Don't you know better than to hit on a woman with whom you've just made a business agreement?" he said. "Nina might get the wrong idea and think you expected special favors in exchange for exhibiting her work, and that would be sexual harassment."

Rob's face turned the color of the maraschino cherries they kept behind the counter for garnishing kid's drinks. "No, of course not," he stammered. "My invitation had nothing to do with that. I only thought . . . I apologize."

Nina looked relieved. "It's all right," she said. "And I'm flattered . . . really I am." She glanced at Danny. "But I'm really not interested in dating anyone right now."

"I'm sorry. Forget I asked." Rob couldn't leave them fast enough.

Danny waited until he was gone before he turned to Nina again. "Sorry about that," he said.

"It's all right. Thank you, though, for coming to my rescue."

He reached into the box and took out another photo. He recognized the Coney Island Ferris wheel he'd admired before. "You should have told him you have a big bruiser of a boyfriend," he said. "That would have made him back off."

"But that isn't true," she said. "I don't have a boyfriend at all."

He knew he shouldn't be so thrilled at this news, but he couldn't hold back a smile. "Have you made it back to Coney Island to take more pictures?" he asked.

"No, I haven't. Why?"

"Maybe you and I could go there this weekend. It's my last weekend before I start work for my cousin. I'd like to do something fun to celebrate."

"What about Renee?" she asked. "I mean, we can invite her to come with us."

Was it his imagination, or did the invitation sound forced? "Renee has to work this weekend. I'm on my own starting Friday afternoon."

"All right," Nina said. No hesitation now.

Danny felt six inches taller and had to refrain from grabbing her in a hug and kissing her cheek. Instead, he handed the photograph of the Ferris wheel to her. "Great," he said. "I'll be looking forward to it."

Nina's footsteps grew slower and slower as she climbed the stairs to Danny's apartment Friday afternoon. She was eager to see him, yes—but reluctant to view the space he shared with Renee. And what if Renee had decided not to go to work this evening after all? Talk about an awkward meeting. Not that Nina and Danny had done anything wrong. They hadn't. They were just friends, and Nina would never do anything to give Renee reason to think otherwise. She was sure Danny wouldn't either. Everything she'd seen of him, everything he'd said, led her to believe he was too kind, too honorable, to deceive or hurt someone else.

At last she reached the right door. Taking a deep breath, she pressed the doorbell, the insect-like buzz echoing somewhere deep in the apartment.

Footsteps sounded heavy on the other side of the door. The lock turned and the door opened. "Nina. Come on in," Danny said. Today he wore a black T-shirt and softly faded jeans. His feet were bare, and she found her gaze riveted on his toes. There was something intimate about bare feet, masculine and sexy and . . . oh God, she must be losing it if she was getting off on a guy's feet!

She forced her gaze up, to the apartment. The room they were in was neat, the furnishings sparce—not in a can't-afford-any-furniture way but in a hip, minimalist-decorator look. What furniture was there was sleek, midcentury modern. A few framed black-and-white photographs adorned white walls, and white sheers let in light through the front window.

No sign of Renee. Nina began to breathe easier. "Let me grab my wallet and we'll go," Danny said. He disappeared into what she assumed was the bedroom.

"Meow!"

Startled, Nina turned and saw a small black cat crossing the room toward her. It was little more than a kitten, really, with a broad, flat face and perfect triangle ears and a long tail with a crook at the end. It came and leaned against her leg, purring loudly. Enchanted, Nina bent to stroke the kitten's soft side.

"That's Mephisto." Danny emerged from the bedroom.

She smiled up at him. "He's adorable."

"He's spoiled rotten." Danny scooped the kitten into his arms and massaged its stomach.

Nina laughed. "You wouldn't have anything to do with him being spoiled, would you?"

"Me? Of course not." He took a treat from a jar on the counter and offered it to Mephisto. "It's Renee's fault he's so rotten."

They said good-bye to the cat and descended the stairs to Nina's red Honda Civic. The little car had been a gift from her stepfather when she graduated college. "Did you bring your camera?" Danny asked, buckling his seat belt.

"Yes." She handed him the camera case. The camera was another graduation gift, from her mother. "The tripod's in the backseat."

"What kind of photographs do you like to take?" Danny looked through the viewfinder of the camera as she pulled the car away from the curb. "Scenery? People? Both?"

"Both." She glanced at him, his face half hidden by the camera. The dimple in his chin stood out and the curve of one cheek.

"Today I want to photograph you and your first time at Coney Island."

"We need props." He looked around the car, as if searching for something. "Me standing around on the boardwalk isn't going to be too exciting."

She laughed. "Props?"

"Sure. A hat. Or sunglasses."

She had an image of him in a straw boater and oversize sunglasses. "Yes," she agreed. "We must have props."

They found a shopping center on the outskirts of Brooklyn and raided the aisles of a dollar store for cheap sunglasses and straw hats. "How about these?" Nina plucked a pair of pink plastic water pistols from a bin near the checkout counter.

Danny grabbed a pistol and stuck the barrel in her side. "Stick 'em up!" he said.

The clerk behind the counter scowled at them, but made no comment as they paid for their purchases and exited the store. Danny wore his hat and glasses, trying them at different angles and studying himself in the passenger-side visor mirror.

"How long have you lived in New York?" Nina asked.

"I came here to go to school three years ago." He flipped up the visor and turned to her. Even in mirrored sunglasses and a pimp hat he was handsome. He would be interesting to photograph, and later, she'd have the photographs to look at. To remember.

"Did you transfer from another school?" she asked.

"No. I graduated early."

"What, are you a genius or something?" She was only half-joking. Clearly, he was a sharp guy.

"I just don't like to waste time. What about you? How did you end up in New York?"

"Like you, I came for school."

"Where did you go to school?"

"I earned my undergraduate degree from Pratt Institute. Then I enrolled in the New York Academy of Art for my MFA."

He gave a low whistle. "Impressive."

"Yes. I am not merely a starving artist—I am a starving artist with a fancy diploma."

She found parking just off the boardwalk and they set out, Nina carrying the camera, Danny with the tripod. They wore the hats and sunglasses and carried the water guns tucked in their jeans. Nina hoped the bright plastic would be enough to reassure passing strangers that the guns weren't real.

Some people thought of New York as Manhattan or the Staten Island Ferry or the East Village on a Saturday night. For Nina, the real New York was here, at the south end of Brooklyn, in the colorful cacophony of Coney Island. Mothers and fathers in Bermuda shorts and flip-flops herded groups of small children past women in saris and tourists in I ♥ NY T-shirts. A group of young Hassidic Jews, with long forelocks and flat, black hats, clustered around a popcorn vendor; while just beyond them, a trio of Arab boys kicked a soccer ball on the beach. The air rang with the calls of carneys at the freak-show and game booths, and music from the carousel and the Wonder Wheel. The aromas of popcorn and hot dogs and cotton candy perfumed the air.

"I can't believe I've lived here all this time and have missed this," Danny said, craning his neck to look up at the lights of Beacon Tower.

"I love it," Nina said. "All the color and light and sound." Art was everywhere she looked at Coney Island, from the garish murals painted on the sides of the freak-show booths to the swirls of light from the rides at Luna Park, to the smiling faces of children playing in the sand beside the water's edge.

"I want to take your picture here," she said, grabbing his arm to stop him.

He lounged obligingly against a post on the boardwalk in a gangster pose, hat low over his eyes, water gun raised in preparation for a shoot-out. Nina laughed and took shot after shot as Danny hammed it up. He alternately smirked and glowered, flirting with the camera—flirting with her? He was so unpretentious, so free and open. Accepting of anything she suggested. His confidence in her—his trust—made her feel stronger and bolder, as if no idea was too outrageous to succeed.

"Watch this." He ran to the edge of the water and filled his water gun, then aimed it at the sand. He guided the stream of water through the sand, tracing the shape of the letters N, I, N, A with the last letter trailing off as the gun ran out of water. "Good thing you have a short name," he said.

She snapped a photo of her name in the sand, then of him aiming his water pistol at the words.

"We need some pictures together," he said. "Doesn't that camera have a timer or something?"

"It does. Stand right there and I'll set up the shot." After a few minutes of fiddling with exposures, she set the timer and hurried to join him. She cocked her hat over one eye and mugged for the camera. He grabbed her arm and stuck his water gun in her side. "Don't move and nobody gets hurt," he said, in a bad gangster accent.

She laughed, but weakly. That's what she wanted, for nobody to get hurt, but was that even possible, when Danny made her feel so many things she shouldn't?

They posed for several more photos, long exposures so they didn't have to use the flash, the lights of the boardwalk blurring behind them. They took aim at each other from behind posts, or posed back to back, guns raised, hats at rakish angles. Nina couldn't remember the last time she'd laughed so much.

"I think I have enough shots for now," she said, returning to the camera and unscrewing it from the tripod. "Maybe we'll take some more later. What do you want to do now?"

"Eat!" he said. "I'm starving."

They hit the food stalls on the boardwalk. Popcorn, pretzels, hamburgers and more beckoned. The lights of [Nathan's Famous Hot Dogs] shimmered down the block, but they decided not to brave the lines at that establishment and to opt for something more convenient. They bought corn dogs and drizzled them with mustard, and ate them as they shopped for a second course. "Funnel cakes!" Danny pointed to a brightly lit booth.

Nina wrinkled her nose. "I've never had a funnel cake."

"You've never had a funnel cake? We'll have to fix that." He pulled her toward the booth. He ordered a large cake, and it arrived on a paper plate, spirals of pastry smelling of hot grease and sugar. "Now this is good eating," he said.

"Isn't it just fried dough?" she asked, amused by his enthusiasm.

"Don't knock it until you've tried it." He held out the plate. "Go ahead."

She tore off a piece and popped it into her mouth. It practically melted, leaving behind a bloom of sweetness. "It is good," she said, reaching for another piece, a cloud of powdered sugar erupting as she tore it off. "Messy though." She sucked powdered sugar from her fingers.

Beside her, Danny grew still. She looked over and saw he was watching her, a slack look of lust on his face. She slowly withdrew her finger from her mouth, self-conscious, yet at the same time thrilled that she'd stirred him this way.

He held out a paper napkin. "Here," he said, his voice strangled.

"Thank you." Smiling to herself, she finished cleaning her fingers.

Danny inhaled the last of the funnel cake, then tossed the empty paper plate in the trash, already searching for his next conquest. "Fried candy bars!" he exclaimed, and pointed to the booth.

"Oh, that sounds horrible!" she said.

"I have to try it." He ordered one fried candy bar. After a few minutes' wait, he was handed a paper tray containing what looked to Nina like a fat corndog dusted with powdered sugar. Chocolate oozed from a crack in one side.

"It looks even messier than the funnel cake," she said. "And all that sugar."

"It's delicious," he said, his voice somewhat muffled by a mouthful of candy bar and fried dough. He swallowed. "You have to help me eat it." He turned it toward her.

She hesitated, then took a small bite. Molten chocolate and caramel flowed around her tongue, along with bits of fried pastry. It tasted much better than she'd expected. "Too sweet," she said. "And too messy!" She felt a blob of chocolate slide from the candy onto her chin.

Before she could wipe it away with her napkin, Danny put out his finger and caught it. As he sucked the chocolate from his finger tips, their eyes met, and once again she felt the heat, searing into her, stealing her breath and making her heart race. They were playing a dangerous game, but one she didn't want to stop.

Danny scarcely tasted the chocolate, his senses overwhelmed by Nina. He smelled the floral undertones of her perfume beneath the food aromas of the midway, and the memory of the velvet softness of her skin made his fingertips tingle. The eroticism of her full, cherry-pink lips sucking the sugar from her fingers had caught him unawares, stripping away any pretense that he wasn't attracted to her. He'd acted instinctively to retrieve that bit of chocolate from her chin, and his own desire reflected in her eyes.

He was in trouble, like a man who dove off the pier and then remembered he couldn't swim. He had no business thinking of Nina this way—wanting her as much as he did. Her pull on him was stronger than any tide. He'd never met anyone so full of energy and joy. Simply being with her made him feel more alive, more aware of the blood pulsing in his veins, of the sensation of salt air on his skin. He felt as if they had embarked together on some great adventure—as if they'd made a trip across the globe rather than a few miles from his apartment. He saw the world differently, through her eyes, and he saw himself differently as well. When she looked at him he felt taller, smarter, *better*. She filled him with an energy that had nothing to do with all the sugar he'd consumed.

She was the first to look away, breaking the spell. "Do you want to ride some rides?" she asked.

He glanced over his shoulder toward the illuminated rib cage of the giant Cyclone roller coaster, and the kaleidoscope whirl of the Wonder Wheel. "That would be fun. What should we try first?"

They rode the Cyclone, waiting in line to board the cars, then screaming with their hands in the air as they hurtled down the wooden track. Nina aimed her camera up among the wooden beams, setting the exposure long, the result a curve of lights like sparklers trailed across the night sky.

On the bumper cars she bashed into him relentlessly, screaming with delight as he backed up, then raced toward her. They took turns trying to puncture balloons with darts at the arcade, then posed for Nina's camera on the carousel, making faces at the animals or posing with their hats and sunglasses on the zebras and lions.

"We have to ride the Ferris wheel," Danny said as they climbed off the carousel. "You've photographed it from below; you should try the view from the top."

"All right." They bought tickets and waited in line for their turn to board the cars.

As soon as they were on, Danny turned to her, his expression solemn. "I should tell you now I'm afraid of heights," he said as the car began to rise.

"Really? And here I thought you weren't afraid of anything."

Did she really think that of him? His heart felt at least one size larger with the idea. "I'm not really afraid of heights," he said. "But what would you do if I was?"

"I'd photograph your panic and use the pictures to blackmail you later."

"Beautiful and cruel. You'd have made a good spy."

The gondolas on the Wonder Wheel were enclosed, the glass scratchy from years of use, but from their front seat Nina and Danny still had a breathtaking view of the boardwalk below and the city before them. Nina watched with all the wonder of a child as the car rose into the air, her eyes wide, lips parted.

The wheel stopped at the top with a jerk. Nina grinned at him, then raised her camera to her eye. He thought she was going to photograph the scenery, but she turned the lens toward him. "Say *fromage*," she said.

"*Queso*," he countered as the shutter clicked.

She laughed and turned the lens toward the view from the car. She was still clicking away when the car lurched and started down. The descent was faster than she'd expected, like plummeting too fast in an elevator. Nina squeaked, and clutched at Danny's shoulder. He put his arm around her, pulling her close.

As the wheel slowed, she relaxed, but made no move to pull away. He savored the warmth of her against him, the soft curve of her breast against his side. Only when they neared the bottom did she pull away, and he reluctantly released her.

She was silent, more subdued as they walked away from the rides. Danny didn't ask her what was wrong; he thought he knew. Being together was magical, but the magic always had to end, reality breaking the spell.

"I've never had a friend like you," she said. Her gaze searched him, as if trying to decipher some hidden message in his expression.

"I've never had a friend like you, either." He shoved his hands in his pockets—it was either that or reach for her. And reaching would be a mistake. "Tonight was the best night I can remember having. And I've had my share of fun times."

"I'll always remember this night." She clutched her camera. Was she thinking of the photographs she'd taken? Or that moment in his arms in the Ferris wheel car?

"We'll do this again," he said. The conviction in his voice surprised him, but as soon as the words were out, he knew they were right. "A friendship like this shouldn't be wasted." To hell with all the reasons they couldn't be together. He wouldn't sacrifice all they'd shared—the fun and spontaneity and zest for life—because of what they couldn't do. They could still enjoy those things without venturing into dangerous territory.

Her smile was brighter to him than any of the midway neon. "Yes. Let's do this again," she said. "I like making art with you."

Is that how she saw it—making art? "I like the sound of that." Making art would have to do, since what he really wanted—making love—was off-limits.

Four

Under stress I froze
Unable to speak to you.
Even books have spines.

WORKING AT HOMBRE, his cousin's clothing company, was a different kind of thrill ride for Danny. Between learning the intricacies of the business at warp speed, dealing with John's mercurial moods, and formulating plans to expand the reach of their brand, he never had time to be bored. He approached new markets and new tasks with the same curiosity and enthusiasm that had drawn him to take film classes and architecture courses in addition to his business studies. Every day brought something new and interesting. When he was on a plane to Miami for a meeting with a new buyer, his days working at the café seemed very far away.

But that magical night with Nina at Coney Island lingered. She e-mailed him some of the pictures she'd taken that evening. He kept them on his phone and as he sat at airport gates waiting to board a plane, or in a hotel room after a long day of meetings, he'd look at them and smile, remembering. In his favorite shot they stood arm and arm on the boardwalk, in those crazy hats and sunglasses, grinning for the camera, so happy and carefree. In that moment, nothing else had mattered—there had been only him and Nina, and the joy of the moment.

Renee knew about the photos, and he'd waited for her to say something, to accuse him of some wrongdoing. But she did not. She pretended not to care about his friendship with Nina. Or maybe she really didn't care, though she continued to make plans to buy a house, despite his protests.

Once a week, whenever his travel schedule permitted, he still did a DJ gig at the Castle. Nina usually came on those nights, sometimes alone, sometimes with her friend Erin. After the club closed, they would go out for breakfast and talk until the sky lightened to the color of pewter and the rattle of delivery trucks shook the mostly silent streets.

"I'm working on a new painting," she told him one night as they sat across from each other in a booth at a diner near the club. "It's of Russia—or how I remember Russia when I was a child."

"Have you been back to visit since you were little?" he asked.

"Oh yes. I've been back several times." She sipped the coffee, which was strong and bitter, but hot and plentiful. "But when you are an adult you see things so differently. In this painting I'm trying to capture the child's point of view—when everything is bigger and mysterious and full of so much possibility."

"I still feel that way about life," he said. "At least the part about it being mysterious and full of possibility."

"Yes." She smiled, a sweet curve of her mouth, a dimple forming in her cheek, a dreaminess about her eyes.

"Would you like pie?" Their waitress stopped beside their table. "We've got two pieces of apple left."

"I would like pie, but I cannot afford pie," Nina said solemnly.

Danny wasn't sure if she meant she couldn't afford the calories or the price tag, though he suspected the latter. He declined the pie also and the waitress moved away, allowing him to turn his attention to Nina once more. "Have any of the photographs from the coffee shop sold?" he asked.

"No. I took samples of my work around to some design firms, but no interest there either." She shrugged. "Art takes time. I know this. And I would rather paint and pinch pennies than work in an office, where I would feel smothered."

"I admire that about you," he said. "That you're so certain what you want."

"Really, I only know what I don't want. As for what I want . . ." Her voice trailed away and the dreamy look returned. "I want to be open and available to all possibilities. I don't want to force my life into a neat little box."

Nina would never fit in a box. Her spirit was too large, her passion too fiery, to be contained by the mundane. Whether she was extolling the perfection of a ripe peach she purchased from a sidewalk vendor or defending her homeland, she put her whole self into the moment.

Once Erin had asked Nina if she'd ever seen a bear on the streets in Moscow and Nina spent ten minutes berating her for her ignorance. Another time, Randy had said there were no great Russian artists, and he'd received an intense art history lesson. Danny had watched Nina, eyes flashing, cheeks flushed, and thought he'd never seen her more beautiful. As if she'd felt him watching, she turned toward him, and the raw longing he'd seen in those blue depths had brought a knot of tears to his throat.

He debated breaking things off with Renee. But he wasn't that kind of man—the kind of man who would abruptly turn his back on the woman he'd been with for five years. He still remembered

all the good things he had with Renee and all her positive qualities. She was beautiful and smart and funny and loyal, and he
couldn't bear to hurt her.

He felt he owed it to Renee to try to make things work. But
she'd changed since graduation. For years she'd been content
with whatever life brought their way at the moment, but now she
was focused on a detailed vision of the future that included a
house in the suburbs, children, a minivan, and summer vacations
by the shore. There was nothing wrong with any of that, of
course, but Danny couldn't see himself living that kind of life. It
seemed so staid and conventional. So boring and suffocating.

"I want to stay in the city," he told her, in hopes of forestalling
an argument. "I need to be close to work."

"We can look at the suburbs later, then," she said. "There are
some fantastic deals right now on condos in Manhattan or
Queens, or even Harlem. I've seen some amazing renovations
there, in beautiful historic buildings."

"Now, really, isn't a good time," he said. "I need to be better
established in my job."

"As if your cousin is going to fire you. If anything, he should
give you a raise. You work all the time. I hardly see you. And
when you are in town, you're out with friends."

Did she mean Nina? But Danny had never hidden their
friendship. Renee was there plenty of evenings at the club, alongside Nina. They invited her to breakfast, but more often than not
she declined, using the excuse that she had to get up early.

All this was on his mind one afternoon in June when he
stopped by the Palette on his way to the office after a meeting
with a new designer he was trying to recruit. As soon as he stepped
in the door of the restaurant the air felt charged with a different
energy. Nina was there. She greeted him with a smile, and threw

her arms around him. "I'm so happy! A customer bought two of my photographs."

"He was interested in one and I talked him into buying two," Rob said, frowning at Danny.

"That was wonderful of you," Nina said, but she didn't take her arms from around Danny.

Rob shook his head and retreated to his office. Danny laughed. "Is he still trying to get you to go out with him?" he asked.

"Yes. I try to let him down nicely, but he won't take no for an answer."

"Why not go out with him?" Rob was an okay guy. A little nerdy, maybe, but okay.

Nina shook her head. "He isn't my type."

"What is your type?" he asked, his curiosity roused.

"I don't know." She straightened one of the remaining photographs on the wall. "I've dated different kinds of men and none of them have worked out. My last boyfriend claimed to be supportive of my artwork and to love how creative I was, but then he complained that I was being unrealistic to try to make a living from my art and that I was too 'flighty.'"

"You need a guy who trusts you to make the right decisions for yourself," he said.

"Yes, but where am I going to find a man like that?" Her eyes met his. Did he imagine the challenge there?

He looked away. She continued to fuss with the photographs on the wall. "Do you want to go to the free concert in Prospect Park on Sunday afternoon?" she asked after a pause. "I thought we could get a bunch of people together for a picnic."

"Can't. I have to be in Miami Monday morning for a meeting with buyers, so I'm flying down Sunday afternoon. I'm going to drop in on my parents while I'm there."

"That'll be nice. Do they live in the home where you grew up?"

"Yeah. They've been married thirty-five years. Can you imagine?"

"I can't. Both my mother's marriages together didn't add up to thirty-five years. It's nice though, to think of finding someone you can love enough to spend the rest of your life with."

"That would be amazing." But was it even possible these days? People had so many more options in life now than they had when his parents were young. It was easier for him to imagine a different relationship for each stage of his life than one person he could never let go. And yet, his parents had kept their love alive through decades of change. This was the ideal that had been his model while growing up. To settle for anything less than a lifetime love was a tragedy in their eyes. Danny didn't believe in his parents' and grandparents' concept of sin, but he'd seen their disappointment when John's marriage had failed and never wanted to be in the position of hurting them that way.

"Love is the most mysterious thing," Nina said. "Like a spider's web that wraps you in its strands, both fragile and strong."

"That doesn't sound very pleasant," Danny said.

"I suppose that depends on if you are the spider or the fly."

He felt the familiar tightness in his chest that came when emotion swelled, too much for words. She enchanted and captivated him, and frightened him a little, too. She saw the world through a different prism; he was standing on the outside, trying to catch a glimpse of her view.

"I'll call you when I get back in town," he said. "We'll get together."

"Of course."

She sounded so certain. As if they would always be good friends. They would always be there for each other.

Nina studied the painting on her easel with a critical eye. She'd raced home from the café the day before to sketch out this idea— a couple in the forest, caught in a silver spider web, a spider hovering in one corner above them. Was the spider God or fate or society, or the couple's own fears? The viewer could decide.

She added a bit of shading around the couple. She needed to work more on the expression on the woman's face. It wasn't quite right.

She'd set up her easel on the fire escape, to take advantage of the light, and conveniently out of hearing of the manager if he should knock on the front door, looking for the rent that was three days late. She would be able to pay him tomorrow, once the check from Rob cleared. In the meantime, she didn't need the hassle.

She dropped her brush in the jar of turpentine. She'd have to think awhile before she worked on the painting more. In the meantime, she should probably buy some groceries; the only thing in the house was a tin of tea and a few cans of soup.

She contemplated her wardrobe choices. A sundress would do for the shopping trip, but what about shoes? Her favorite ballerina flats had badly scuffed toes. She was tempted to spend part of the money from the sale of the photographs for new shoes, but no—she had rent and groceries to think of. If she bought anything more, it would have to be paint.

She put on the shoes and contemplated the scuffed toes. A little black paint might cover the scuffs. Excited by the idea, she raced to the fire escape and her box of paints. A few minutes later, she'd transformed the worn leather with a coat of black acrylic. Inspired, she added a trail of red roses and green leaves. Who needed new shoes when she had custom-painted ones?

She was admiring her handiwork when the tinny cascade of a xylophone being played filled the apartment. She grabbed up her cell phone and studied the read out. Smiling, she slid open the phone. "Hello, Mom."

"Ninochka, how are you?"

"I'm good."

"What are you doing?"

"I'm painting my shoes."

"Really. You can do that?"

"I just did. They look great." She smiled at the roses scattered across the toes of the shoes.

"That's wonderful, Nin. I called to ask if you remember Alex Lessing."

"Alex Lessing. Who is he?"

"He was the boy who lived three doors down when we had the house over on Falcon Ridge," Natasha said. "You were in seventh grade together."

Nina had a vague recollection of a skinny boy with a blond buzz cut. "What about him?" she asked.

"There was an article about him in the paper today. He has his own company, making macrobiotic energy bars."

"That's nice." Did Natasha think Nina needed to eat macrobiotic energy bars?

"The article said he is very successful," Natasha said. "He has a beautiful home and races bicycles as a hobby. And he is single."

"That's nice."

"I thought if you came home for a visit, you could call him up, maybe arrange to get together."

Nina smothered a laugh. Natasha wasn't known for subtlety, but this attempt at matchmaking was too much. "Mom, I really don't think Alex is my type."

"How can you say that? You have not seen him in years."

"He used to pick his nose and eat the buggers. That's all I need to know."

"Well really, Nin. You can't hold what a man did in seventh grade against him."

"I just don't think I could look at him without remembering that," Nina said.

Natasha sighed. "Well, even if you do not want to get together with Alex, I wish you would come back to Boulder. You're up there in that horrible little apartment, all alone and so far from family."

"Geeze, Mom, I didn't realize my life was so pathetic until you pointed it out."

"All I'm saying is that I sense you are not happy."

"Of course I'm happy. I'm especially happy today. Two of my photographs sold and this morning I started a new painting."

"That's wonderful. You should go out and celebrate. Are you dating anyone?"

As if the only way she could celebrate would be with a man. Though Nina had to admit it would have been nice to have one special someone with whom she could share her triumph. "I have lots of friends," she said. "You of all people should know I don't need a man to be happy. You taught me to be independent."

"Of course. But you are such a warm, loving person, Ninochka. You would make such a good mother."

This surprised a choked laugh out of Nina. "Are you saying you want to be a grandmother?"

"Really, Nin, I am much too young to be a grandmother. I am only saying you cannot let what happened with that last man—what was his name, Ryan?"

"Sam." She'd dated Sam for two years, her longest relationship to date.

"You cannot let what happened with Sam turn you sour on all men."

"I'm not soured on men. I have plenty of male friends." She thought of Danny, who was, if truth be told, her best friend.

"You cannot let fear of what might happen keep you from getting out there and trying," Natasha continued. "You are in the prime of your life. This is the time you should be exploring and experimenting, discovering what you truly like and dislike. Romance is like anything else in life—the more information you have, the better you will be able to make the right decision."

Was that true? Was love a science—a matter of experimenting until you found the right formula, of gathering all the facts in order to make an informed choice? Or was it more like art—heady inspiration mixed with instinct, and a deep internal sense that yes, this was right? "I appreciate the advice, really," Nina said.

"I just want you to be happy."

"No one can be delirious all the time, Mom."

"I'm not talking delirious, Nin. I want you to be satisfied. Fulfilled."

"My art fulfills me. My friends fulfill me. I'm okay."

"I am very proud of you, Nin. At your age I'm sure I was not so confident."

At Nina's age, Natasha had been a single mother studying for her masters in botany. She'd gone on to earn her Ph.D., all while caring for Nina, and remaining on good terms with Nina's father and his family. Her mother had accomplished so much—Nina felt like a slug in comparison. "Thanks, Mom. That means a lot to me, coming from you."

"I miss you, dear. Come see me soon."

"You could come see me."

"New York City in the summer?" Natasha sounded horrified.

"The humidity would kill me. The mountains are much nicer this time of year. You should come see me."

"I'll think about it." Going home was always fun at first, but after awhile it was hard not to feel a little smothered.

She hung up the phone and set her shoes on the fire escape to dry. Another hour or so and she ought to be able to wear them, if she was careful. She busied herself straightening the tiny apartment, but her mother's words kept replaying in her mind. Was she letting her breakup with Sam keep her from dating other men?

Or was it that the only man who interested her was off-limits? She sighed. Pining for Danny was getting her nowhere, and she was sensible enough to know not every man was like Sam. Dating someone new might even make it easier for her to be just friends with Danny. She might even come to think of him as more like a brother.

Right. A totally hot brother with smoldering eyes and a killer smile.

She laughed. Oh, she was a mess. But she was also her mother's daughter. If she had a problem, she'd find a solution, whether it was painting her old shoes or getting out of her dating rut. She needed to go out with someone new. A practice date, to get back into the swing of things.

She searched her mind for a likely candidate and thought of Rob. He'd asked her out more than once. He was a nice guy. Cute, and close to her age. They could probably have a good time together. Before she could lose her nerve, she picked up her phone and searched the directory for the number for the café.

A woman answered. "Hi, may I speak to Rob? This is Nina."

He was on the line in a flash. "Nina? How are you?"

"Great. I was wondering if you'd like to go to the concert at Prospect Park with me on Sunday."

That was what she meant to say. But when she opened her mouth to speak, what came out was "I was wondering if I should bring in a couple of photos to replace the two that sold?"

"Actually, I was thinking you should take some of the older ones home with you," he said. "Bring in some new ones, but not as many. I have another girl who's asked to display some of her work. I like to offer my customers more variety, you know?"

Had this other girl agreed to go out with him? Nina wondered. "Sure," she said. "I'll pick out a few new ones and rearrange them to make room for another artist's work."

She hung up the phone, dismayed at her own impotence. She hadn't been able to ask Rob for a date—not because she was afraid or anything like that. She simply didn't want to go to the concert with him. She wanted to go with Danny.

She groaned and sank onto the daybed, head in her hands. So much for being proactive and solving her own problems. She was in a mess she didn't think she could paint her way out of.

Five

Frustration builds up
Spilling over in the most
Uncalled-for moments.

NINA AND ERIN AND A GROUP OF FRIENDS met at the Castle on a Saturday night in late June to celebrate Erin's twenty-fifth birthday. Randy was there with his new girlfriend Tawny. Danny joined them, along with Renee, who looked happy and gorgeous in a lace-trimmed top and fashionably ripped jeans. She sat next to Danny, sipping a margarita and talking with Tawny, occasionally smiling at Danny, who was entertaining them all with stories about his visit back home to Florida. "The moment I arrive, my mother is pushing food at me," he said, "Telling me I'm too skinny, I'm too pale, and what is that I'm wearing? I half-expected her to tell me to sit up straight and that I had to be in bed by nine. It's like time travel. I step into my parents' house and I'm ten years younger and two feet shorter."

"You'll always be her baby," Renee said. "And you don't really hate it as much as you let on."

"Well, my mom is a good cook," he conceded. "But three days of that is about all I can take. And we won't even go into the arguments my dad and I can get into about politics."

A new DJ was in the booth that night, so both Randy and Danny were ready to party. They ordered pitchers of beer, then hit the dance floor. Like Nina, Erin was unattached at the moment, but she made up for it by dancing with as many men as possible. Nina made her share of trips to the dance floor, trying very hard not to watch Danny as he grooved with Renee. He was a great dancer, fluid and graceful. And he clearly loved to dance.

He danced with Renee, but also with Erin and Tawny. At last it was Nina's turn. "Oh, I think I'm ready to rest a little," she said, trying to put him off gracefully.

"You don't need to rest." He grabbed her hand and pulled her from her chair.

So there she was on the dance floor, following Danny's footwork, laughing as he spun her around. She improvised moves of her own, and he applauded her efforts. "You're great," he called above the loud music.

"You inspire me!" she answered.

If this was a romance novel, she thought, *the music would shift into a slow number, and Danny would take me into his arms and hold me close. I'd be bold enough to look into his eyes and let him see everything I'm feeling, and at the end of the dance, he wouldn't be able to help himself. He'd kiss me. . . .*

But this wasn't a novel, and neither one of them was foolish enough to behave that way in front of their friends—especially in front of Renee. Instead, the song ended and Danny patted her on the back the way he would any buddy, and they returned to their table and ordered another round of drinks.

"I'm thinking we should do something fun to celebrate the Fourth of July," Danny said.

"What'd you have in mind?" Randy asked. "Buying illegal fireworks?"

"We could get tickets on a boat to watch the fireworks under the Statue of Liberty," Erin said.

"That would be cool, but I was thinking of getting out of town for a few days, maybe going camping," said Danny.

"Camping?" Randy leaned forward. "You mean like with tents and sleeping bags and campfires and all that?"

"What other kind of camping is there?" Tawny asked. "It's all too much dirt and too many bugs for me."

"No, it would be a blast," Danny said. "A bunch of us hit the road and go up through New England to Canada. We can hike and sit around the campfire at night, drinking wine and telling stories or singing. I could bring my guitar."

"You make it sound like fun," Tawny admitted.

"Are you kidding? This guy could sell snow to Eskimos." Randy clapped Danny on the back. "I'm in. I can probably even borrow a tent and some gear from my parents."

"I could go for a few days running wild in the great outdoors," Erin said. "As long as you promise me wine and music . . . and decent coffee in the morning. You don't want to see me without my coffee."

"You in?" Danny looked at Renee.

She shrugged. "Sure."

"What about you, Nina? Will you come camping with us?"

As a girl in Colorado, she'd spent plenty of time camping in the mountains, hiking, and sleeping out under the stars. Going with a group of friends sounded like a great vacation. "Sure. I'll go."

"We can share a tent," Erin said.

Not Nina's preferred tent mate, but in this case, Erin was probably the better choice. "Sure. I think I even have my old sleeping bag somewhere in my apartment."

"We should rent a van or something, to carry all our stuff," Randy said.

"We'll need plenty of food," Danny said.

"And booze," Tawny said. "We'll need a big cooler."

They spent the next hour discussing plans for the trip: when they would go, where, what they should bring, what they should do, how much fun they would have. Everyone contributed to the conversation, even Nina, who offered suggestions for routes they could take for the best scenery.

"We should see Niagara Falls," Erin said.

"We should spend time in Toronto," Randy said. "Maybe take in some concerts."

"We'll need at least a week to do all this," Tawny said.

"Maybe ten days," Randy agreed.

"Can you take that much time off work?" Renee asked Danny.

"John promised me two weeks vacation this summer, and I intend to hold him to that promise."

"Nice cousin," Tawny said.

"He's great." Danny's smile was so warm and genuine. No wonder everyone loved him so much. He returned that love in spades. He didn't waste time with anger or regret or any of the negative emotions that stifled people.

Nina had never been able to look at life so lightly. As much as she saw the beauty and joy in every day, she saw the darker side too. When bleak moods overwhelmed her, she sought therapy in painting. Whether it was worrying about the future of her career, or overdue rent, or her nonexistent love life, she found solace in the paints and brushes, in trying to bring the pictures in her head to the canvas.

"I'll bring my sketchbook with me and my paints." Some plein air painting might give her a fresh perspective.

"You know, Nina, this is the twenty-first century," Randy leaned toward her, his face shiny from dancing in the heat and drinking too much beer. "You don't have to draw your own souvenirs of your vacation. They have these things called cameras."

He laughed, and the others with him, not because the joke was so clever, but because he was Randy being Randy. Nina joined in the fun, knowing there was no malice behind the words. Her mother had worried about her being alone in New York with no family. But the people around this table were her family—the goofy cousins and beautiful sisters and protective brother. "I'll be sure to paint a special portrait of you," she told Randy. "Dancing around the campfire, in your mountain man costume."

"That's me," he said, clearly pleased. "Randy the wild man."

"Oh please!" Tawny rolled her eyes, but let him pull her into a hug.

"You love it that I'm a wild man," he said.

"You two get the tent farthest from the rest of us," Danny said.

"Maybe you could do a painting of me and Danny."

Renee's request startled Nina. "A painting?"

"Yeah. A portrait of the two of us together." Renee put her arm through Danny's and squeezed closer to him.

"Oh. Well, sure. I could probably do that," Nina said. What else could she say?

"It would be wonderful to hang in the new house," Renee said.

"You two are buying a house?" Erin's face lit up. She devoted whole weekends to marathon viewings of reality shows involving people hunting for houses, selling houses, remodeling houses, or decorating houses. She'd once persuaded Nina to dress up and spend a day attending open houses of swanky Manhattan condos whose monthly payment exceeded Nina's annual income. She talked about getting a realtor's license, though so far she hadn't done anything about it. "Where?" Erin asked. "Tell me all about it."

"We're not buying a house," Danny said, his smile vanishing.

"We're seriously thinking about it," Renee said, serene as ever. "Danny doesn't like change."

Nina knew this wasn't true. Danny welcomed new experiences and new ideas. But, judging by the tightness around his mouth, he clearly didn't welcome the idea of buying a house. Or at least . . . buying a house with Renee.

"I like this song," Danny said. He stood and grabbed Renee's hand. "Come dance with me."

She smiled and offered no resistance. Danny led her onto the floor and pulled her into his arms to dance to Kate Bush's "Hounds of Love." Erin leaned close to Nina. "Buying a house together—that's a big step," she said.

"Yes, it is." Nina choked out the words.

"Renee told me they'd been dating since high school and all through college. That surprised me."

"Why does it surprise you?"

Erin shifted in her chair. "I don't know. Maybe because he doesn't act like a man who's that settled into a relationship."

Nina watched Danny and Renee as they danced in tight circles, close together. Renee was saying something; Danny was frowning. Nina felt an ugly ache in her chest she recognized as jealousy. She'd been lying when she told herself she was okay with just being friends, but in the back of her mind she'd been holding out hope that that could change. If Danny married Renee—which seemed the next logical step if they bought a house together—he'd be lost to her forever.

Suddenly, he turned and walked away, leaving Renee alone in the middle of the dance floor. "Uh-oh," Erin said. "Lover's quarrel."

She made a tsking noise with her tongue. "Renee pushed too hard on the house thing, I'll bet. She ought to know you've got to reel them in slowly—give them plenty of line to wear themselves out, then scoop them up in the net when they're tired of fighting."

Nina stared at her friend. "What are you talking about?"

Erin laughed. "My dad's a big sports fisherman. I used to go on fishing trips with him. One day I was watching him land a marlin and I realized going after trophy fish wasn't that different from a woman catching the guy she wants."

Nina didn't want a man she had to play games with, as if he was a reluctant fish who had to be lured into her clutches. No wonder so many men didn't want to marry, if that was the way women made them feel.

Danny headed toward the back of the club. Nina stood. "I have to go to the ladies' room," she said, and left before Erin offered to come with her. Or before common sense forced her to stay in her seat.

Danny pushed through the crowd toward the bar, fighting to rein in his anger. As soon as they heard Renee had reached the dance floor, Renee had brought up the house again. "You're being so silly about this," she said. "There's no reason we shouldn't buy a house, or at least a condo, now that we're both working good jobs. You know it makes financial sense, and you don't want to rent apartments for the rest of your life, do you?"

"The rest of my life is a long time. I have no idea what I do or don't want to do for that time. But I do know right now I don't want to buy a house."

"You don't want the house—or you don't want to buy it with me?"

He wondered if she already knew the answer to that question

and was pushing him to make a declaration. But what if the answer she thought she knew was the wrong one? "I'm not going to talk about this now," he said, and stepped away from her.

"Danny, really, I—."

"Not now," he said, and turned away. He hated when other couples he knew fought in public. He hated fighting in general, but especially with strangers and friends looking on. Better to leave this alone for now, and give them both time to calm down.

He reached the bar and ordered a gin and tonic, then looked back to make sure Renee wasn't following. He didn't see Renee, but another familiar figure was making her way toward him. "Nina," he said, moving over to make room for her beside him at the crowded bar.

"Don't think I'm an awful person," she said. "But I don't want to paint you and Renee." She looked behind them, toward the dance floor, as if searching for someone—Renee? Her expression was troubled.

"It's all right," he said.

"It's just that I don't like doing serious portraits of friends," she continued, the words pouring out in a rush. "There's the danger they won't like the way I portray them and that would interfere with the friendship, plus I wouldn't know what to charge you and . . ."

"Nina." He put his hand over hers and she fell silent, full lips still slightly parted, cheeks flushed. He had never seen her more beautiful, and he tightened his hand over hers, fighting the urge to pull her close, to cradle her head on his shoulder and feel the steady beat of her heart against his own. "It's all right," he said. "I don't want you to paint our portrait."

Her hand fluttered under his, like a trapped bird. Reluctantly, he started to pull away, but she clutched his arm, stopping him.

Her eyes met his, dark and glittering. He hoped that was a trick of the nightclub lights, and she wasn't close to tears. "You don't? Really?" Nina asked.

"Maybe one day you can paint a portrait of me." The idea of seeing himself as she saw him intrigued him. "But not now. And not with Renee."

She pulled her hand away, and her gaze dropped to the floor. He looked down also and noticed she was wearing shoes with roses painted across the toes, as if she'd walked through one of her own paintings and caught some of it on her feet.

"It's none of my business, I know," she said. "But it looked like you were arguing just now."

He turned to accept his drink from the bartender. "We argue a lot lately."

"I'm sorry to hear that."

Was she sorry, really? "Renee is unhappy because I'm not giving her what she wants."

"What does she want?"

He couldn't be certain, because he'd never bothered to ask. He didn't want to know the answer. "I think she wants a house in the suburbs. She wants marriage and probably children."

"And you don't want those things?"

"Some day, yes. But not now. And I'm not sure I want them with Renee." He'd avoided admitting that truth, even to himself, but it felt good to confide it now, to Nina.

"You ought to be very sure about the person you marry," she said solemnly.

"Yes." He wasn't sure about anything in his life at the moment. Even the new job, for all he enjoyed the challenges, could be overwhelming. And confining. He missed having the freedom to set his own schedule, to come and go as he pleased. Which is why he looked forward to their upcoming camping trip.

"I'm glad you can be part of our camping trip," he said, eager to change the subject to something more uplifting than his floundering relationship with Renee. "Have you camped much before?"

"Growing up in Colorado we camped a lot in the Rocky Mountains. Have you ever been there?"

He shook his head. "I'm a Florida kid. It's all about the beaches there."

"The mountains are beautiful too, in a different way. I think you'd like them."

"There are a lot of places I'd like to see. The mountains. California and New England. I want to be able to travel—to Europe and Africa and Asia and all over the world. I even thought about taking off a year between college and work, to travel." The idea still warred with the need to be a responsible adult, supporting himself and fulfilling the unspoken family expectation that, like his cousin and sister before him, he would "make something of himself."

"I've been to Tuscany and to Russia, of course," she said. "I want to travel more, too. To photograph and paint all the beautiful places of the world."

"When you travel, do you plan a strict itinerary or do you keep things loose?"

"Keep things loose, of course," she said. "If I see something I want to sketch, I want to be able to stop and sketch it. And if I hear about an interesting sight or a good restaurant, I want to be able to detour to see it."

"Me too," he said. "We should do that on this camping trip— keep things loose so we can do whatever looks interesting."

"More difficult to do with a lot of people along," she said.

"Agreed." Especially people like Renee, who did prefer a

definite schedule and plan, though over the years Danny had persuaded her to be more flexible. Still, her current mood had the potential to take some of the fun out of the adventure. "We'll have a good time," he said, as if saying it out loud could make it so.

"We will," Nina agreed. Her expression grew serious. "Don't stop being my friend, Danny. No matter what happens, promise?"

"What's going to happen?" he asked. Did she know something he didn't?

"Nothing. I hope nothing's going to happen. I just can't imagine not having you for a friend."

Another time, with another person, he might have chided her for being overly dramatic, but Nina spoke with such earnestness, and he felt a prickle of unease in his chest at her words. "I promise," he said solemnly. "We'll always be friends."

"Good." She flashed a smile, then walked away, a tall, graceful figure he never tired of watching. The idea of an end to his friendship with Nina caused a physical pain, yet the relationship felt so fragile at times. They were balanced on the thin line men and women walk between friends and lovers, hormones and past experiences and the expectations of others threatening to push them over the edge, in one direction or the other. But falling either way might end in disaster.

Nina unpacked her old sleeping bag from the storage unit in the basement of her apartment and hauled it upstairs. She'd hang it out on the fire escape to air out for a bit. As she unrolled it she inhaled the scents of moth balls and dried pine needles and was transported back to summer evenings lying in a tent across from her mother and stepfather, the darkness cool and comforting around her little family. It was probably only because she was worn out from a day spent exploring the woods and trails around their camp, but on those nights, snuggled in the tent with her parents so nearby, Nina slept better than she did anywhere else in the world.

She tried to recall the last time she'd used the bag. She thought it was a trip with her mother and stepfather to Colorado's western slope. They'd rented four-wheelers and explored narrow dirt roads high in the mountains, and camped in a field of wildflowers, awakening the next morning to find frost on the tents, even in August.

Canada in July probably wouldn't be as spectacular, but she was excited about the trip. She hadn't been out of New York, other than a few trips back to Boulder, in years.

A knock on the door interrupted her thoughts. She went to answer it and found Erin and Tawny. "We came to tell you we can't go on the camping trip," Erin said, as soon as the two women stepped into Nina's apartment.

"What? Why not?"

"My parents are having a big barbecue at their place on Long Island on the Fourth and I have to be there," Tawny explained.

"You're skipping the camping trip for a barbecue?" Nina asked.

"It's not just a barbecue. It's to announce my brother's engagement. The whole family's going to be there. If I don't show up they'll never forgive me. And I really want to be there, too. It's not every day my brother gets engaged. I want to help him celebrate."

"I guess I can understand that." Nina didn't have a brother, but if she did, she'd want to be a part of the special moments in his life, and engagement certainly qualified. She turned to Erin. "What about you?"

"This guy at work invited me to come with him to a party on a boat in the East River." At Nina's disapproving look, she rushed on. "I know it's lousy of me to bail on you all, but I really like this guy. He's good-looking and successful. He drives an Audi and has his own condo in lower Manhattan. And he's really good-looking."

"You said that already," Nina said.

"It was worth repeating."

"How old is this guy?" Nina asked.

"Thirty-two. So not too old. I just couldn't pass up this chance."

"Especially not to go camping." Tawny made a face.

"You'll still have Renee and Danny and Randy," Erin said.

"Randy's not going to the barbecue with you?" Nina asked Tawny.

Tawny made a face. "Randy's a fun guy but, no offense, he's not the type I'd take home to Mom and Dad. Besides, if I brought anyone to a family party like this, they'd take it as a sign that things were serious between us."

"And you're not serious," Nina said.

"Not at all."

"Say you forgive us," Erin said.

"I forgive you," Nina said. She'd been hoping for Erin to serve as more of a buffer between herself and Renee, but maybe this was a good thing. She could get to know Danny's girlfriend better. "I'll have the tent all to myself," she said.

"I knew you'd understand." Erin kissed her cheek. "Tawny and I are going shopping. Want to come?"

Nina shook her head. "I don't think so."

"Come on," Tawny said. "I have to find a dress to wear to this barbecue."

"And I'm looking for an outfit that will wow Thad."

"I don't need anything special for this camping trip," Nina said.

"At least you don't have to worry about keeping up appearances for a guy while you're out there," Tawny said. "I was dreading Randy seeing me when I didn't have access to my flat iron and makeup for three days. He'd probably run screaming in the other direction."

"I always figured a man ought to see the real me sooner or later," Nina said.

"Maybe after you're sure he's in love with you," Erin said. "But it's like my dad always said about fishing: to be successful, you have to start with good bait."

Nina shook her head. "Are you saying women are like bugs and worms?"

"More like those fancy spinners, with mirrors and feathers." Erin fluffed her hair and laughed. "We'll have to get together when you get back and compare notes on our holidays."

The two friends left and Nina opened her closet and contemplated her wardrobe. What, exactly, should she wear camping? She wanted to look nice, but not as if she was trying too hard.

The phone rang and she went to answer it.

"Hey, Nina, it's Randy. Is Tawny there?"

"She and Erin just left. Why?"

"I was trying to get hold of her. She mentioned she might stop by your place."

"Why don't you call her cell?"

"I did. But it goes straight to voice mail. She probably forget to charge it again. If you see her again, tell her to call me."

"All right. But I probably won't see her for awhile. She told me she and Erin aren't coming camping with us."

"Yeah. That's why I was calling. I can't make it either."

"You can't?"

"Nah. I got a chance to do a gig on Long Island that weekend. Really good money, too. I couldn't pass it up."

"I guess not."

"Anyway, you'll have fun without me. Talk to you later."

Nina set down the phone, stunned. If Tawny and Erin and Randy weren't going, that left Nina—and Danny and Renee. She sank into a chair. The phrase "three's a crowd" rang loudly in her ears. She'd have to cancel. That's all there was to it. She couldn't go along and spend all week playing third wheel to Danny and Renee's happy couple. Or, if they weren't so happy at the moment—as Danny had hinted at the club Saturday night—this trip might be what they needed to draw close again. It would be the right thing to do for her to step out of the way and give them that chance.

When the phone rang again, she figured it was Erin, calling to give her the news about Randy's cancellation. Frowning, she snatched up the receiver. "Hello?"

"Hey, Nina." Danny's voice never failed to make her heart flutter, but today she felt as if she had a bird trapped in her chest.

"I was just going to call you," she said.

"Yeah? That's good 'cause we need to talk about this camping trip."

"I already talked to Randy and Tawny and Erin. I know they aren't going."

"Yeah, that's why I was calling."

Nina took a deep breath. Better to get this over with. "I think it would be better if you and Renee went by yourselves," she said. "It would probably do you good to have some time away together."

"I don't think it would," he said. "In fact, she's not going."

"She's not?"

"No." His voice sounded grim.

"Why not?" she asked.

"She says she can't take off work that long. She actually said I was selfish for expecting her to drop everything and come with me. I reminded her that I asked her, right there in the club in front of everyone, if she wanted to come and she said yes. If she didn't want to come, why did she lie?"

Nina winced. "I guess she didn't care for that."

"No. We had a fight. Anyway, I wanted to see if you were okay with just the two of us going on the trip."

"You mean . . . you and me?"

"Yes. I still want to go. I think we could have a lot of fun."

She wanted to ask him what Renee thought about this, but sensed now was not the time to pose that question. "I want to go, but . . ."

"But what?"

"Do you really think it will be all right?" Could the two of them spend a week together, mostly alone, and not end up doing things they might have reason to regret later?

"You and I always have a good time together, Nina. Being with you always relaxes me. And it'll be good to get out of the city for awhile, don't you think?"

She wouldn't say she ever felt completely relaxed when she was with Danny, but he definitely made her feel good. More energized and daring. She'd act on that daring feeling now. "All right. I've really been looking forward to this trip."

"Fantastic. Don't worry about anything. I'll get the food and some camping equipment. Just bring your clothes and other things you'll need and any special goodies you want."

She was glad he couldn't see the smile on her face as she hung up the phone. She laughed to herself. Goodies she wanted, indeed. He might not know it yet, but Danny would be bringing those, too.

Six

Matters of the heart
Make little sense to the mind;
Its caprice triumphs.

DANNY MET NINA AT THE CURB IN FRONT of his apartment early Saturday morning, camping gear stacked on the sidewalk around him. "You have enough here for an army," she said as she opened the trunk of the car.

"We'll use it all." He hefted a large cooler into the trunk beside Nina's sleeping bag. They stuffed in tents, tarps, a duffle bag, and assorted boxes and bags. Danny's guitar case went into the back seat next to Nina's portable easel and sketch pad. Danny was quiet as they worked, but Nina put this off to the early hour.

She kept watching the door of the apartment building, expecting Renee to come down to say good-bye. But maybe she and Danny had already said their farewells in private. Or maybe she was still angry with him for taking this trip at all.

Car loaded, they set out, Nina driving east on I–278 out of Brooklyn. Their plan was to head up the coast toward Nova Scotia, detouring around Boston and spending the night wherever they felt like stopping. They had no agenda for the next week or so, only the agreement that they would stop when they felt like it and explore whatever sights caught their fancy.

Danny slumped in the seat beside her, staring out the window, but he had the attitude of someone who isn't seeing his surroundings, but is focused instead on some mental scenery. Nina thought of all the hours they'd spent together, in coffee shops and cafés—hours filled with conversation. She and Danny always had so much to talk about; this silence felt awkward and uncomfortable. She let him brood until they were out of Brooklyn, then she could stand the silence no more. "Is something wrong?" she asked.

"No. Nothing's wrong."

"Then why are you being so quiet? You're never this quiet."

"Are you saying I talk too much?" The hint of a smile at the corners of his mouth let her know he wasn't angry.

"You don't talk too much," she said. "But you talk. *We* talk. We're going to spend the next week together . . . and those are going to be very long days if you've run out of things to say to me."

He sat up straighter. "I'll never run out of things to say to you."

Then tell me what's wrong, she thought. But before she could say this, he said. "Tell me about a camping trip you took in the mountains."

It wasn't the conversation she wanted to have, but it would do for now—anything was better than his silence. She searched for an appropriate anecdote. "One of my favorite trips was in Rocky Mountain National Park with my mother and stepfather when I was twelve. My stepfather was a climatologist but he knew a lot about plants and birds and trees and he would tell me the names of flowers or what parts of plants I could eat if I was ever lost in the woods."

"And you liked that?"

"I think it was the lost in the woods part I liked most," she said. "Not that I wanted to be lost, but the thought that I could survive by my wits pleased me. I liked to imagine my rescuers being amazed that I was so competent and courageous."

"So you got along well with your stepfather?"

"Yes. He's a wonderful man. My own father was so far away, in Russia, so my stepfather was like a father to me. He and I are still close, though he and my mother divorced a few years ago."

"Was that hard, when they divorced?"

"I was grown and living in New York. It made me sad in a way, but he and my mother are still friends, so it doesn't affect me much."

"I think I'd lose it if my parents ever split," he said. "They're such a team—I can't imagine them not together."

"It's wonderful that they have that kind of relationship."

"It's the kind of relationship I want," he said. "That's why I don't want to rush into anything. I don't want to make a mistake. My mom and dad's marriage is so perfect."

Was he repeating an argument he'd had with Renee? "Every couple has problems sometimes, I expect," she said. "Those who stay together learn how to work out their problems."

"Some problems are too big to work out," he said.

"I don't know if I believe that." Her hands tightened on the steering wheel. "Not if the two people involved really love each other. I think what happens is that sometimes they reach a place where they no longer love each other enough to work out the problems."

"The secret, I guess, is learning how to make the love last," Danny said. "I haven't figured that out."

"I don't think it's anything you can know in advance," she said. "You have to learn as you go along."

"I asked my parents once how they had managed to stay together so long," Danny said. "My mother told me that, being Catholic, divorce was never a possibility, so they had to make things work."

"What did your father say?"

"He said he got lucky when he met my mother."

"Aww, that's sweet."

"Sweet. But not very helpful." He shifted in his seat. "I need more coffee. When you see a good place, pull in."

When they emerged from the coffee shop half an hour later, Danny walked to the driver's side. "Do you care if I drive for awhile?" he asked.

"All right." She handed him the keys, only a little nervous about turning over the car to him. But he turned out to be a good driver, careful but not overly so, guiding them smoothly through the moderately heavy traffic. He turned the radio to an alternative music station; and Nina found herself growing drowsy in the heat of the sun pouring through the windshield, lulled by the hum of the tires on pavement.

She woke with a start as the car rocked in a dip in a gravel pull out. "Where are we?" she asked, looking around at the unfamiliar surroundings. "Is something wrong?"

"It's lunchtime," Danny said. "I thought we'd have a picnic."

She saw now that they were in a roadside park, with picnic tables set among the trees. She followed Danny around to the back of the car and helped him unload the cooler and a bag of plates and cups.

"What is all this?" she asked, as he arranged plastic containers of food on one of the picnic tables.

"Chicken satay and Thai noodle salad." He handed her a paper plate. "Sodas or water to drink."

Nina hadn't realized she was hungry until she tasted the food. "This is great," she said. "Where did you get it?"

"I made it."

"Then you get to do all the cooking on this trip," she said.

"If I cook, you clean."

"That's only fair."

He lay back on the picnic bench. "It's nice here, isn't it?" he said.

She looked around the little park. Tall oaks shaded the tables and benches and a children's play set with swings, a slide, and jungle gym. Two little boys raced around the jungle gym while a smiling woman looked on. A stone hut housed restrooms. "It is pretty," she said. Already they seemed worlds away from the bustling city. "I'm going to check out the restroom."

Danny's answer was a grunt. She gathered up the trash from their meal and carried it to the trash can in front of the ladies' room. When she returned to the table, he was asleep, hands folded on his stomach, mouth slightly open. Smiling to herself, she retrieved her sketch pad and charcoal from the car and took a seat on a bench nearby.

She had sketched many people before, in art classes and coffee shops, in parks and on the street, both strangers and people who were known to her. She strove to capture their form, but also their personality—the quirk of a smile, the glint in the eye, the expressive gestures they made with their hands. The drawing became a kind of partnership between artist and subject.

But never had a drawing felt so intimate to her. Perhaps it was because Danny didn't know he was being sketched, placing her in the role of voyeur spying on his sleeping form. She traced his limbs with her eyes, then transferred what she saw to the page, freed by his slumber to allow her gaze to linger over the muscular curve of his shoulders or the pleasing flatness of his stomach or the graceful length of his fingers clasped there.

She spent the most time on his face, recreating the soft curve of his cheek, the dimple in his chin, the full lips. Her own lips tingled as she worked, imagination working overtime. What would happen if she walked up now and kissed him as he slept? When he opened his eyes and saw it was her, would he pull her into his arms or push her away?

A car door slammed and Danny woke with a start. He yawned and sat up and blinked at Nina. "How long have I been asleep?" he asked.

She shrugged. "Half an hour or so."

He wiped his hand across his face. "I guess I was more tired than I thought. I didn't sleep well last night."

"Excited about the trip?" She'd had a restless night herself, torn between anticipation and dread for the outing.

"Right." He nodded to the sketch pad. "What are you drawing?"

She felt a blush heat her cheeks, and she cradled the pad to her chest, taking care not to smudge the charcoal.

"Let me see." He stood and came to stand beside her, reaching for the pad.

Curious to see his reaction, she moved the pad away from her, revealing the sketch of him asleep on the bench. She'd shown him from the waist up, the bench a bare outline beneath him.

He stared at the portrait a long moment—so long she began to get nervous. "You were a very good subject," she said, trying to lighten the moment. "You hardly moved at all."

"That's amazing." He put a hand on her shoulder. "What are you going to do with it?"

"I don't know." She'd thought she might hang the drawing in her apartment, where she could look at it and think of him. But maybe that was a bad idea. "Do you want it? Renee might like to have it."

"Renee won't want it," he said.

"Do you think she'd be upset because I didn't want to paint the two of you together?"

He took his hand from her and moved to the table, where he began gathering up the rest of the picnic supplies. "Renee and I split up. She's moving into a place of her own this week while we're gone."

Nina put a hand to her chest, as if to hide the fierce beating of her heart. She wondered for a moment if she was the one who had fallen asleep. This was a dream—Danny telling her so calmly that the main obstacle to the two of them being together was now gone.

But no. She was sure she was awake. "What happened?" she asked.

He shook his head. "We didn't want the same things anymore." He picked up the cooler. "I don't want to talk about it right now. Are you ready to go?"

"Sure." She followed him to the car and restowed her art supplies.

He handed her the keys. "You drive for awhile," he said. "I'm still pretty sleepy."

Was he really sleepy after his nap, or was that merely an excuse not to talk? It didn't matter. She wasn't necessarily in the mood for conversation, either. She had too much to think about. Renee and Danny had split up. Renee was moving out of their apartment. He was a single man. For so long she hadn't allowed herself to think of him that way—as available.

Not so fast, she told herself as she pulled the car back out onto the highway. *Single does not mean available. He's obviously upset about the way things ended with Renee. The last thing a man like that wants is another relationship. Right now, he needs a friend, not a girlfriend. Nothing between us has changed. And it may never change.*

But she couldn't completely quell the happiness blossoming inside her. Danny's news had been unexpected and shocking, but it had given her a wonderful gift. He'd given her hope that one day things could be different between them. One day maybe they could be more than just friends.

When he was honest with himself, Danny could admit he'd seen the storm coming. He'd known Renee wasn't happy—and he certainly hadn't been happy, either. When she'd announced she wasn't coming on the camping trip he'd felt relief, not regret. In that moment he'd realized he'd fallen completely out of love with Renee. All that was left was to find a way to end things between them as gracefully as possible.

But of course, endings seldom come gracefully. Yesterday afternoon, as he'd packed for this trip, he'd searched his mind for the right words to say. But how do you tell someone you once loved that your feelings have changed? He'd braced himself for anger and tears, and vowed to let her rail at him as long as she needed to, with no anger on his part.

Instead, she'd made the first move, startling him with her directness. "If you go on this trip, don't bother to come back," she said.

He'd stared at her a long moment, not sure if he'd heard her right. "Are you throwing me out?" he asked. "Over a camping trip?"

"This isn't about a camping trip and you know it." Her expression had softened a little. "We used to have such good times together, but lately you've been so . . . distant."

He shoved aside the duffle bag he'd been packing and sat on the side of the bed. "You're not happy," he said. An obvious statement, maybe, but one he wanted to make.

"Neither are you." She sat down beside him. "I thought things would be so different after graduation," she said. "That we'd buy a house and get married and have children—that we'd be partners and have common goals."

She made love sound like a business contract—all plans and practicalities. What happened to spontaneity and creativity and fun? "That's not what I want right now," he said.

"I've given you five years," she said. "I'm tired of waiting."

He risked looking at her, at her eyes, red-rimmed from crying. When had she cried, and why hadn't he noticed? He hated this feeling that he'd failed her, yet at the same time a weight had been rolled off his shoulders. "I'm sorry," he said. "I never meant to hurt you."

"You may not have meant to, but you have."

"I'm sorry," he said again, then stood. "I'll move out when I get back from this trip."

"Don't bother." She stood also. "My sister's offered to let me move in with her, until I can find my own place."

"All right." Again, that sense of relief. She was making this easy. Probably easier than he deserved.

"I'm taking Mephisto with me," she said, in a voice that offered no room for argument.

What did it say about him that he felt more regret over losing the cat than losing Renee? "All right," he said again. He would give her that much. Maybe it was some relic of his Catholic upbringing that made him feel he ought to suffer a little for his sin of falling out of love with her.

That guilt had lingered as he'd carried his gear to the curb the next morning. The door of the bedroom had remained firmly shut against him. He'd spent an uncomfortable night on the sofa, kept awake by his warring emotions and the uncomfortable design of the furniture. He'd gone downstairs earlier than he needed to, after kissing the cat and giving it a farewell treat. He preferred the humid dawn stillness on the sidewalk to the cold silence of the apartment.

Not until he saw Nina did the full impact of his new status hit him. He was a single man again. Available. And he was about to embark on a week-long vacation with a woman who stirred him in a way no woman had in a long time. In a few hours the whole tenor of the trip had changed for him, but was that good or bad? Could Nina see him as more than buddy and pseudobrother? Would she think he was taking advantage if he made a move on her?

And what kind of jerk did it make him if he went straight from the arms of one woman to another?

This last thought brought him up short and made him promise to himself that he'd be on his best behavior this week. He wouldn't screw up a good friendship for the sake of lust, and he'd cut off his arm before he'd do anything to make Nina think less of him.

That had been this morning. Now it was late afternoon and he was slumped in the passenger seat of her car, eyes firmly shut, pretending to sleep. Eyes shut, because the only alternative was to open them and stare at her, because he couldn't get enough of looking at her.

Closing his eyes may have prevented him from seeing her beautiful face, but it didn't make him any less aware of her a scant three feet beside him now. With every breath he inhaled the faint aroma of her perfume. Beneath the music on the radio he listened to the squeak of the seat as she shifted position or the chime of her bracelet against the steering wheel. Every sense was keenly attuned to her, rendering every other stimulus only so much outside interference.

He couldn't believe he'd slept through her sketching him. How had he not felt her gaze on him? She'd captured him so perfectly, from the quirk of one eyebrow to the way his T-shirt had wrinkled under one arm. The drawing had been executed with great skill, but also with great tenderness. That tenderness was almost his undoing. Only fear that she'd think he was crazy had kept him from declaring his feelings for her on the spot.

"You can't possibly be sleeping all this time," she said.

He opened his eyes and found her looking at him. The car was stopped at a red light in some smallish town that had a vaguely New England look to it, with half-timbered store fronts and stone saltbox houses fronting narrow, shaded streets. "What did you say?" he asked.

"You can't have been sleeping all this time. Are you avoiding me?"

"I forgot my sunglasses and the light hurts my eyes," he lied. A pitiful lie, he could admit.

"Look in the glove box. I think the sunglasses we wore that night at Coney Island are still there."

He opened the box and found the glasses he'd worn that night. Was it really only five weeks ago? He put them on and thought he caught the faint aroma of funnel cakes and cotton candy. "I had such a good time that night," he said.

"Me too." She put on her blinker and made a right turn.

"Where are we?" he asked.

"Waltham, Massachusetts. I'm tired of driving. I thought we might stop and look around."

"Good idea."

She found a parking spot at the curb and they got out and made their way down the sidewalk, past shops selling books and boots and women's clothing. The storefronts were draped in red, white, and blue bunting in anticipation of the Independence Day holiday, and flags fluttered from light poles at every corner. In silent agreement they turned into a coffee shop, then took their drinks to a table on the sidewalk. "You didn't answer my question," she said. "Are you avoiding talking to me?"

"No." He stared into the brown swirl of coffee and milk. "Yes. Only because I don't know what to say."

"About what?"

"Do you think I'm a jerk for breaking things off with Renee?"

"I don't think you could ever be a jerk."

"I doubt Renee would agree with you."

"Would it have been better for you to pretend something you didn't feel, just because it's what some people expected of you?"

"When she talked about the future she had planned for us, she never mentioned love. She said we should be partners, with the same goals."

Nina was silent for a moment, her full lips pursed, brow furrowed in concentration. "I think . . . " Her voice trailed away and she started again. "I think I would rather go through the pain of finding out someone I cared about didn't feel the same for me, than go through life pretending things were all right when they really weren't. Inside, I would always know something was missing, no matter what other people saw on the outside."

"She said I'd grown distant. There was no reason for us to stay together when neither one of us was happy."

"At least now she'll have a chance to find someone who can make her happy," Nina said.

"I hope she does. She deserves to have all the things she wants, but I couldn't be the man to give them to her."

"You deserve happiness too," Nina said.

"No one can be happy all the time, but I think we're at the point in our lives where we should be experimenting . . . trying out new things to see what it is that truly makes us happy. Maybe some people come out of college knowing everything they need to make their life complete, but the rest of us need to discover that as we go along."

"Sometimes you don't know what you like until you try it," Nina said. "Like funnel cakes."

"Or jazz. Or Thai food. Or even camping." Or spending a week in another country with a woman who's become your best friend.

"I want to try all sorts of new things this trip," she said. "I've never been to Canada before."

"Me either." He drank the last of his coffee. "Let's start by checking out Waltham."

"Let's."

They spent the next hour poking around in antique stores and souvenir shops. Nina retrieved her camera from the car and took pictures of a dog on the sidewalk in a red, white, and blue scarf, and of Danny posed beside a stern-looking cigar-store Indian in front of an antique store. They watched workmen in the town park set up chairs in front of the bandstand in preparation for the next day's concert.

"Hialeah has a huge Fourth of July celebration," Danny said. "A parade and music and barbecues. In a city of so many first- and second-generation Americans, the holiday means a lot."

"My first Fourth of July in the United States, I didn't really understand the significance," Nina said. "I liked the parties and music—and I especially liked the fireworks."

"Bombs bursting in air. You have a violent streak."

"No." She shoved him. "I liked the light and color—the spectacle of it all. It made the holiday seem more . . . significant, somehow. Something to shout about."

"I like the fireworks, too. And it is one of the things that sets the Fourth of July apart from, say, Labor Day."

"I guess you'll be celebrating your own Independence Day this year," Nina said.

"I hadn't really thought of it that way, but I guess so."

"We'll drink a toast to freedom, and all the possibilities that holds."

Seven

Life is more dazzling
Through the lens of remembrance,
Its flaws glossed over.

THEY CAMPED THAT NIGHT IN A PARK outside of Portland, Maine, the Atlantic Ocean crashing on the rocky beach below. Danny grilled burgers and they washed them down with bottles of dark beer. After supper, he built a campfire and they spread their sleeping bags beside it to sit. A soft breeze brought the smell of saltwater and fish, and a damp chill that made Nina wrap a sweater around her shoulders and sit closer to the flames.

She studied Danny's face as he leaned forward to add another stick of wood to the fire. Light flickered across his sculpted cheeks, casting his eyes in shadow so she couldn't read his expression. A dark dusting of beard showed along his jaw, rough and masculine. She had always thought of him as a man of the city, always perfectly groomed and at home in nightclubs and cafés, smart and sophisticated. Yet here he was in the middle of nowhere, competent and calm as any experienced woodsman. She had the sense there was no environment he wouldn't make his own. He looked up and caught her staring at him, and she was grateful for the darkness to hide her blush. "Would you play your guitar for me?" she asked.

"All right." He rose and fetched the guitar case from the car, then spent some time tuning it, plucking at the strings and turning the pegs while she watched. He strummed a few chords. "What would you like to hear?" he asked.

"Whatever you want to play."

He nodded, and played a few notes of a tune that wasn't familiar to her. She had expected a pop song or maybe one of the folk tunes she'd heard around campfires in her youth. Instead, this was a simple, lilting melody that was neither folk nor pop. "You looked at me and I was lost," he sang, and a chill danced up her spine.

The song was a love song, simple and sweet and heartfelt without being cloying. Danny had a soft, low singing voice. A sexy voice, but then, in her current mood, lulled by the firelight and slightly buzzed from the beer, she thought everything about him was sexy.

The man just broke up with his girlfriend, she reminded herself. *Even if it was the right thing to do, they were together five years. It's bound to be a shock. I will not be the pushy woman who goes after him just because he's suddenly single.* She could be strong and assertive when she needed to be, but that was too pushy. Too predatory.

For all she knew, he'd chosen this song because it reminded him of Renee. This thought was a wet blanket smothering her desire. He finished the song and she applauded. "That was beautiful," she said.

"Thanks. I wrote it."

"You wrote it?" Was there anything he couldn't do?

He shrugged. "When I was twelve I started a band with some

friends. We got to be pretty good. We played parties and festivals and stuff in our neighborhood and even did some low-budget recording."

"Why didn't you pursue singing as a career?"

"I really got into listening to other people's music. I started getting jobs as a DJ and discovering new bands or obscure cuts from familiar bands and sharing them with others became more important. Now I only play for my own amusement."

"Will you play some more for me?"

"Of course."

He did play a pop song then, and she sang along. Then they ran through a string of campfire songs, laughing when they couldn't remember all the words. He finished with another song he wrote—a love song.

"Are all your songs love songs?" she asked.

"Love is such a universal emotion," he said. "And the experience of love—whether it's love of family and friends, or romantic love—is the most important experience we ever have. It colors and influences everything we do."

"Yes," she agreed. "Yes." Even if she and Danny never became lovers, she would always love him as one of her dearest friends. Knowing him had changed her.

He set aside the guitar and leaned back on his elbows, looking up at the stars. "This is beautiful," he said. "One thing I miss, living in New York—you can't really see the stars."

"When I was little I would visit my grandparents' summer house in the country, in Russia. At night my grandfather would sometimes set up a telescope and show me the stars. When I was very little, I thought the stars preferred the country, too, since there were so many more of them there."

"If you could live anywhere, where would it be?" he asked.

"Anywhere?" She lay back beside him, conscious of him so close by, but not quite touching her. "I don't know. Italy is beautiful and there's so much art. I sometimes miss Russia, but it would be hard to make it as an artist there, especially having been away so many years. I love New York, though it can be very expensive sometimes. Where would you live?"

"I don't know. Sometimes I think it would be fun to throw a dart at a map and go wherever it lands."

"What if it was some horrible place like East Armpit, Nowheresville?"

"That would be part of the challenge—to make a go of it wherever you ended up."

"Do you really think you could do that?"

"I think there are good people and good things every place you go. In some places you might have to look harder to find them, but I believe I could."

"I never thought about it that way, but I probably could too," she said. "I'm just not sure I would want to."

"Then here's another question." He rolled onto his side, facing her. Firelight illuminated half his face, the other thrust in darkness, like a harlequin mask. "If you were stranded on a deserted island and could have only one other person with you, who would it be? It could be a family member, a friend, or even a famous person or a person from history."

"So I could pick a famous engineer who could get us off the island," she said. "Someone like Leonardo da Vinci?"

"You could. Or you could pick the person you thought would be the best company."

"That one is easy," she said. "I would pick you."

An emotion she couldn't read—or maybe one she didn't want to read—flashed across his face. They'd moved into dangerous territory once more. Time to tread lightly.

She rose, and gathered up her sleeping bag. "Good night, Danny. I'll see you in the morning."

Then she crawled into her tent where she lay for a long while, staring into the darkness and trying, but failing, to stop imagining what it would be like if Danny were in here with her, sharing her sleeping bag and more than conversation.

They made an early start the next morning, awakened by the drone of a foghorn just off the coast. Danny felt as if he'd hardly slept; Nina's last pronouncement, along with her abrupt departure from the campfire, had kept him awake much of the night. At one point he'd debated getting up and calling at the door of her tent, but what if she took the gesture the wrong way? What if she thought he was imposing himself on her, that it was only his own ego that made him think she'd welcome such a gesture?

He finally dozed off to a restless sleep and woke feeling groggy and ill-used. But the crisp morning air and Nina's appearance beside him as he coaxed the campfire to life restored him somewhat. She was fresh scrubbed and pink cheeked, a colorful scarf tied in her hair, a peasant blouse accenting her curves. He definitely had nothing to complain about with company like this.

He made breakfast burritos, and they repacked the car and set out. The drive up the coast was breathtaking rock cliffs and wheeling sea birds and white-capped waves on one side, green woods or farm meadows on the other. They stopped often to take photographs of the rugged coastline, and at lunch Nina filled several pages of a sketchbook with drawings.

At the Canadian border, they compared passport photos as they waited for their turn to present their documents to the border guard. "You look all serious and mysterious," Danny pronounced as he studied the photograph of her taken five years before. Her hair had been longer and her bangs fell over one eye, à la Greta Garbo. "You look like a movie star." He grinned. "Or a Russian spy."

He expected her to bristle at this. Instead, she gave him a knowing look. "You look like the lead singer in a boy band," she said.

"A boy band!" He put a hand over his heart, pretending to be wounded.

"Yes. All boyish grin and clean-cut good looks. The kind of face teen girls would have on posters in their rooms." Not the masculine image a man hoped to convey to the woman of his dreams, but he heard no disdain in her voice, so counted it all good.

Fog set in almost immediately after they crossed the border, obscuring the view. "My first time in Canada and I can't even see it," he said as he piloted the car down the coast highway.

"Maybe the fog will burn off later."

"Maybe it will." For now, the white curtain around them was like a veil, separating them from the world, making the interior of the little car even more intimate. With nothing to focus on outside the window, their attention was forced inward. He wondered if Nina felt this, too, and if that was why she turned the conversation to the friends they'd left behind. "I wonder what our friends are doing right now," she said.

"Randy should be setting up to DJ at the gig on Long Island," he said.

"What was it—some kind of corporate function?" she asked.

"No. I think it was a big family barbecue for folks who could afford to hire a DJ for the occasion."

"You don't think it was Tawny's family's party, do you?" Nina said. "Their barbecue was on Long Island. And people might hire a DJ for a big engagement party."

He laughed. "Stranger things have happened. What do you think Tawny will do if it is him?"

"I don't know. She said Randy wasn't the kind of guy she wanted to bring home to her parents."

"Yeah, I can't picture Randy with that tony crowd. Then again, he might liven up a dull party."

"I'll definitely have to call Tawny and find out how things went. But the person I really want to hear from is Erin."

"Ah yes. Partying on the river with the rich, older, potential boyfriend."

"He's not that much older. And he doesn't have to have that much money to be richer than Erin. And don't forget handsome. She was very clear on that point."

"I hope they live happily ever after," Danny said. "Though I'm always suspicious of women who focus so much on a man's wallet." Not that he'd had much experience with that, but he'd seen it enough at the clubs where he'd worked as a DJ—women who started conversations by asking about your job and where you lived, and dismissing you if the profession and address didn't fulfill their monetary expectations.

"Erin's not a gold digger." Nina defended her friend. "But when you're broke all the time in a city like New York, a man who isn't in the same position does hold a certain attraction."

"I thought women wanted to be independent and pay their own way."

"If I have to choose between pride and a nice steak dinner, I'm choosing the steak dinner," she said. "But only if I already like the guy anyway. And Erin clearly likes this guy."

"Then I wish her luck."

That left Renee, the only one who was originally supposed to be on this trip that they hadn't discussed. Danny didn't want to bring up something that might be awkward for Nina, yet he didn't want to imply that there were any subjects off-limits between them, either. "I imagine Renee is out of the apartment by now," he said.

"You really think she's leaving so soon?" Nina frowned. "When she has at least a week?"

"She's moving in with her sister in Queens, then I think she's going to look for a house."

"At least she'll have her house."

"Renee will be fine," he said. "She knows exactly what she wants in life and I have no doubt she'll get it."

"Sometimes I think I know what I want," Nina said. "But then the picture changes."

"I like being flexible," Danny said. "Open to whatever comes along." He glanced in the rearview mirror and switched on his blinker to change lanes. "I'll have to advertise for a roommate when we get back to the city," he said. "To help with the rent."

"You won't have trouble finding someone. People are always looking for roommates. If my place weren't so tiny, I'd have one myself."

"Your place *is* tiny."

"It was all I could afford if I wanted to live on my own. Though lately I've been thinking I might be better off splitting rent with a couple of other people."

"Privacy is worth something though, right?"

"Yes. But when I have to ask my mother for money to pay the rent, I'm not so sure."

They decided to spend a couple of days at Fundy National Park, on the Bay of Fundy, which was known for its dramatic changes of tides. "Not that we can see them in this fog," Danny said as he pounded tent stakes into the ground.

"I don't know. I like it here." She glanced around the fog-shrouded campground. "It's all so mysterious," she said. "Like Russia, when I was little, and I was too small to see around all the trees in the forest."

He imagined her as a little girl, big blue eyes set in a doll-like face, standing in a forest of tree trunks, leafy branches a canopy high overhead. "Like those fairy tales you draw," he said.

"Yes!" She smiled, clearly pleased he understood.

They hiked, camera in hand, and she collected some interesting stones and lichen. "I might make a collage," she said.

"Or a disguise." Danny held a bit of the lichen to his lip and arched his brow and mugged a melodrama villain smile. Nina laughed and snapped a picture.

The park featured a small restaurant and he proposed they splurge on dinner out. "After all, it's a holiday," he said. "And too damp for a barbecue."

Nina knew she should stick to her budget, but the invitation was too tempting. She'd save money somewhere else on the trip. They shared a meal of mussels and crabs, eating off of each other's plates and talking about everything from old Dudley Do-Right cartoons (they'd both watched reruns as children) to Canadian hockey (about which she knew nothing) to the best seafood restaurants in New York (they were torn between an Italian place he knew in the East Village and a Vietnamese specialty shop in their own neighborhood). They shared a bottle of wine and lingered over coffee.

When they left the restaurant it was full dark. The sky had cleared enough for a few stars to show through the clouds, tiny glints of silver against a soft-black wash. They walked arm in arm back to camp, the crash of the waves providing background music for their stroll. They stopped at a scenic overlook on the cliffs, staring out at the buoy lights.

To Danny, the air shimmered with expectation. Even as he looked out at the ocean and listened to the pounding surf, he was focused on the woman beside him—on the warm curve of her hip against his and the soft perfume of her hair. His heart raced as if he'd run up a flight of stairs, but he was determined not to let this moment pass. "If we'd been planning this right, we'd have spent one more night below the border," he said. "That way you'd have been sure to have fireworks tonight."

"It doesn't matter," she said. "It's beautiful here."

He turned to look at her profile. He loved that she was almost the same height, so that he never had to look down on her, but always directly at her. "I've been thinking about what you said last night," he said.

She frowned, just a tiny wrinkling of her brow. "What did I say?"

"You said the person you'd most like to be stranded with on a desert island would be me."

"Oh, that." Her eyes met his, and his heart leaped in his chest. Why was she looking at him that way, as if she was trying to see inside of him?

"I think the person I'd most want to be stranded with is you."

Nina held her breath, unsure at first she'd heard Danny correctly. He touched her cheek, his skin as heated as the smoldering look in his eyes. She leaned toward him, swaying a little with the effort of holding back.

Kiss me, she thought. She wondered later if she'd whispered the words out loud. He obeyed the command, covering her lips with his own, his arms encircling her, holding her tightly against him.

She slid her hand up between them, to his chest. Not to push him away, but to bunch the fabric of his shirt in her fist, holding him to her. All the months of wanting and waiting and wondering melted away in the heat of that kiss. His lips against hers were firm and sure, with none of the awkwardness of most first kisses. They'd been anticipating this moment too long, the kiss rehearsed too often, in dreams and the subconscious, so that when the moment came they knew exactly what to do. They kissed, not like friends exploring new territory, but like experienced lovers revisiting favorite terrain.

She slid her hand up to the base of his throat, and felt the pounding of his pulse there, matching the rhythm of her own thudding heart. He gave a soft groan and tore his mouth from hers, and stared into her eyes.

"You've gone and done it now," she said.

With an anguished look, he closed his eyes and pressed his forehead against hers. "Don't tell me I've ruined it," he said.

"No." She touched the dimple in his chin with the tip of her finger, pleased to find it a perfect fit. "You haven't ruined it. But you don't think I'm going to stop at one kiss, do you?"

His answer was another kiss that had her arching against him, jelly legged and grateful for his arms supporting her. "You can forget about sleeping in your own tent tonight," she said when they were forced to come up for air.

"We'd better go now before I undress you right here in public."

She was tempted to run back to camp, but instead they walked, pausing often in the shadows to embrace, taking advantage of the darkness to grope each other like horny teenagers, running hands up under each other's shirts, teasing then pulling away, drawing out the moments of discovery.

Back at camp, Nina felt suddenly shy. She followed Danny into his tent, where they sat side by side on his sleeping bag. "You're sure about this?" he asked, smoothing his hand down her arm.

"Yes." She kissed his cheek. "Yes."

He reached for the hem of her T-shirt and pushed it up, over her bra. She held up her arms and let him peel it off, then was surprised when he leaned away from her. "I only wanted a light so I could see," he said, returning to her side with a battery-powered lantern. He set this by the head of his sleeping bag, where it cast a yellow glow over his pillow, dimly illuminating the space beyond.

"That's better," he said, and reached around and unhooked the clasp of her bra.

A chill overtook her as the bra fell away, and she fought the urge to cover herself. She felt so vulnerable with him still dressed. But then, that was the beauty of intimacy, that you could be so vulnerable, and yet so safe. She would always feel safe with Danny. Cherished.

"You're so beautiful," he said, cradling her breasts in his hands. He swept his thumbs across her nipples, and she gasped and arched toward him, and reached for the hem of his shirt.

His shirt came off, and the rest of their clothes soon followed, though undressing in the confines of a small tent required more contortion than she would have thought. They laughed as they wiggled out of jeans and skimmed off underwear, the humor breaking the tension some.

But then they were both naked, facing each other, stretched out on his sleeping bag, and Nina was shaky with desire once more.

"I should paint you like this," she said, running her hand along the strong line of his hip and thigh.

"I'll let you do that," he said. "I'll let you do anything you want."

He pulled her close and she reveled in the feel of him, fitting so perfectly against her, hot and supple and muscular. They explored with lips and hands, tracing the indentation beneath the collar bone or the curve of a bicep, letting the tension build.

"We need to stop for just a minute," he said, covering her hand with his own to still her.

"Why?"

"I need to get a condom out of my pack." He reached across her and dragged the backpack closer. She watched him fish out the foil packet and tear it open.

"You brought condoms?" she asked. Which, of course, wasn't the real question at all.

The look he gave her sent a fresh wave of arousal through her. "You have to know how much I've wanted you," he said. "I couldn't do anything about it before, but now that I'm free I wasn't going to waste an opportunity because of the lack of a condom."

"Oh." The knowledge that he'd been thinking of her as much as she'd been thinking of him sent a shudder of delight through her.

He sheathed himself, then moved over her. "Are you ready?" he asked.

"I've been ready for you for a long time."

He moved tentatively at first, as if afraid he might break her. But passion soon overcame caution, and they found a satisfying rhythm between the urgency that drove them and the need to savor this moment. Nina kept her eyes open, watching the play of emotion on his face, almost overwhelmed by the intensity of her own feelings. Then the needs of her body pushed aside coherent thought and she closed her eyes and rode the waves of sensation upward. She came with a cry of pure joy, and he followed with a guttural moan, then lay atop her, a comforting weight.

Eventually he slid over to lay beside her, and pulled the top of the sleeping bag over them to shield them from the night chill. "Danny?" she said as he settled against her.

"Mmmm."

"What you said earlier about not having fireworks tonight? You were wrong."

He chuckled. "I guess I was." He pulled her closer, and she was sure she'd lay awake for hours, reliving the magic of this night. But she fell asleep within minutes, cradled in his arms.

Eight

The best mementos
Are those carried in our minds
Wherever we go.

NOVA SCOTIA MIGHT BE HOME to grizzly bears and hockey greats, but Nina would always think of it as the place she had well and truly fallen in love with Danny. They spent their days exploring the scenery along the Canadian coast and their nights exploring each other. More than the physical closeness, she treasured the time spent in uninterrupted conversation, about everything from religious philosophy to favorite childhood television shows. She supposed this was what a honeymoon was like—days spent focused almost exclusively on each other, learning that person inside and out.

On the fifth day of the trip, Erin telephoned. When Nina saw her friend's number on her cell phone display she felt a stab of guilt. Erin would be dying to share the details of her Fourth of July with Thad, and Nina had scarcely thought of her in days. "Hello," she answered.

"Thank God you answered. I was about ready to send out the Royal Mounted Police, or whoever is responsible for tracking down missing persons up there."

"Hi Erin." Nina glanced at Danny. "How are you?"

Danny waved and gestured that he'd give her some privacy, then set off down the trail away from the spot where they'd set up camp. "We'll get to me in a minute," Erin said. "How are *you*? And how is Danny? No one I've talked to has heard a word out of either of you. What are you two doing up there in Canada? Or can't I guess?"

Nina thought of what they'd been doing—particularly the sessions of heated lovemaking in Danny's tent. "Oh, we've been keeping busy," she said. "Nova Scotia is beautiful."

"*Busy*? Is that all you have to say for yourself? I know he and Renee split up before he left New York. Tawny talked to her the other day and got the whole scoop."

"What did she say?" Nina braced herself for accusations that she'd stolen Danny from Renee.

"Just that things didn't work out between them, and she had to move on with her life."

"Did Tawny say if she sounded very upset?"

"I think she was upset, but not devastated. I think the relationship had merely worn itself out—maybe because he realized you were a better match for him."

"Oh. Well, I don't know about that. . . ." Nina struggled for the right words, even as she was secretly pleased with Erin's assessment.

"So what have you two really been up to?" Erin asked.

"Well . . ." Nina stalled. Not that she had any intention of keeping her new relationship with Danny a secret, but she hadn't imagined breaking the news to Erin—and by default, to their entire social circle—over the phone.

"You don't even have to tell me," Erin said. "I hear it in your voice. The two of you are having wild monkey sex morning and night."

This wasn't that far from the truth. Could Erin really tell all of that just from Nina's voice? Or was she a good guesser? "Let's just say we're sharing a tent now," she said. "And a sleeping bag."

Erin squealed so loudly Nina had to hold the phone away from her ear. "I knew you two would get together," Erin said, her voice ringing with triumph.

"You did?"

"Of course. Didn't I tell you the first night you met him at the Castle? You two were meant for each other. "

"You couldn't have known that," Nina protested. "He was with Renee."

"He was with Renee, but he wanted you."

"But he never did anything." Danny had always been the perfect gentleman. The perfect friend.

"He didn't have to do anything. You two are such a perfect match—not just physically, but intellectually. Creatively. Didn't you ever notice how when he talked about some obscure film or new music group, you were practically the only one who had anything intelligent to add to the conversation? None of the rest of us could keep up."

Thinking back, Nina could admit that even when they were in a group, she and Danny often ended up having a private conversation. And long after everyone else would drift away to go home or to another bar or restaurant or coffee shop, she and Danny would sit and talk—or sometimes merely sit in companionable silence, each with a book and a cup of coffee, content to sit across from each other for hours. Sometimes she would look up and catch him watching her, and they'd both smile, as if sharing a special secret. Could the secret have been that they were already in love? "Danny and I have always been good friends," she said.

"You know they say the best love matches start out as friend-ships," Erin said. "So what are you going to do now? Elope?"

Nina almost dropped her phone. "No! We're nowhere near ready for that."

"Why not? I'm seriously considering it, myself. A quick trip to Vegas seems so much less a headache than planning a big wedding."

"Erin! Are you engaged?"

"Not yet, but the way things are going, it won't be long. Thad has let me know he's ready to settle down, and I am definitely ready to be Mrs. Thad Coffman."

"But you've only know him a few weeks, and dated him scarcely a few days. Tell me everything."

Erin needed no prodding. "It was magic, Nina. He picked me up for our date on the Fourth and brought me flowers. Red, white, and blue mums, can you believe it? The party was with a bunch of people he knew: old friends, some family, and some business associates. I usually don't like that sort of thing for a first date because you know how it can be—the guy leaves you alone at the buffet table while he mingles with everyone else, and you end up standing there by the onion dip trying not to look as mis-erable as you feel. But Thad wasn't like that at all. He stayed by my side all day, made sure I always had a drink or food or shade or someone to talk to. He was amazing."

Erin went on for another ten minutes about the amazing Thad. He and Erin had been practically inseparable since the Fourth. "He's taking me to meet his parents this weekend," Erin gushed. "Can you believe it? That's always a good sign, don't you think?"

"Sounds like it."

"You should feel Danny out about introducing you to his folks."

Nina blanched. Telling their friends they were a couple was a big enough step for her and Danny. She wasn't ready to get their parents involved. "Tell me what everyone else is up to," she said. "Did Tawny have a good time at her parents' barbecue? Did Randy's gig go well?"

Erin let out a whoop of laughter. "I forgot you didn't know. Randy definitely had a good time this weekend. He was the DJ Tawny's parents had hired for their barbecue."

"You're kidding." Wait until she told Danny.

"I'm not kidding. You remember how Tawny was all worried what her family might think of Randy so she was secretly glad he had to work this weekend. But it turns out, her family loves him."

"So that's great, right?" Nina said.

"Not so great. Tawny isn't sure she's that into Randy now that her parents want to adopt him. I think part of the attraction for her before was that she was so sure her mom and dad wouldn't approve."

"Awkward," Nina said.

"Who needs soap operas, right?" Erin said. "Anyway, I can't wait for you to get home. I want to introduce you to Thad . . . and to hear all about you and Danny."

When Danny came strolling back into camp a few minutes later, he found Nina seated in a folding chair beside the remains of last night's campfire, her phone in her lap. "How's Erin?" he asked.

"In love."

"Things went that well with Thad, huh?"

"Apparently so. Oh, and Randy's gig on the Fourth on Long Island? It *was* Tawny's parents. And now they love him, but Tawny isn't so keen on him anymore."

"Randy's never dated a woman more than a few months in the three years I've known him," Danny said. "I didn't get the sense he was serious enough about Tawny to be heartbroken if she dumped him."

Talk of breaking up—even of other people's break ups—made Nina uncomfortable. "Where did you go?" she asked. "See anything interesting?"

"I walked up to the little camp store. I checked my voice mail. I've been putting it off for a few days, so the message box was full."

"Oh?" Who had called him? Renee, begging him to take her back?

"Most of the calls were from John. He's already regretting agreeing to give me this much vacation."

"He really depends on you," she said.

"Too much." He sank into the chair beside her. "Things are really starting to take off for us. John worries we won't be able to keep up. I tell him not to worry, but that's the way he's always been. He says I'm too laid back, and I tell him he pushes too much."

"Who is right?" she asked.

"There's truth on both sides," Danny said. "It's not so much that I'm laid back, but that I like to approach problems at my own pace, in my own way. If someone pushes me too hard, I push back in the opposite direction. John knows this is true and he tries to give me space, but he can't help slipping into the role of bossy, older cousin sometimes."

"So you're stubborn," she said.

He nodded. "Sometimes. But that's not a bad thing. When I really want something, I go after it with everything I have."

"What is it you want?" she asked.

His smile sent heat curling through her. "Right now, I want you."

"It's the middle of the afternoon," she said. Not protesting, merely teasing, drawing out the inevitable moment.

"We haven't made love in the afternoon yet," he said. "We've done it in the morning and at night." He stood and took her hand and pulled her up to stand facing him. "We don't want to leave our experimentations incomplete."

"Is that what this is—an experiment?"

"One with endless permutations," he said. "And no definite ending."

"And what have you concluded from all this experimenting so far?"

He kissed the corner of her mouth. "That I love you." Another kiss. "And I'll never tire of being with you."

She slipped her arms around his neck and melted against him. "I'll never tire of you," she said. "Not when there are so many sides of you to get to know." And so many sides of herself with him to discover.

"I could live like this," Danny said as they packed the car after yet another night camping under the stars. The past seven days with Nina had been an amazing escape from his everyday life. Twice already they'd postponed their return home. Nina had no commitments and Danny had managed to put off work. Predictably, John protested the delay, but Danny ignored his complaints, reminding him he'd promised two full weeks of vacation. Danny wanted to prolong this time alone with Nina as long as possible—and he wanted time to think about what he really wanted for his life. He loved the city and everything there was to do there, but too often lately he didn't feel in control of his own time.

"I love the freedom of travel," Nina said. "But I do miss a comfortable bed." She stowed her easel behind the seat.

"All right, I wouldn't want to spend my life like a gypsy, living out of a tent," he said. "But to have the freedom to come and go when and where you please—that would be ideal."

"All you have to do is make enough money to support that kind of lifestyle," she said.

"That's what I want to do," he said. "Working for John is fine for now, but I've always wanted to make a go of it with my own ideas, to be really independent."

"Like an artist," she said. "Supporting yourself through your own creativity."

"Exactly." He slammed the trunk shut. "Want to take the ferry over to Prince Edward Island this morning? The fog's lifted, so we should have some terrific scenery."

"How much is the ferry?" she asked.

"About sixty dollars, I think, with the car."

She shook her head. "My budget for this trip is already blown. I need to cut back."

"You're on vacation," he said. "You can cut back at home."

"I don't have the money, Danny."

"Thirty dollars? You sell one photograph and you'll have five or ten times that much."

"I can't just sell a photograph because I decide I want to," she said. "You know that."

"You just need someone to help you. I can do that." He put his arm around her. "When we get home, I'll help you set up a website for your work. And we'll put together some advertising— maybe a brochure, or a video."

"You'd do that?"

"Yes. I really believe in you. I want to help you."

"That would be good."

"So stop worrying about the money for the ferry. When are

you going to be in Nova Scotia again? You should see everything you can."

"All right," she relented.

Buoyed by his ideas for helping Nina promote her artwork, he drove the car toward the ferry landing. "One of the things I'm learning with the fashion business is half the battle is making people aware of your product. It must be the same with art."

"But people need to have clothes to wear," Nina said. "They don't need to have paintings and photographs on their walls."

"You're wrong," he said. "People need art. But not all of them realize it."

"You almost make me believe that."

"You have a gift, Nina. You could be a big success."

"It would be easier for me to believe that if I wasn't always worrying about paying the rent."

"How much is your rent every month?" he asked.

"Eight hundred dollars a month."

"My place is twelve hundred for two bedrooms." He glanced at her. "You should move in with me. You'd save two hundred dollars a month."

"You want me to move into your second bedroom?" She frowned.

"No. I want you to move into *my* bedroom." He reached over and squeezed her hand. "We can turn the second bedroom into a studio for you."

She stared at him, eyes wide. "Are you serious?"

"Absolutely." He felt the rush of energy that always overtook him when a new idea seized him. "I need a roommate. You need to save money. And we get along great. It would be perfect."

"We do get along well," she said. "But I don't want to ruin that by rushing into anything."

"We're not rushing. This week together proves we can live together."

"A camping vacation is different from sharing an apartment," she said.

"We have similar personalities. We could make it work."

"When I'm working on a project, I can't drop everything to cook or clean house," she said.

"I don't expect you to do any of that," he said.

"Sometimes I like to sleep late," she said.

"So do I, especially if I've been up late the night before. But even if I have to get up early for work, I don't expect you to get up with me."

"What if it doesn't work out? What if we fight?"

"If we have a fight, we'll work things out." He stopped the car at an intersection and turned to her. "Come on, Nina. You know this is a good idea."

She nodded, but her eyes still held a troubled expression.

"What's bothering you?" he asked.

"I think I just need time to get used to the idea," she said. "I promise to think about it."

A car behind them honked, and he was forced to pull ahead. "You think," he said. "And I'll do my best to persuade you." Now that he'd spent so much time with Nina, he didn't want to be apart from her any more than necessary. Living together was the perfect solution.

Nina hadn't expected a marriage proposal—that would definitely have been too much, too soon. But Danny's proposal that they live together had disappointed her. He'd talked about how well they got along, and what a practical solution it was financially— all true, but not the romantic words a woman wants to hear.

Of course, he'd already told her he loved her. But Danny loved all his friends. His openness about his feelings was one of his most endearing qualities.

Nina couldn't help feeling that if one of their other friends had mentioned financial problems, Danny might have invited them to share his apartment, too. Though not, she had to admit, to share his bed as well.

The thought of spending every night with Danny once they returned to New York definitely appealed to her. And his offer to help her market her artwork touched her. He was gifted about promoting himself and his ideas. Mostly, she appreciated that he understood and supported her art and her ambitions. On the ferry to Prince Edward Island, Nina handed over her portion of the fare for themselves and their car with only a small wince. She wished she could adopt the attitude of "it's only money" but she suspected that was a luxury only the truly financially secure could pull off well.

Once on board the ferry, she and Danny exited the car and went up on deck and took their place at the railing. A chill spray blew back on them as the ferry cut through the choppy waters of the bay. When Nina stumbled to keep her balance, Danny put his arms around her. "Don't want you going over-board," he said.

His arms tightened around her as the boat shuddered in the waves and she leaned against him, the hard plain of his chest and stomach comforting against her back. "I wouldn't have made a very good sailor, I'm afraid," she said. "The ocean is beautiful, but a little frightening."

"I've never sailed," he said. "But I think I'd like it."

She looked back at him. "Is there anything you can't do?" she asked.

He laughed. "Probably. But my parents raised me to believe I could do anything I wanted, and I guess that really sunk in."

"You're the one with the gift, then," she said. "To believe in yourself that way."

"I believe in you that way, too." He kissed her lightly on the lips. "Move in with me, Nina. I want us to be together."

"Not merely because it's practical and will save us both money?"

"Is that what you thought?"

"It's true."

"Yes, but that's not the only reason I want you to move in."

"It's not? Then what other reason do you have?" She challenged him to say it out loud.

"Because I love you, and I don't want to be apart from you any more than I have to. I want to see your face when I wake up in the morning and know that you'll be there waiting when I come home from a trip out of town."

She had a vision of him walking in the door of the apartment, suitcase in hand, and her, dressed in a paint-smudged smock, running to greet him. She'd be eager to tell him about her latest project, and he'd be just as eager to hear her news. They'd talk and kiss, and make love sprawled across his bed, and afterward they'd drink wine and talk long into the night about everything that had happened while they'd been apart.

The image was so real in her mind she could almost believe it had already happened. The idea filled her with such happiness, and her earlier fears receded like the tide. "Yes," she said. "I'll move in with you, Danny. Because it's practical, but also because I believe we will be happy together."

"We will be happy," he said. "Much happier together than I would be if we were apart."

What better declaration of love could a woman ask for? she thought, as they kissed, salt spray washing over them, arms tight around each other, a steadying embrace that would keep them both safe.

Nine

"Home" is all details:
The way the sun hits, the fog
Rolls, and the air smells.

DANNY REPORTED BACK TO WORK upon his return to New York to find his desk papered with memos and notes from John. His cousin had a habit of dashing off notes whenever an idea occurred to him and leaving them for Danny to find. After almost two weeks away, Danny could hardly see his desk for the blizzard of paper. Shaking his head, he began collecting the notes and sorting them. "What does 'lightning bolt' mean?" he asked.

John snatched the paper from him and scowled at it. "I don't know." He tossed the note in the general direction of the trash can; it landed beside the can, in a pile of similarly crumpled papers. "That's the trouble with you being gone so long. I can't remember what I wanted you to do."

"Then it must not be important." Danny pulled out his chair and moved aside a stack of magazines so he could sit. "Maybe you're the one who needs a vacation," he said. "You're getting forgetful in your old age."

John muttered an obscenity. Danny laughed. When they were younger, John enjoyed lording over his younger cousin all the privileges that came with being older, but now Danny had the advantage and John hated it. "Tell me what you think of those new designs," John said, indicating a folder of drawings in the center of the desk. "And follow up with our supplier in California."

"I'll do that. And I'll touch base with that buyer in Houston, too," he said, opening the folder. He felt the familiar rush of energy that came with every new project. As much as he'd enjoyed his time off, he'd missed this too—the urgency of new ideas and the excitement of knowing success was just around the corner. His heart beat a little faster and he felt a little lighter, the way he did when he put together a killer playlist for a night of working as a DJ, or when he discovered a brilliant new independent film to share with friends. He wanted to share his discoveries—whether music, film, or new clothing designs—with others. Being able to do that made this more than a job and worth the long hours and the sometimes grueling travel.

By lunch time, he'd scheduled appointments to meet with contacts in Houston, Dallas, and Chicago, and suggested design changes for two new products to add to the line. He strode into John's office to find his cousin hunched in front of the computer, staring at a spread sheet. "Let's grab some lunch," he said.

"Good idea." John pushed away from the computer. "You can tell me about your trip. Did you see anything interesting?"

"Everything was interesting," Danny said as they headed toward the elevator. "Nova Scotia is beautiful. I'll have to get copies of the photographs Nina took so you can see."

"How did that go—all that time with just Nina?"

"It went very well." He couldn't hold back a grin. The almost two weeks discovering Canada with Nina—and discovering each other—ranked as possibly the best vacation of his life so far.

"I'm not sure I like that look," John said as they stepped into the elevator.

They rode in silence to the lobby surrounded by others, but as soon as they stepped onto the sidewalk, John picked up the conversation. "You're not getting involved with that woman, are you?"

"She isn't 'that woman.' She's Nina. And yes, I'm 'involved.' I love her."

"You just broke up with one woman and already you're in love with another?" John snorted. "You didn't even let your bed get cold."

"It wasn't like that," Danny said. "Renee and I have been drifting apart for months. I've been in love with Nina for a while, but I couldn't do anything about it because I was involved with Renee."

"How do you even know what you feel if you don't give yourself time to cool off from one relationship before you rush into the next?"

"I didn't rush," Danny said. "Love isn't like that."

"Since when are you an expert?"

"I don't tell you what you should feel, so don't you tell me what I should feel," Danny said. He followed John into a Vietnamese café, where they ordered sandwiches and bubble tea.

"Just don't screw things up by rushing into something too fast," John said. "Don't make the same mistakes I did."

Danny's annoyance at his cousin's interference evaporated. So that's what this was all about. "How is Tomas?" Tomas was John's son, who lived with his mother, John's ex-wife, in Queens.

"Tomas is fine." He swallowed, his lips compressed. "Caridad wants to move back to Miami and take Tomas with her."

Danny's heart clenched in sympathy. He put a hand on John's shoulder. "Can you stop her?"

"I can. But I don't know if I should. He'd be closer to his grandparents there, and most of his aunts and uncles. She could afford to live in a better neighborhood. She says I could see him whenever I liked, and he could spend the summers here with me."

"I'm sorry," Danny said. He felt bad now, spouting all his talk of love when his cousin was hurting so. "You know Tomas loves you. You'll always be a big part of his life."

John's expression remained grim. "I know." He took a long sip of tea. "She's taking him down there this weekend to look at houses. He's excited about living in a house instead of an apartment."

"You should get out and do something so you won't sit at home and brood all weekend," Danny said. In his position, Danny would have been out clubbing with friends, but John was prone to dwell on his misery.

"You're right," John said. "Want to catch a Mets game?"

"I can't. I have to help Nina move her things over."

"She's moving in with you?"

"I need a roommate to help with the rent anyway, now that Renee has moved out. And Nina needed a cheaper place to live. She was able to find someone to sublet her apartment. This was the perfect solution."

John shook his head. "I don't like it," he said. "How do you know she isn't just taking advantage of you? She doesn't have a job, does she?"

"She's an artist. She sells photographs and paintings and does some graphic design."

"She doesn't have a job. And she has to know you're bringing in good money now. Next thing you know, you'll be paying all the bills."

"Nina isn't like that," he protested.

"You don't know. You never know what women are really like. Did you expect things to go bad with Renee?"

"No, but that was different."

"How was that different? I know you, Danny. Every relationship starts the same. You're in love and things are good, and then they go bad."

"Every relationship does not go bad."

"What about that first girlfriend you had—the stalker?"

"She wasn't a stalker. Just a little possessive." The relationship had ended, yes, but only because she didn't have realistic expectations. His next girlfriend had moved to Brazil to be with family. Other relationships had moved from passion to platonic friendship in a process that felt very natural—part of life evolving. He'd suffered a few pangs of regret about some of those women, but no great heartbreak, and he liked to think he hadn't left them brokenhearted, either. "I've stayed friends with all my girlfriends," he said. "What's wrong with acting on your feelings and letting things progress naturally in a relationship? You can't avoid enjoying what's happening right now because you're worried about the future. You have to just let things happen."

"Hmmph." John took a savage bite of his sandwich.

"If you knew Nina better, you wouldn't think she's some gold digger or something like that," Danny said. "Come have dinner with us Saturday night. I'll cook and you'll see—she's the sweetest woman. Very smart and funny and really wonderful."

"The last thing I want to do is sit at the dinner table and watch the two of you make googly eyes at each other," John said.

"You'd rather sit at home and pout."

"I don't pout."

"And I don't make googly eyes. Come on. I really want you and Nina to be friends. And at least you'll get a good meal out of it."

"All right. But I still think you're moving too fast with her."

"I like to move fast." With work or women, he'd never been one to hesitate. He threw himself headlong into projects and relationships, giving them his all. He didn't fret about the future because he was too busy enjoying himself right now. Right now he loved Nina, and she loved him. What more did a man need?

Saturday afternoon Nina bustled about Danny's apartment, trying to clear out some of the packing boxes and other clutter before John arrived for dinner. "I wish you had waited to invite your cousin until I'd had time to unpack," she said.

"It'll be fine," Danny said, sliding a box of books behind the sofa. "John won't even notice. And I had to invite him this weekend. His ex-wife and his son are in Florida, getting ready to move there, and I know John's been sitting home all weekend, depressed. I wanted to do something to cheer him up."

"And you think having dinner with me is going to make him happy?" She'd only been around John a few times, but he always seemed so stern and solemn, so much older and nothing like Danny. And though Danny denied it, she had the impression his cousin didn't care much for her.

"It'll do him good to get out of the house and have a good meal and get to know you better," Danny said. "I know once he gets to know you he'll love you as much as I do."

Nina had her doubts about that, but kept those thoughts to herself. Danny always thought the best of everyone, especially those he loved. It was one of his most appealing qualities, but it made him unable to understand when people he cared about didn't get along.

She opened another box and carefully unwrapped the set of Russian nesting dolls—a gift from her grandmother before Nina and her mother moved to the United States. She set the dolls on a shelf on the wall that divided the living room from the apartment's tiny kitchen.

"No, no, not there," Danny said, rushing to take the dolls from her.

"No?" She took the dolls back and frowned at him.

"They don't really go with the rest of the decor on this wall," he said.

The decor consisted of a sleek black vase, a black-framed poster advertising a noir film, and a silver-framed mirror. Very sophisticated and spare. The nesting dolls would have added a quirky note and some color, she thought, and started to say so when Danny took her hand and led her across the room to a blank wall by the door.

"I left space here for your photographs," he said. "And cleared off a shelf in that bookcase for your books."

He was trying. She could see that. Attempting to make room for her in his spare, masculine decor. "I'll put the dolls in my studio," she said, referring to the spare bedroom he'd turned over to her art supplies and the little bit of furniture she'd brought with her.

He looked relieved. "That's a great idea."

She went to put the dolls away in the studio and he followed, carrying another box. "We'll put everything in here and finish unpacking tomorrow," he said. "Then I'd better start cooking."

"What are you making?" she asked.

"Just some chicken and vegetables," he said.

"Do you need any help?" she asked. "I can chop vegetables or something."

"That's all right. The kitchen's a little small for two people. You relax and make yourself at home."

Nina wasn't so sure how "at home" she could feel in a place where she wasn't allowed to help in the kitchen or decorate as she saw fit, but she told herself she and Danny would work out these little details. Every relationship required compromise and adjustments.

By the time John arrived an hour later, Nina had changed clothes and done her hair and makeup, then set the table while Danny sautéed chicken breasts and seasoned vegetables. When the doorbell rang, he called for her to answer it. She peered through the peephole and saw John, wearing khakis and a polo shirt, arms crossed over his chest, as if he was already shielding himself—but from what?

She unfastened the locks and opened the door. "Hello, John," she said, her smile as friendly as possible.

"Hello, Nina." He moved past her into the apartment. "Where's Danny?"

"He's in the kitchen. Can I get you anything?"

But the last words fell on dead air, as John was already striding into the kitchen. She followed him and found the two cousins embracing. "I brought some wine." John handed Danny a bottle of red.

"Go ahead and open it so it can breathe," Danny said. "Dinner's almost ready."

"Where do you keep your corkscrew?"

"Nina, get John the corkscrew." Danny threw something into a pan, creating a cloud of fragrant steam.

She looked around, hoping to spot the elusive corkscrew. She hadn't been in the apartment long enough to know where such things were.

"Never mind," John said, and began jerking open drawers. He found the corkscrew and held it aloft, victorious.

Nina did know where the wineglasses were, so she took out three, and set them on the counter beside the wine. Then she and John stared at each other, like two animals who were unsure if the other was predator or prey.

"Did you go to the Mets game?" Danny asked.

"I stayed home and watched it on television. Glavine pitched a great game."

When they started talking baseball, Nina fled to the living room. She wouldn't even pretend to like sports and besides, the two cousins probably needed time to relax together without the tension of her presence.

"Dinner's ready," Danny announced half an hour later. Nina had spent the time in the spare bedroom-cum-studio, venting her frustrations on a sketch pad, drawing half a dozen different versions of frowning expressions both male and female.

The food was delicious, so much so that it occupied their complete attention for the first few minutes of the meal. But when they had all filled their plates and exclaimed over the first few bites, Danny raised his wine glass. "A toast," he said. "To Nina, and our new adventure together."

She smiled. How like Danny to characterize their moving in together as an adventure—new and exciting and full of possibility. She clinked her glass to his, and John, after a moment's hesitation, joined them.

"Speaking of new living arrangements, Tomas called right before I left to come here," he said.

"Tomas is John's son," Danny explained to Nina. "What did he have to say?"

"They found a house he likes, near a school, with a big back yard. Caridad has promised he can get a dog."

"How wonderful for him," Nina said. "I always wanted to have a dog, but my parents never wanted pets. Of course, apartments are rather small for dogs." She looked around the room. "Cats would be better here. Two, so they could keep each other company."

"Danny's allergic to cats," John said.

"Oh. But he and Renee had a cat." She'd been under the impression he missed Mephisto, and thought getting another kitty—or two—would make him happy.

"Her idea," Danny said. "Not that I didn't love him, but I had to learn to live with a stuffed-up head."

He was willing to do so for Renee, but not for her? She pressed her lips together.

"Anyway, Tomas sounded excited about the move." John looked thoughtful. "He said I should get webcams so we can talk and see each other at the same time."

"That's a great idea," Danny said. "I can help you set them up."

"Yeah. I'm just glad he wants to stay in touch."

"Of course he wants to stay in touch." Danny refilled their wine glasses. "You're his father."

"Why is your ex-wife moving to Miami?" Nina asked.

John's look of annoyance returned. Did he think she was being too nosy? She stiffened, waiting for him to tell her so. "She has a good job offer there, and she wants to be closer to family," he said. "It'll be good for Tomas to see more of his grandparents."

"Divorce is hard on families," she said. "But children manage. It's not so unusual these days."

"Nina's parents are divorced," Danny said. He turned to her. "What did you do when you were little and moved to the United States? How did you keep in touch with your father?"

"He wrote letters," she said. "And made phone calls. Every summer I would go to Russia to visit him and my grandparents." She didn't point out that after awhile, her father had seemed more like a distant relative of whom she was very fond, while her stepfather, the man who was a part of her everyday life, became more like her real father.

"How's the art career coming?" John asked. "Are you really able to make a living with photography and painting?"

"Some months are better than others," she said. "I'm also look-ing for work as a graphic artist. I have a degree in that, though I prefer fine art."

"Nina's done graphics for websites," Danny said. "I think together we could put together a couple of online business ideas I've been working on."

She glanced at him, surprised. "You do?"

"We'd work great together, don't you think?" he asked, with that smile that made her melt.

"Freelance projects here and there aren't the same as a steady job," John said.

Nina tried not to be offended. John was understandably con-cerned about his cousin, and protective. "I'd love to show you more of my work sometime," she said.

"I'm sure it's very nice." But he said it dismissively, as if appeas-ing a child. But he didn't seem to notice Nina's hurt. He was cut-ting into his chicken. "What do you put in this sauce?" he asked.

The sauce was so spicy it burned Nina's tongue, but at least if Danny asked, she could pretend her eyes were watering because of hot peppers and not her hurt at his cousin's indifference. Had she made a horrible mistake, moving in with Danny, blithely believing she could make a place for herself in his already crowded life?

Danny left town three days later on a business trip, leaving
Nina to finish unpacking and settle into the apartment. She determined she would update her portfolio and compile a new list of
design firms to contact seeking work. And she would organize the
photographs she'd taken on their trip to Nova Scotia, and perhaps
sketch a few ideas for paintings.

Before she could do any of this, however, Erin called. "I've got
some fabulous news to share," she said, her voice high-pitched
with excitement.

"Come on over," Nina said. "You can see my new place."

She scarcely had time to shove extra boxes back behind the
sofa and make a fresh pot of coffee before Erin arrived. Erin
threw her arms around Nina in a hug. "It's so good to see you!"
she said, though the friends had had lunch the day after Nina
returned from Nova Scotia. "I have so much to tell you."

"So tell." Nina laughed and ushered her friend to the sofa.

"Nice." Erin stroked her hand along the leather. She surveyed
the room. "Very nice. Danny always did have classy taste."

"I'm going to put a bunch of my photographs over there,"
Nina said, indicating the blank wall Danny had set aside as her
gallery.

"They'll look great," Erin said. "So, how's it going? Are you
settling in well?"

"I've never lived with anyone before, so it's taking a little getting used to." Not that Danny wasn't considerate and neat—
maybe a little too neat. She sometimes felt guilty if she left the
bathroom a mess, though she was trying to get over that. This
was her place as much as his now, and she had every right to
make herself at home.

"I suppose he's at work right now."

"He's out of town. Houston, I think." He'd thoughtfully e-mailed her his schedule, but she hadn't bothered to memorize it.

"That must be hard," Erin said. "Him going away just when you've moved in together."

"Well, I do miss him." True enough, especially at night. Amazing how quickly she'd grown used to him lying next to her—his arms around her as they cuddled before falling asleep. But during the day, when she was lost in her work, she admitted she liked having the apartment to herself.

"I'm glad you're happy," Erin said. "I always did think you two were perfect for each other."

"Enough about me. What is this fabulous news you wanted to tell me?"

"I thought you'd never ask." Grinning hugely, Erin extended her left hand to display a diamond the size of a tooth on the third finger. "I'm engaged."

Nina squealed and the two women embraced. "Let me see," she demanded, and Erin extended her hand once more so that Nina could admire the large diamond set in platinum. "It's gorgeous," Nina said.

"It is, isn't it?" Erin admired the ring. "Thad is the sweetest man." She sighed and smiled at Nina, her expression dreamy. "I was so excited when he asked me."

"Tell me everything," Nina said.

"He asked me to dinner and took me to this fancy new place in lower Manhattan—Pierre's. We sat at a table in the corner. We had steak and lobster, my favorite, and *crème brûlée* for dessert, then Thad pulled out a ring box and proposed, right there in the restaurant. The waiter was in on it because, as soon as I squealed yes, he brought over a bottle of champagne. It was magical."

It sounded magical. The perfect evening of every woman's fantasy. But was it the fantasy, or the man that Erin found so enchanting? "You don't think this was a little sudden?" Nina ventured. "I mean, you've only been dating, what, three weeks?"

"We've spent almost every minute of that three weeks together," Erin said. "And don't forget, he's older than I am. He's ready to settle down."

Nina thought of Erin's love of parties and dancing. Erin was always up for a night of hitting the clubs, even if she had to rise early the next morning to get to work on time. "But are *you* ready to settle down?" Nina asked.

"With Thad, I am." She grabbed Nina's hand and squeezed. "He's promised we can go looking for houses next week."

"Houses? Already?"

"We have to start looking right away. The wedding's in only three months. Even if we find a place we like right away, we'll probably want to redecorate and that takes a little time. We want the house ready to move into when we come back from our honeymoon. What do you think? Should we go to Hawaii or Paris or somewhere more exotic? Thad says it's my choice."

"I . . . I don't know," Nina said. "It just seems so sudden."

"Hey, when you know you've found the right man, you know. So why waste time?"

But how do you know? Nina wondered. If anyone had asked, she would have said she loved Danny—she loved him very much. But even living with him had been a scary proposition, one she was still trying to get comfortable with. The idea of marriage, of pledging to spend the rest of your life with someone, seemed much too risky at this point.

Did that mean their love wasn't real because they weren't already certain of the future, as Erin and Thad were after only three weeks?

"I want you to help me with the wedding," Erin said. "I hope you'll be my maid of honor, of course, but I really need your artistic eye to help me with the planning. I want this wedding to be beautiful and perfect."

Every bride wanted a beautiful, perfect wedding, Nina was sure. She smiled and nodded. "Of course I'll help. Do you know where it's going to be held?"

"His parents are members of a big church in Westchester, so Thad wants the wedding to be there. He's taking me down this weekend to see it—and to meet his folks." She put a hand to her stomach. "I don't have to tell you how nervous I am about that. Though he swears his family will love me."

Nina thought of John's solemn expression whenever he was around her. How much more would he dislike her if Danny had announced they were getting married, as opposed to just moving in together? No matter how much a couple loved each other, families were less predictable. "I'm sure they will love you," she lied. "How could they not?"

"I hope so. You'll have to help me pick out what to wear."

"Be sure to take plenty of pictures of the church so we can plan decorations for the ceremony," Nina said. "Do you know where you'll have the reception?"

"Their country club. It's not too far away. I think we're supposed to have dinner there on Saturday."

Country club dinners and weekends in Westchester. Erin was definitely moving up in the world. But she was sweet and pretty and would no doubt charm Thad's parents and their friends. If she didn't, Nina prayed Thad would stand up for her and prove himself worthy of being her husband.

Erin pulled a small spiral notebook and a pen from her purse. "I'm thinking about blue and silver for the wedding," she said. "Or maybe I should go with black and white. That's so elegant, don't you think?"

"Blue and silver could be elegant, too," Nina said. "Though black is very easy on everyone. Most people already own a nice black dress." She thought of the dress she'd have to buy if Erin went with blue.

"That's what I was thinking," Erin said. "Of course, you and I are almost the same size, so if we choose a dress and color we both like, you can wear it in my wedding, and then I can turn around and wear it in yours."

"In my wedding?" Nina stared at her. "I'm not getting married."

"Maybe not right away," Erin waved her hand. "But you will. You and Danny are clearly so much in love. I predict it won't be long before you're wearing one of these." She tapped the diamond.

The idea sent a rush of feeling through Nina. Her heart fluttered wildly as a sudden image of Danny on his knees before her, holding a ring and pledging his love eternal, filled her vision. Tears stung her eyes and she swallowed. It was the most beautiful image, and she heard herself saying "yes" even as part of her told herself she was being ridiculous. Hadn't she been thinking only moments before that it was far too soon to be dreaming of forever when she and Danny were only just getting to know each other?

"I almost forgot to tell you," Erin exclaimed. "I ran into Renee last week at the big shoe sale over at Macy's. She told me she was buying a condo in Queens. She's cut her hair and she looks great. Really happy. So I guess she's not too torn up about Danny."

"Oh. That's good." Nina still felt a little guilty about Renee, even though she was sure she'd had nothing to do with her and Danny's split. "Did you tell her I'd moved in with Danny?"

"Oh no. I'd never do that," Erin said. "But I imagine she already knows. You know how word gets around." She laughed. "But it wouldn't surprise me if she forgives him for that. Danny's so charming and sweet, I don't think a woman could stay angry with him. And the two of you did wait until she was out of the picture before you got together—right?"

"Absolutely," Nina said. "You don't think . . ."

Erin patted her hand. "Of course not." She turned her attention back to the pad and paper. "Black and white, I think for the wedding. As you said, it's easiest and very elegant. And maybe with red roses for a punch of color."

"Red roses," Nina mumbled, and sagged back against the couch, weak from the whirlwind of emotions. She was relieved to hear Renee harbored no hard feelings toward Danny—and she hoped none toward her. But it was also a bit unnerving to think that she and Danny had been together for five years and things had ended between them with scarcely a whimper. They'd spent so much time as a couple and as far as she knew had never contemplated marriage. Or at least, Danny had never contemplated it. If he hadn't asked Renee to marry him in all that time, any prospects of marriage for him and Nina seemed very far away indeed. She told herself that was a good thing. It was what she wanted. She certainly wasn't ready to marry anyone right now. She needed time to devote to her art and to establish herself in the city. Danny was her dear friend and her lover, but she didn't need him to be anything more.

Ten

Being powerless
To live your dreams is the worst
Punishment of all.

AFTER TRAVELING TO THREE CITIES IN A WEEK, Danny was
jet-lagged and looking forward to sleeping in his own bed. And
he was anxious to see Nina. He'd missed her more than he'd anti-
cipated, though they'd talked every day on the phone. At night,
when he had trouble falling asleep in unfamiliar hotel rooms, he
found himself thinking of her, remembering the way her eyes
shone with laughter when something amused her or the funny
faces she made when she was concentrating on her work.

When the taxi dropped him in front of the apartment, he
grabbed his bag from the trunk and took the stairs two at a time.
Nina had offered to pick him up at the airport, but he hadn't
wanted to put her to so much trouble. And he'd liked the idea of
surprising her, of walking into the apartment to find her waiting.

He liked this moment of returning, of stepping into familiar
surroundings and seeing them, at least for a moment, with fresh
eyes. The first thing he noticed as he set his bags on the floor was
how different the room smelled, like oil paints and turpentine

and fresh coffee and feminine perfume . . . like Nina. A magazine lay open on the sofa, a coffee cup on the floor beside it. A pair of her sandals sat by the door. A dozen framed photographs filled the once-empty wall to his right. He recognized some of the pictures they'd taken that night in Coney Island. He remembered how much he'd wanted to kiss her that night and the desire returned, stronger now that he knew how wonderful kissing her could be.

The door to the guest bedroom opened and she emerged, hair tousled, a smudge of blue paint on her chin. "Danny!" Her eyes lit with welcome. "I wasn't expecting you until tonight."

"I was able to get an earlier flight." He held out his arms and she came to him, all soft curves and silken hair and tender lips and the perfume and paint smell that was Nina. They kissed for a long time, until both were breathless.

"I missed you," she said.

"I missed you, too." He wiped at the smudge of paint with his thumb.

She laughed. "I'm working on a new painting."

"Show me."

She led him into the bedroom, and he admired the work on the easel, a shore scene from Nova Scotia. But they couldn't keep their hands off each other, and soon they were rolling around on the bed that had been in her apartment, clothing tossed to the floor a piece at a time, like wrapping torn from birthday gifts. They made love with the passion of two people determined to make up for lost time. Afterward, when they lay twined together atop the rumpled bedclothes, she grinned at him. "Welcome home."

"I'm glad to be home." He kissed the tip of her nose and snuggled closer. He might have fallen asleep, but his stomach growled.

Nina laughed and pushed him away. "You'd better feed that monster before it frightens me away."

They ate takeout Chinese on the sofa, the souvenirs of Danny's travels scattered around them: new music CDs he'd picked up in a specialty store in Houston, postcards of art prints from a gift shop in Dallas, and the ticket stubs and other paper work that were the inevitable detritus of any long trip.

"So it was a good trip?" Nina asked.

"I think so." He fished lo mein noodles from a carton with a pair of chopsticks. "I have to go back next month to oversee the opening of a couple of new stores."

"What will you do, exactly?"

"Everything—from overseeing construction to hiring staff and placing ads in the papers." He smiled. It was amazing, really. Only a few months ago he'd been a college student working part time in a café. Now he supervised dozens of people, some twice his age. And he did a good job; no one could deny that.

"I hope John appreciates how hard you work for him," she said.

"He does. I remind him every chance I get." He set aside the lo mein and picked up a carton of spicy beef. "What did you do while I was gone? Besides the new painting, of course."

"I went shopping with Erin for decorations for her reception."

"I still can't believe she's marrying a guy she's known all of three weeks." Nina had shared the news with him one night on the telephone. She'd sounded as shocked by the news as he'd been.

"It will be three months by the time they marry," Nina said. "And she really does seem to be head over heels in love with him. The more I hear about him, the more I think he might really be the perfect man for her."

"Oh? And what is the perfect man for her?" Erin was Nina's friend; he didn't know her as well, though she'd struck him as the typical New York party girl—fun loving and sweet and not the least bit interested in settling down. Clearly he'd been wrong.

"He has money, and money is very important to her. Not that she's shallow—she's definitely not." Nina looked thoughtful. "She doesn't come from money. In fact, I think she was pretty poor growing up, so she likes the security money represents. And he's a little bit older, well established in his business. Erin's not clingy, but I think she enjoys being taken care of and Thad will offer that."

"So she's marrying him because he's a meal ticket?" Danny made a face.

"No!" Nina swatted at him. "She loves him. I believe she really does. But so many other things are important to making a marriage work: common goals, a similar way of looking at life. A commitment to taking care of each other."

"It sounds to me like Thad's doing all the taking care of in this situation," Danny said.

"That's not true. He wants a home and family and Erin will give him that."

"I suppose some men see that as a fair trade."

"And you don't?"

Nina's tone wasn't exactly accusing, but the words made him shift in his seat uncomfortably. "I guess I'm a romantic. I don't like to see marriage reduced to a financial balance sheet. People should marry because they want to commit to a life together. Because they want to be together."

Her expression softened, growing almost dreamy. "I think Erin and Thad will have that. I hope they will."

She looked so beautiful in that moment, and he thought again of how much he'd missed her while he was away. "I love you," he said, and leaned forward to kiss her.

"Watch out. You're going to spill the lo mein."

"We can clean it up later." He pressed her back against the sofa.

"*You* can clean it up." She put her arms around him.

"Mmmm." He buried his face in her neck, hands sliding under her shirt. "I don't have anywhere to be all weekend," he said, kissing his way along her collarbone. "We might have to spend it in bed."

"What if I want to go out?" she asked, her voice muffled by the shirt she was pulling over her head.

"I'll do my best to persuade you to stay in." He stripped off his own shirt and sent it flying.

"Maybe I could be persuaded." She kissed his shoulder. "Or maybe not. After all, you have to tire out sometime."

"That's what you think." But he didn't give her a chance to answer, we merely covered her mouth with his own. He was going to make the most of every minute of this weekend. Leaving her was difficult, but almost worth it for the experience of coming home.

Nina woke early the next morning, the familiar weight of Danny beside her in the bed, his breathing a soft rhythm barely audible in the still air. Slowly, careful not to wake him, she slid into a sitting position and studied him in the pale light that seeped around the window blinds. He slept on his stomach, arms curled to him, face buried in the pillow. The dark shadow of beard dusted his jaw, his usually impeccably styled hair tousled. He frowned in his sleep, so serious she had to stifle a laugh. In his waking hours, he was seldom so serious. The contrast intrigued her. What was he dreaming of that put that frown on his face?

She might have sat, watching him sleep for hours, but she had to pee; and she really would like a cup of coffee. She eased her way out of bed and padded into the bathroom.

When she emerged, he was sitting up in bed, smiling at her. "Good morning, beautiful," he said.

"Good morning." She slipped on a robe. "I'm going to make coffee."

"I'll come with you." He threw back the covers and reached for a pair of shorts. "I'm starved. What do you want for breakfast?"

While he made omelets, she brewed the coffee and thought how comfortable they were together in this kitchen, where only a week ago she'd been worried she'd always feel like an intruder. His going away for a week had been good in that respect, giving her time to make herself at home in this apartment.

"What did you want to do today?" he asked.

"I thought you had plans to stay in bed all weekend," she teased.

"There is that option." He slid a perfect, fluffy omelet onto her plate.

"I thought we might visit the animal shelter," she said, watching out of the corner of her eye to see how he received this suggestion.

"The animal shelter?" He sent her a questioning look.

"I really would like to adopt a pair of kittens," she said. "I've always wanted pets, and they'd be good company when you're away."

He hesitated only a moment, then nodded. "All right."

"Are you really allergic?" she asked. "Or was John just saying that?"

"Why would he make something like that up?"

Because he doesn't like me and wanted to thwart me, she thought. But she didn't want to argue with Danny about his cousin. Not now when things were so good between them. "Then it's true?" she asked.

"It's true. But it's nothing I can't live with."

"Maybe we'll find cats that won't make you sneeze," she said. She knew nothing about such things. The reason she'd never had pets growing up was because her mother always said she was allergic, though sometimes Nina had wondered if this was simply her mother's way of saying she didn't like animals, at least not in her home. That clearly wasn't the case with Danny; she'd seen him with Mephisto, and when they were out on the street he would stop and pet dogs that approached him with their owners. Animals were drawn to him, as if they sensed his innate goodness.

The animal shelter bustled with activity this Saturday morning, and Nina and Danny had to wait for their turn to visit with a counselor. The kittens were housed separately from the older cats. A shelter worker showed them several groups of squirming bundles of fur. "They're all so adorable," Nina exclaimed.

"Look at this one." Danny held up a fat orange tabby.

"What a cute little snuffleupagus," she cooed, scratching its chin. The kitten responded with a loud purr.

"We'll take this one," Danny told the counselor, cradling the contented kitten in his arms.

They chose a white, yellow, and black calico female as a companion for the tabby and paid the discounted adoption fee. Laden with a cardboard carrier and a bag containing food, collars, and cat toys, they headed for the subway. They were scarcely out the door when Danny sneezed loudly and so forcefully he almost dropped the carrier.

"Danny!" Nina grabbed his arm. "Are you all right?"

He sneezed again, then sniffed. "Just allergies," he said.

Guilt filled Nina as she stared at his reddened eyes and suddenly dripping nose. "The cats?" she asked, dreading the answer.

"Probably just because we were around so many." He sneezed

again. "We'll stop on the way home and buy some antihistamine."

They stopped at the first drugstore they saw, and Nina waited on the sidewalk with the kittens while Danny went inside. He came out, tearing open the package of antihistamine as he walked. "I'll be fine soon," he promised as he downed a pill, dry.

She winced. "I hope so." She didn't want to have to choose between Danny and the kittens. Not that the choice wouldn't be obvious, but she was already falling in love with the little fluff balls, and she hated the thought of taking them back to the shelter.

Back at the apartment, they let the kittens out of the carrier to explore their new home. While Nina set up the litter box, Danny collapsed on the sofa. Nina fed and watered their new companions, whom they'd decided to name Snuffleupagus and Chickadee. She cleaned up the first "accident" and showed them their litter box, and returned to the living room to find Danny asleep on the sofa. At least he wasn't sneezing, and his nose was a little less red.

He really was the sweetest man to inconvenience himself for her sake this way. She'd do her best to make it up to him, starting tonight, with a dinner she cooked. She wasn't a pro in the kitchen, but she could prepare an edible meal. When he woke from his nap, they'd enjoy a romantic dinner and play with the kittens. Still later, they could retire to the bedroom . . . for dessert.

Nina and Danny settled into a comfortable routine. During the week he worked long hours, often out of town. She spent her days painting, talking to galleries and coffee shops about displaying her photographs, and looking for work. She missed him when he was away, but the kittens provided endless amusement and good company and, really, she was used to living alone, so how was this any different?

But, of course, it was different. Since he'd taken his job with John, Nina sometimes felt she saw him less than she had before she'd moved in with him. In those days they'd spent several evenings a week together, at the café or the club or out with friends. Now he rarely had time for any of that.

When he was home she found it hard to really relax, knowing he'd be leaving again soon. Practical tasks warred with the desire to spend the time making love and lounging around the apartment, playing with the kittens, and talking. Nina told herself they'd eventually find a balance, but for now everything felt so off-kilter.

One Sunday afternoon, about six weeks after Nina had moved in, they shopped together for groceries. Danny pushed the cart while Nina read from the list they'd compiled. Danny was scheduled to be home all week and he planned to cook dinner at least five nights, so much of the list consisted of ingredients for those meals, as well as cat treats, tea and coffee, and staples for Nina's lunches at home. Nina's biggest indulgence was fruit, she loaded up the cart with fresh peaches and nectarines from upstate orchards.

She hummed to herself as she helped unload their purchases at the checkout counter. There was something so happily domestic about shopping together—the perfect end to the perfect weekend.

"Ninety-four sixty-two." The clerk announced their total.

Nina felt a jolt of alarm at the sum. She couldn't remember ever spending so much on a single trip to the store. Was feeding two people really that much more expensive, or had they both gotten carried away?

Danny opened his wallet and counted out bills. He dug in his pockets for some coins to add to the pile. "That's forty-seven, thirty-one," he said.

Both the clerk and Danny looked at Nina expectantly. Flushing, she opened her purse. A search of her wallet yielded seven dollars and eighty-two cents. She opened her checkbook and, aware of two pairs of eyes on her, wrote out a check for her half of the groceries.

"I didn't realize we'd bought so much," she said to Danny as they left the store, arms laden with bags. "I'm afraid it's going to leave me a little short."

"All that fruit adds up," he said.

"What about all those spices?" she said. "Spices are expensive."

"They'll last a long time," he said. "And wait until you taste my curried chicken."

"I might have to borrow a little from you for my half of the rent," she said.

"That's not due for another two weeks," he said. "We won't worry about it now. You might get another commission in the meantime or find a great job."

Easy for him to say. He was making plenty of money working for his cousin. Would it have hurt for him to offer to pay for all of the groceries or to forgive the difference in the rent? Not that she wanted to be dependent on him or even that she'd have accepted the offer—but the gesture would have been a thoughtful one.

Aaargh! For all she loved art and wanted not to care about things, being poor was a pain in the ass sometimes. And it was especially a pain when it affected her love life. There had to be a way to balance romantic dreams and practical reality, to be equal partners in a relationship even when they didn't have equal incomes.

Back at the apartment, they unpacked the groceries. "Watch this," Danny said, and shook the carton of cat treats. Snuffleupagus and Chickadee looked up, heads cocked. Danny opened the package and held a treat aloft. Two pairs of furry ears stood erect, whiskers twitching. Danny tossed the treat and Snuffleupagus pounced. Chickadee jumped on him, until Danny distracted her with a second treat.

"My turn." Nina fished a treat from the package and offered it to Chickadee. The kitten stood on her hind legs, reaching toward the treat. Nina laughed and rewarded the kitten for her efforts, then did the same for Snuffleupagus.

Danny tucked the carton of treats in the cabinet next to the cat food. "I have a couple of hours before I have to start dinner," he said. "I'm going to get some work done."

"But it's Sunday afternoon," Nina protested. She'd been hoping he'd want to watch one of the new DVDs he'd brought back from his latest trip.

"I've gotten behind while I was away," he said. "If I don't spend at least a little time catching up, I'll be drowning next week."

He pulled out his laptop and booted it up. Nina curled up on the end of the sofa and watched him. "Do you still have your music website?" she asked.

He made a face. "The site is still up, though I haven't had much time to work on it lately."

She didn't have to ask the last time he'd screened one of the independent films he loved or had time to take in a concert or photo exhibition—all things he used to enjoy. All he did lately was work and travel for work.

"John can't expect you to work for him twenty-four hours a day, seven days a week," she said.

"He doesn't expect it of me. But right now, it's what's required to do a good job." He pecked at a few keys on the computer. "We're building something really big here. It's exciting to be a part of it."

More exciting than the art and music he'd always loved? More
compelling than spending time with the things he'd once avowed
were most important in life—than spending time with *her*?

She was all for independence, for each person having indi-
vidual interests. But she hadn't moved in with Danny solely to
save money or even because she wanted to share his bed. She'd
moved in so they could share their lives—so they could explore
the creative synergy they'd experienced on that night in Coney
Island, and in all those days exploring the Canadian coastline.
She'd been sure Danny wanted that too. "Do you remember
when we were in Nova Scotia and we talked about working on an
art project together?" she asked.

"What was that?" He looked up from the computer, expression
distracted.

She scooted toward him on the sofa. "We talked about doing
some kind of creative project together, putting together a website
with music and art and writing."

He smiled. "I do remember that. I even have some ideas."

A thrill ran through her at the knowledge that he'd been thinking about the project—about her. "I want to see them."

"All right." He opened a directory on his computer and pulled
up a file. "I was thinking we might work with poetry or short nar-
rative and line drawings or photography to tell stories. Something
that would keep people coming back. Maybe even interactive."

"Illustration, I think," she said. "Something colorful."

"Those fairy-tale characters you do so well," he said. "And writing. Something enigmatic people could interpret for themselves."

"Yes." Heads together, they leaned over the computer, ideas
tumbling out almost as quickly as they could speak. Nina felt a
delicious warmth of creativity and companionship and com-
munion. This was the Danny she loved and missed—the man

she'd come to believe might be *the one*—the one who loved her and believed in her and made her life and her art better by his presence. She didn't need Danny in order to live, but she liked the view of life through his eyes and the way both of them together were able to see things from a brand new perspective. If this really was love, it was a kind she'd never experienced before. One she didn't want to lose to the demands of his job or the realities of her finances or any of the petty ways the mundane world insisted on intruding.

Eleven

Holding on is tough,
Much tougher than letting go
Or simply quitting.

"I'VE NARROWED THE CHOICE FOR the invitations down to these three." Erin handed three envelopes across the table to Nina when the friends met for coffee two weeks later. October had made its entrance with a cold rain and Nina had dug her coat from storage and borrowed Danny's umbrella to make her way to the coffee shop where she and Erin had agreed to meet. "Thad says he doesn't care, so you have to help me pick," Erin said.

Nina studied the invitations, all white or cream-colored cards with black engraving. "They're all nice," she said. "But we could make something more personal—perhaps with a pen and ink drawing of you and Thad—or roses, since you're going with a rose theme." One day, when she married, she wanted everything about the event to reflect her and her future husband's personality and talents. The invitations would be little works of art the guests would want to keep.

"That would be beautiful, but not practical, since I need four hundred of them."

"Four hundred!"

"I know, I know." Erin spread the invitations out in front of her like a hand of playing cards. "We don't expect all of them to show up, of course, but Thad has a lot of relatives and friends and business associates. He doesn't want to leave any of them out."

"How many do you think will come to the wedding?" Nina asked.

"Thad's mother says to plan for 250 to 300. My mother about died when I told her, but Thad's parents are picking up part of the tab, since most of the guests are their friends or family."

"That was good of them." Nina sipped her coffee. "So you're getting along well with his parents?"

"Well enough. I'm not sure they really approve of me, but they're too polite to say anything, and I'm doing my best to charm them. They're thawing a little bit."

"Everyone likes you," Nina said. "You'll be their favorite daughter-in-law."

"I'll be their only daughter-in-law. Thad only has sisters—one older and one younger. I haven't met them yet, but I've heard plenty about their accomplishments. One is a lawyer in some big firm in Boston. The other is raising the world's most perfect grandchildren in Maryland. Her husband works for some D.C. think tank." Erin rolled her eyes. "I'm sure they're secretly appalled their only son is marrying a woman with no connections, no family, and a mere liberal arts education from a public university, but they're too afraid of alienating Thad to say anything."

Nina wondered what Danny's parents would think of her. John certainly hadn't warmed much to her, but Danny had never mentioned his parents' opinion of his new living arrangements. Natasha hadn't approved of Nina moving in with Danny, but mostly because she thought if Nina moved anywhere, it should be back to Boulder. She was sure if her mother actually met Danny, she'd be completely charmed. Danny had that effect on people, especially women.

"I'm not sure, but I think Thad might have said something to his parents about not interfering with his choice or something," Erin continued. "He can be very forceful when he wants to be."

The romance of a man defying his family for the love of a woman wasn't lost on Nina. "You're very lucky," she said.

"Yeah." Erin's face took on the dreamy look Nina was growing accustomed to. "I really am the luckiest girl. Thad's so wonderful."

Nina braced herself for another cataloging of Thad's wonderfulness, but Erin snapped out of her daze. "I almost forgot! Randy's going to DJ at the reception. Thad's parents wanted to hire a live band, but I wanted Randy so it would be like old times at the Castle. Thad backed me up there, too."

"So you're in touch?" As she and Erin had predicted, Tawny had broken off with Randy shortly after her parents' barbecue. Having a boyfriend her parents approved of so heartily was apparently too much for her. The last Nina had heard, Tawny was dating a bicycle messenger with multiple piercings and a green mohawk.

"We saw him just the other night at the Castle. He's still a DJ there."

"You were at the Castle? When?" Since Danny had given up working there, Nina hadn't been to the club.

"Thursday. Everyone said they missed you."

"You should have called," Nina said, trying to hide her hurt. "I would have come."

"I guess we all figured you were busy with Danny or something."

"He was out of town. I would have loved to have come by myself."

"Next time I'll call, I promise," Erin said. "I would have asked Danny to do the music for my wedding, but he's so busy with work I figured he wouldn't have time."

"He probably wouldn't," Nina agreed. Danny didn't have time for anything lately. The website they'd both been so excited about—the one that would pair Nina's drawings and Danny's poetry—still languished half finished on Danny's hard drive.

"Anyway, Randy said he'd do the job, so that's one more thing checked off my list." She frowned at the invitations, then plucked the one from the middle. "What do you think of this one?"

"That one is beautiful," Nina said.

"It'll have to do." Erin returned all three samples to her purse. "I have to get the invitations out this week. I'm already terribly late. And I have to meet with the caterer and the florist and find some time to speak with the church organist and have another fitting for my gown." She gave Nina a desperate look. "Sometimes I think you and Danny might have the right idea after all, living together instead of getting married."

"You don't really think that," Nina said.

"Well, no, I don't. But I do wonder sometimes if I wouldn't be better off eloping." She laughed. "What am I saying? I've waited all my life for this wedding. I'd never forgive myself if I skipped out on the whole production."

"It will be a beautiful wedding," Nina said. Early on, she'd decided her chief job as maid of honor was to keep repeating this phrase.

"At least I don't have to worry about the photographs," Erin said. "You're sure it's not too much for you—being in the wedding and taking the pictures?"

"Danny will photograph the ceremony. He's very good."

"You two make such a great team."

"We do work well together." When they were actually together, Nina couldn't have been happier. It was only when Danny was away that she struggled. How was it she felt lonelier in the apartment they shared than she had in her own place? She still spent her days the same way, with the addition of the kittens for company. She still had the same friends, though now they apparently thought of her as part of a couple, absent if Danny was absent.

Maybe she was like her friends in that respect. Now that she was living with Danny, she expected them to be together more instead of less. When he was away, it was as if part of her was missing. A terrible feeling—but that was the thing about emotions. They were unpredictable and not easily controlled. Her mother had often accused her of being moody, but Nina saw no profit in suppressing one's feelings. Better to embrace emotions as part of really living. They came from the same place as creativity and inspiration. They were part of yourself that always told the truth, whether you were ready for that kind of honesty or not.

Home. Danny hadn't really thought of his New York apartment that way before, but now that he was on the road so much, he looked forward to returning to this space where he could be surrounded by everything he loved most, to catch his breath and get his bearings.

Or maybe it was Nina who had transformed the space into a real home. She was responsible for the presence of the kittens that were fast growing into cats. Her artwork on the walls added color to his heretofore Spartan decor. She'd added other things too—quirky little sculptures on a side table, a comic coffee mug in the kitchen, a silk robe hanging on the bathroom door. He'd lived with a woman before and was used to feminine things around, but these items were so uniquely Nina—decorative and artistic and slightly exotic like the woman herself. Though he thought he knew her well, she continued to surprise him, and with each return home he was more reluctant to leave.

This time, after a week-long sojourn in Detroit, she greeted him at the door with a smile full of pure joy. She bounced on her toes as he set down his bags, then threw her arms around him. "I have a new commission to paint a portrait," she said. "A woman saw my paintings on a website and contacted me to do a painting as a gift for her husband."

"That's fantastic." He squeezed her tight, loving the feel of her body against his. More than that, even, he loved seeing her this happy. Too often lately she was down about her stalled career or depressed over her lack of money. This sale was just what she needed. "We should celebrate."

"Erin and Thad and Randy and some others are getting together at the Castle tonight. We could join them."

It felt like years since he'd hung out with his friends at the club, though only a few weeks—well, maybe a few months—had passed since they'd gotten together. Where had the time gone? "We'll go," he said. "It'll be fun."

He sank onto the sofa. Snufflupagus immediately crawled into his lap. "How was your week?" Nina asked. "Is the shop in Detroit ready to open?"

"It will be as soon as all the stock is in," he said. "I have to go back in two weeks for the grand opening."

Nina sat beside him, bare feet curled beneath her. "You look exhausted. Why doesn't John ever go to these things? Why does it always have to be you?"

"He goes to some of them, but I'm better at managing people than he is. Besides, in two weeks he's going to Miami to pick up Tomas and bring him back here for a visit."

"We should have them over while Tomas is in town."

"That's a great idea." He was glad Nina didn't hold John's some-times gruff attitude against him. He patted her leg. God, he'd missed her. Maybe next time he left for a week long trip he'd sug-gest she come with him. They could have fun exploring a new city together.

"Don't forget Erin and Thad's wedding next month," she said. "You have to be there to help take photographs."

"I remember." He really didn't want to talk about Erin and Thad right now. He leaned over to kiss her, suddenly not as tired.

He brought his hands up to caress her neck, and his fingers tangled in her earrings, long strings of beads hanging from her lobes. "Where did you get these?" he asked, fingering the color-ful wooden beads.

"I found them at a shop Erin and I visited this week, looking for decorations for her wedding." She touched the beaded dan-gles. "I think they are supposed to be for hanging from lamp chains, but I turned them into earrings."

"You're amazing," he said. "You make art out of everything."

"You're the same way," she said. "Art and music and poetry. You have so many talents."

"Mmmm." He pulled her close once more, and kissed the silken hollow at the base of her throat. She smelled of floral shampoo and vanilla body lotion and a spice that was uniquely Nina. Yes, he had definitely been away too long.

He slid his hand beneath her shirt, but she caught his arm, stopping him. "I'm serious, Danny. You could do anything you want. I remember when you used to have so many ideas for busi-nesses, creative things you would do yourself."

"I'll still do those things," he said, with only a pinch of guilt. "One day."

"When?" Her gaze searched his, her blue eyes so full of concern. "Are you really happy, building shelves and hiring employees and planning marketing campaigns for your cousin's business?"

"This is a fantastic opportunity for me right now," he said. "I have more responsibility, and am making more money, than most guys my age."

"But are you really happy?" she asked again.

He opened his mouth to say he was happy, but he couldn't lie. Not to Nina, who knew him better than anyone. "I miss working as a DJ at the club," he said. "And I miss working on my websites and finding new music and all the things I used to do. But right now John needs my help. I can't desert him."

"Just don't lose sight of what's really important." She put her hand on his chest over his heart. "Don't lose yourself."

"I won't. You'll make sure of that." When he was with Nina he knew exactly what he wanted in life. She kept him grounded to that essential part of himself that traveling and making business deals couldn't change. That part of him had to take a backseat for the time being, while he helped his cousin and made some money. But one day he'd come back to it. He'd have more time for music and art and all the things he wanted to do. Nina would be a part of it all.

Why did I ever agree to entertain Danny's cousin and his son right now, when I have so many other things to do? Nina wondered as she hurried to change clothes before their guests arrived. She'd spent most of the day working on the commissioned portrait, which was coming along wonderfully well. She'd been tempted to lock herself in the spare bedroom for the evening and keep working, but she knew John would never forgive such rudeness, and she wasn't sure even Danny would understand.

So she'd raced the clock, painting as long as she dared, then running to scrub paint from her fingers and comb her suddenly uncooperative hair. She was standing in bra and panties in front of the closet, trying to decide what to wear, when the doorbell rang.

"Nina, can you get that?" Danny called from the kitchen.

"I'm dressing!" she answered.

The doorbell rang again, insistent.

"Nina!" Danny called.

Grumbling to herself, she snatched up her robe and threw it on, then stalked to the living room and threw open the door. John's expression of surprise quickly morphed into a smirk. "If we're interrupting something . . ."

"Come in." She opened the door wide. "Danny's in the kitchen."

"Hello?" A slim, brown-haired, brown-eyed boy who had been standing behind John gave her a tentative smile. "My name is Tomas."

"Hello, Tomas," she said, charmed. "I'm Nina."

"Were you taking a bath?" he asked.

Behind her, Nina thought she heard John choke back a laugh—a surprise in itself, since he'd never seemed to have a sense of humor around her. She ignored him. "I've been painting all day," she said. "I had to change out of my work clothes into something nicer to meet you."

"The robe is nice," he said sincerely.

She laughed. "I think jeans and a shirt would be more appropriate. Can you wait just a moment for me to change? I promise I'll be right back."

"I'll wait," Tomas said.

"We'll go into the kitchen and say hello to your Cousin

Danny," John said, and steered the boy in that direction.

When Nina joined them a few minutes later, she found the men drinking beers while Tomas had a can of soda. She helped herself to a beer and leaned against the counter.

"Uncle Danny says you're an artist," Tomas said shyly.

"Yes. Do you like art?"

He nodded. "I like to draw. I haven't painted much, but I think I'd like that, too."

"Would you like to see my studio?"

His smile showed a gap between his front teeth. "Would you show me?"

She led him to the spare bedroom and opened the door to her workspace. Chickadee looked up from the bed, where he'd been curled in a ball. "That's Chickadee," she said, as Tomas approached.

Chickadee obligingly rolled onto his back. Tomas laughed and rubbed the cat's tummy. Then he turned to the painting on the easel. "Who's the lady?" he asked.

"A woman who hired me to paint her portrait."

"You're doing a good job."

Praise from the city's most esteemed art critic couldn't have pleased Nina more. She showed Tomas her paints and sketch-books, then gave him a little modeling clay to play with. "If you pinch and poke at it you can make a little animal," she said, thinking of the afternoons she'd spent on the floor of her grand-mother's studio shaping her own clay menagerie.

He bent over the chunk of clay, his brow furrowed in concen-tration and his lip stuck out. Nina felt her heart tighten and had to refrain from reaching out to stroke his hair. He had Danny's hair, that straight, deep brown that fell perfectly into place. Is this what Danny had looked like as a boy? And would his children look like this?

"Tomas, are you in there?" A tap sounded on the door and then it opened and John stood studying them.

"Look, Papa. I made a dog." Tomas held up the lump of clay, which did indeed resemble a dog.

"That's great, son. Good job."

"I'm going to show Uncle Danny." He sped out of the room, leaving Nina and John alone.

John looked around the room. "So this is where you work?"

"Yes." She put her hands behind her back, a bit defensive. She didn't expect a big businessman to think much of her creations. After all, she didn't have a lot of money to show for her efforts.

"Danny said you were talented," he said. "I can see he was right."

This praise caught her off guard. "That means a lot, coming from you," she said.

His eyes met hers. Maybe Tomas had led her to look at John differently, but today she was struck by the sadness behind his solemn facade.

"I know you think I don't like you," he said. "But that's not true."

"You haven't exactly been friendly," she said.

"You're Danny's girlfriend, not mine. I don't see what difference it makes."

"But I want us to be friends."

He shifted from one foot to the other. "I don't like to get close to people who might not be around for the long-term," he said.

The words were like a little dart, piercing her skin and making her wince. "What do you mean by that?"

"You and Danny haven't been together that long. I know how relationships work. Not every one lasts."

"Are you saying you don't think Danny and I will stay together?" Had Danny said something to his cousin? A hard knot formed in her stomach.

"I have no way of knowing," John said. "So I like to keep my distance until I do. Nothing against you; it's just the way I prefer to handle things."

He turned and left her to stare after him. Were he and Danny really related—Danny who was so open about his feelings and quick to make friends, and John who seemed determined to armor himself against the possibility of more loss?

It was true she and Danny hadn't been together very long, but their feelings for each other went deep. Nina couldn't imagine loving anyone more than she loved Danny, and she was sure he felt the same. *So what does anyone else's opinion matter?* she told herself as she left the room, closing the door behind her. But the conversation left her feeling a little queasy.

She was crossing the living room toward the kitchen when her cell phone rang. The display showed Natasha's number. Nina had called earlier in the day but she hadn't left a message. She slid open the phone. "Hello, Mom."

"My caller I.D. showed your number. Is everything all right? Why didn't you leave a message?"

"I'm fine, Mom. How are you?"

"You don't sound fine. You sound upset about something. What is it?"

Could her mother really hear all that over the phone? Or was she merely a good guesser? The last thing Nina wanted was to be psychoanalyzed by her mother. "We've got company right now," she said. "Danny's cousin and his son are here for dinner. I've got to go."

"Not until you tell me why you called in the first place. You know I don't like playing these guessing games, Nin."

Nina sighed, and slipped back into the studio and sat down on the edge of the bed. She might as well get this over with. "I need to borrow money to make my share of this month's rent," she said.

"What about that portrait you just sold?"

"It isn't finished yet." She glanced at the portrait of the woman emerging from the canvas. "And I had to spend part of the money she gave me up front for supplies."

"I thought Danny was making all kinds of money at his job," Natasha said. "Why doesn't he pay the rent?"

"He pays his half, but our agreement is that I'll pay the other half."

"Are you two roommates or lovers?"

"Mom! What do you mean by that?"

"I mean all this splitting hairs and dividing everything down the middle sounds more like roommates than lovers," Natasha said. "If he makes so much more money than you, why can't he be more supportive of your work? Why is he so focused on the bottom line?"

Hadn't Nina asked herself those same questions? Somehow, coming from her mom they hurt more. "Are you suggesting I let Danny support me?"

"If you were married it's what he'd do."

"But we aren't married. And this is the financial arrangement we agreed on."

"Darling, I know this is the twenty-first century, but give me one reason the man should ever marry you if he's free to keep all his money for himself while you struggle to make ends meet? He has all the benefits of your companionship without the least sacrifice. It hardly seems fair."

"What would be fair about him paying more than his share of expenses?"

"I'm not talking an accountant's assessment of fairness," Natasha said. "I am talking about love." She drew out the syllables of the word love, making it sound exotic. "When two people love each other, numbers don't matter and each partner is willing to give one hundred percent to make the relationship work. If only one person is making all the sacrifice, things will never work."

"I don't want Danny to sacrifice for me," Nina said. "I just want to be able pay my half of the rent."

Natasha made a tsking sound. "How much do you need?"

"Two hundred dollars."

"I'll wire the money to your bank in the morning. But you can't make a habit of this. If New York is too expensive, you should come home."

"You want me to leave Danny." The rock in her stomach felt even larger, weighing her down.

"If he really cares for you, he won't let you go."

"Are you suggesting I test him? Make him prove his feelings?"

"At least then you will know for sure where you stand," Natasha said. "Of course, you might not like the answer."

"That's ridiculous. I won't play games like that."

Natasha chuckled. "You don't think relationships all have an element of gamesmanship?"

"Danny and I will figure things out our own way," Nina said.

"I should have known you wouldn't listen to me. You've always been so stubborn. Just like your father."

"Thanks for sending the money," Nina said. "I really do have to go now."

"Go. But think about what I said. Your room here is still waiting for you whenever you need it."

Nina hung up and shoved the phone back into the pocket of

her jeans. What did her mother know about successful relationships? Could a woman who'd been divorced twice really give advice about love?

She returned to the living room, and found everyone sitting down to dinner. "I was about to come looking for you," Danny said.

"My mother called. I couldn't get her off the phone."

"How is Natasha?" Danny asked.

"Fine. She says hello." It was a lie, but she wanted him to think the best of her mother. She'd like him to have a positive view of her before they actually met. Natasha was a wonderful woman, but she could be a bit overwhelming at first.

"Your parents live in Boulder?" John asked.

"My mother does. My father is in Russia. They divorced when I was very young."

John frowned at this news. Was he thinking of his own divorce or of his parents' long marriage?

"This steak is good," Tomas said. "Nina, do you cook?"

"Danny is a better cook than I am," Nina said, glad of the change of subject.

"Nina cleans," Danny said. "It works out."

Nina hadn't really thought of it that way, but she saw Danny was right. When it came to household chores, they didn't divide everything strictly down the middle. She and Danny each did whatever they were best at or disliked the least. So why couldn't they handle finances the same way? Danny could pay more of the bills to make it easier for Nina to stay here in New York, while she did more of what? Shopping? Taking care of the cats and the house? She already did more of those things since she was in town more. This could be used to make the argument that she should pay more of the rent since she made more use of the apartment.

These mathematics made her head hurt. Maybe her mother was right. You couldn't sum up a relationship in terms of accounting. Trying to do so was a recipe for trouble.

"I'm going to be Spiderman for Halloween," Tomas said. "I already have my costume."

"Are you going to go trick or treating?" Nina asked, glad to focus her attention on something besides her own problems. "Or to a party?"

"There's a party at my school. I guess I'll go to that." He shoved another piece of steak into his mouth and chewed thoughtfully.

"We should have a Halloween party." Nina turned to Danny. "A costume party. We could ask everyone to bring food, and you could pick out music for dancing."

"That's a great idea." He turned to John. "You're invited. What costume will you wear?"

John frowned. "I don't want to wear a costume."

"You can come as a bear," Nina said. "I'll make you a mask out of papier-mâché and you can wear a brown suit."

"A bear!" Tomas giggled. "Daddy is a grouchy bear."

John's scowl deepened, but Nina joined Tomas in laughing. Really, John was such a bear sometimes. And now that he'd confessed his wariness of getting close to people, he didn't seem nearly so forbidding.

"What will you come to the party as?" Danny asked Nina.

"I don't know," she said. "I'll have to play around and see what kind of costume I come up with." She wanted a mask—something with feathers and sequins. Maybe an exotic cat or a fantastical figure. Her palms literally itched, and it was all she could do not to leave the table immediately to rush to the studio to begin work. "What costume will you wear?" she asked Danny.

Danny grinned. "You have to wait until the party to see. It'll be a surprise. I'll make it really creative."

John made a snorting noise. "I'd rather you put your creativity into designing the new marketing campaign for Hombre."

"No, it'll be good to have something else to focus on," Danny said. His gaze met Nina's across the table and he winked. "The party is a great idea. We'll have fun planning it together."

Together. That was all she wanted for them. She didn't have to define what that togetherness looked like—where they lived or how much money they made or what they did—only that they do it as a team. Two people creating their own works of art out of the raw materials of life.

Twelve

Sooner or later
Every flame is extinguished.
All fires burn out.

"FANTASTIC PARTY!" Erin, dressed as the Bride of Frankenstein, complete with towering black and white beehive and artfully ripped wedding gown, shouted to be heard over the dance mix blaring from the stereo.

"It's really great," Thad, said. Dressed as a neck-bolted Frankenstein, he handed Erin a glass of the potent punch Nina had mixed up in a punch bowl she'd borrowed from a neighbor. "Like your costume." He nodded at Nina's rendition of a wood nymph—green and black tights twined with silk vines and flowers, topped with a papier mâché half mask adorned with feathers and sequins.

"Thanks. Danny and I had a lot of fun putting this together." Danny had even neglected his work to spend hours sorting through his CD collection for the perfect soundtrack for the evening, then stayed up late locked in her studio, working on his costume.

He joined them now, resplendent in a crimson-lined cloak and stark-white face paint, an elegant, sexy vampire. He grinned to show gleaming fangs. Nina, in a nod to his costume, had painted a discrete but noticeable pair of fang marks onto her own neck. "Have you see John?" he asked.

"Last time I saw him he was talking to a zombie in the kitchen," Nina said. As a joke, she'd made the bear mask and sent it to the office with Danny one day. To her astonishment, John had actually worn it tonight, with a brown tweed suit that made him look like the result of a bizarre nuclear accident or cloning experiment—the head of a bear grafted onto the body of a businessman. The persona suited him, though she wasn't sure he appreciated the irony.

"Best party ever!" Tawny said. In a brief-nurse's costume streaked with fake blood, she danced by with Lawrence, her bicycle-messenger boyfriend who was dressed as a mad scientist in a lab coat and green rubber gloves.

"We should have parties more often," Danny said, pulling Nina close. "Pulling this together was a blast."

"Maybe we'll start a business as professional party planners," she said.

"Or costume designers." He adjusted the collar of his cape.

"No, photographers," Erin said. "Don't forget you're going to photograph my wedding."

"As if we could ever forget," Nina said.

"I may have to be in Santa Fe that week," Danny said.

Erin, Thad, and Nina stared at him. His expression was sober. "You can't be in Santa Fe," Nina said. "You have to be at Erin and Thad's wedding."

"I'm pretty sure I'm supposed to open a store there," Danny said, still grave.

"Then they'll have to open without you." Erin took a sip of her drink, surprisingly calm, Nina thought, for a bride whose carefully made plans were in danger of unraveling. "Or I might have to live up to this costume and go on a rampage."

Danny laughed. "I really had you going there for a minute, didn't I? Of course I'll be at your wedding. I wouldn't miss it."

Nina joined in the laughter, though weakly. "You'd better be there," Erin said. "Or I really will make your life hell."

She and Thad moved off to dance. Nina turned to Danny. "That wasn't a very funny joke," she said. "Erin's stressed out about the wedding as it is."

"You don't really think I'd miss out on the ceremony because of work, do you?" he asked. "You know I'm not that kind of guy."

The problem was, the Danny she'd seen lately was in danger of becoming that kind of guy. He'd set aside practically his whole life in pursuit of his job. The Halloween party was the rare activity that could distract him these days. Nina liked knowing the creative, fun Danny she loved still lurked beneath the surface of his businessman's facade, but even as she enjoyed playing with him tonight, she knew tomorrow he'd be back at his computer, and next week he'd be back on a plane, racking up frequent flyer miles and moving farther away—both physically and emotionally—from her.

She tapped his chest with a long fake fingernail she'd donned for the party. "Will the real Danny de Zayas please stand up? Is he the menacing vampire? Or the dynamic, young businessman? Or the creative genius, musician/writer/web designer?"

"I'm all those things and more," he said.

But his answer didn't please her. How could the businessman and the artist happily coexist? And where did she fall into the picture?

"I'm the wood nymph's lover," he whispered, low and sexy in her ear. A shiver danced down her spine as he pulled her close.

"That would make a strange fairy tale," she said. "The wood nymph and the vampire."

"You ought to write it," he said. "I hear vampire books are very popular these days."

"I don't like books with sad endings," she said. "That's why I prefer fairy tales. In them, everyone lives happily ever after."

"Then write a fairy tale," he said. "The vampire and the wood nymph live happily ever after."

"Yes, but only after he becomes a vegetarian."

"Or he teaches her to enjoy roaming the forest at night."

"So much compromise," she protested, only half in jest.

"But they love each other in spite of their differences," he said. "And because of them. They'll find a way to work things out. They really want to be together."

Was he talking about the fairy-tale characters—or about the two of them? She wanted to ask him, but another party guest called him away. She stood with one hand to her throat, on the bite marks she'd painted there, wondering if real people could ever navigate the challenges of life as skillfully as the characters in fairy tales. Or was happily ever after just another kind of myth, one that couldn't be summed up in a painting or a photograph?

As he'd promised, Danny made sure he was in town the weekend of Thad and Erin's wedding. He and Nina drove to Westchester County that morning, Nina's camera equipment in the back seat. They spent the morning photographing the bride and groom and preparations for the wedding. Nina was in charge, but Danny was able to offer his input. Together, they got some great shots. Then he took over to photograph the ceremony while Nina took her place with the wedding party.

Shooting from the balcony overlooking the altar, Danny focused the camera on the bride and groom exchanging their vows, but his gaze kept straying to Nina. She stood to one side of the altar, a simple black sheath showing off her tall, shapely figure, a bouquet of red roses in her hands. Seeing her in this setting, the air scented with candles and roses, the refrains of the familiar vows echoing in the ornate sanctuary, did funny things to his insides. "Do you take this woman to be your lawfully wedded wife, to have and to hold, in sickness and in health . . ." He closed his eyes and took a deep breath, trying to shake the dizzy, out-of-control feeling.

He opened his eyes again and forced his attention to Erin and Thad. She really was beautiful in her white gown and gossamer veil. Radiant. And Thad looked happy. Confident. He showed no signs of the nervousness Danny would have expected from a man about to pledge himself for life to a woman he'd known three months. Clearly Thad had money and came from money. Danny would think a man with a background like that would think even harder about marrying the wrong woman. A divorce would put a healthy dent in his finances.

Of course love was about more than money, but true love wasn't going to disappear because you delayed the proposal a few months. It seemed smart to take the time to be sure you were making the right choice.

He looked at Nina, and saw a single tear slide down her cheek as she watched Erin and Thad exchange rings. What was it that led so many women to cry at weddings? He could hear the mother of the bride sobbing on the front pew. Then again, it was just like Nina to be moved by her friend's happiness. She was such a sweet, sensitive woman. It was one of the reasons her paintings were so filled with emotion and meaning.

Even John had admitted to Danny after dinner last month that Nina had talent. John still held himself aloof from Nina, but Danny was sure he was thawing. He'd tried to explain to Nina that John was merely a very reserved man, but she couldn't seem to help taking his coolness personally. Probably because she was so warm and friendly herself.

At least Tomas had been utterly charmed. Nina had given the little boy her undivided attention, had listened to his stories and praised his creation with the bit of clay she'd given him, until the boy had been almost hyper with happiness. Danny was certain all John would hear from his son for much of the remainder of his visit would be *Nina, Nina, Nina*.

"I now pronounce you man and wife."

Danny clicked off several pictures of the bride and groom kissing, then picked up the camera and hurried downstairs to photograph the processional. When Nina had made her way down the aisle after the happy couple, she met Danny on the front steps of the church. "I got some great shots," he said. He kissed her cheek. "You were beautiful. I couldn't stop looking at you."

Her cheeks glowed a warmer pink. "You're not supposed to be looking at me."

"You're irresistible. I can't help myself."

She made a face, but when she took hold of his arm and squeezed, he knew she was pleased.

They drove to the reception and set up the cameras once more. They'd circulate among the tables, photographing the guests, then they'd be free to enjoy the rest of the evening.

Randy was already at the country club manning the sound system. He played "How Sweet It Is" as guests arrived. Danny shook his head. "Couldn't he had chosen something less predictable?" he whispered to Nina.

"Maybe the family wanted predictable," she said.

"I'd have persuaded them to think differently," he said.

"Of course you would have. But you're not in charge."

She was right, of course. But that didn't stop him from thinking about how he would have done things if he were calling the shots. One of the best things about his job with John is that when he went out of town to oversee the opening of a new store, he got to be in charge. John left him free to make his own decisions, something that had always been important to him.

He and Nina split up to take more photographs. Danny drifted toward a group of younger guests at the bar. "Danny!" he heard.

He looked up from the camera to see Tawny and her boyfriend Lawrence hurrying toward him. She'd also been a bridesmaid, and wore bright red heels with her black dress. "Wasn't it a gorgeous wedding?" she gushed. "Like a fairy tale."

"Women think every wedding is gorgeous," Lawrence said amiably.

"No we don't." Tawny frowned at him. "My cousin's wedding was an absolute disaster. My uncle got drunk and picked a fight with the groom's brother. The bridesmaids wore these horrible, unflattering orange dresses, and the reception hall was so hot the cake melted."

"I stand corrected," Lawrence said.

"When I get married, I want it to be just like this," Tawny said, the dreamy look seeping into her eyes once more.

"You told me you didn't have any interest in getting married." Lawrence looked alarmed.

"Well . . . not for ages." Tawny took his arm once more. "Right now I really do want to have fun. But one day . . ."

Danny said good-bye and continued his foray through the crowd. He photographed the bride's grandparents and a group of cousins, then made his way to the seat reserved for him next to Nina just as the best man rose to offer a toast. He told some rambling story about Thad, then held his glass aloft. "To Thad and Erin and their happy life together."

The clink of glasses sounded like chimes around the room. Danny touched glasses with Nina. "It's so romantic," she whispered.

"Yes." It was romantic, but was it real, or only a fantasy? He liked the thrill of romance, but long-term, you needed something more. Something sure.

After dinner the guests took to the dance floor. Nina photographed the bride dancing with her new husband, then with her father. Afterward, Danny approached Nina where she stood on the side of the dance floor. "May I have this dance?" he asked formally.

"All right." She looked around and spotted Tawny. "Will you watch my camera?" she asked.

"Sure."

Danny and Nina moved onto the dance floor and he took her in his arms. He remembered the first time they'd danced. He'd wanted to hold her like this then, but hadn't dared. He'd already been falling in love with Nina then; maybe he'd always loved her. He knew he'd felt something special almost from their first meeting.

"I love you," he said now, and pulled her closer.

She looked at him, eyes shining. "I love you, too." They danced on, through one song, and then another, both unwilling to break the spell of closeness. He was away so much lately; he wanted to savor this chance to be with her without other demands on his time and attention. "Do you know what your cousin said to me when he came for dinner last month?" Nina asked.

"John?" He wasn't sure he liked his cousin intruding on this romantic moment.

"Yes. He said I shouldn't take offense at his not wanting to get close to me because he never got close to someone when he wasn't certain they'd stay in his life."

"John takes awhile to warm up to people. I told you that."

"Did you say something to make him think I wasn't going to stay a part of his life . . . of your life?"

"No!" The crazy, out-of-control feeling he'd experienced while watching Nina at the front of the church returned, and he gripped her more tightly. "John was burned by his ex-wife, so he's skeptical of all relationships. But you're not like her, and I'm not like my cousin. I have no intention of letting you go."

She smiled and relaxed against him. "Good," she said, and lay her head on his shoulder.

But it was awhile before Danny's heart stopped pounding. What was John thinking? Danny loved Nina, and the two of them were made for each other. Of course he and Nina were going to stay together.

After the excitement of the wedding, Nina felt let down. Erin left on a two-week honeymoon to Fiji, and Danny flew to Las Vegas to open Hombre's biggest store yet. Nina worked on the commissioned portrait, which was shaping up nicely. The woman had requested a depiction of herself on the subway—yet the subway wasn't really the subway, but purgatory, the other passengers were lost souls. The painting had a mysterious, dreamy quality Nina loved—not to mention the dark humor in the idea of the a train as Purgatory.

But other than the painting, Nina felt dissatisfied with everything else in her life. She berated herself for this attitude; she had no reason to be unhappy. A few sales of photographs had fattened her bank account and life was good.

But then she would pull out the photographs she'd taken of the wedding. She was supposed to be assembling an album to present to the happy couple when they returned from the honeymoon, but as she flipped through shots of the bride and groom exchanging vows or standing with members of the wedding party she only felt more depressed. The day had been so romantic, and Erin had been so happy. Thad—rich, handsome Thad—had been willing to risk everything based on only a few month's acquaintance to pledge to spend the rest of his life with Erin. Part of Nina knew it was crazy; she'd never have acted so impulsively herself. Yet another part of her thrilled at that kind of certainty that you were meant to be with the one you loved, no matter what the cost.

As much as she adored Danny, she couldn't imagine him making such a sacrifice for her. She told herself she didn't even want him to sacrifice for her; why should she want the man she loved to suffer? But she wanted to know he would if she needed him to. "I am such a stupid romantic," she told Snuffleupagus as the cat lay cradled in her arms one evening. "I want to be strong and independent, yet I want Danny there to support me too. And I would be there to support him also." She knew if Danny needed anything from her she would give it—money, her car, a kidney. She wouldn't hesitate. But knowing Danny, he'd never even ask. He'd been doing things on his own, to great success, for so long she couldn't imagine a scenario where he'd ever need her help.

She shoved these thoughts aside and focused on happier things. She'd finished the portrait and would deliver it Saturday morning. Danny was flying home Friday night, and Saturday night they'd planned a dinner with friends to celebrate. Erin and Thad, home from the honeymoon, would come, along with Tawny and Lawrence and Randy and his latest, a woman named Morgan

music stands, and crates of DVDs, CDs, and band T-shirts.

"Nina doesn't care about the mess," Melissa stepped over a duffle bag and took hold of one side of the painting. "Get the scissors so we can unwrap this masterpiece. I want to see."

Joe rummaged around in a kitchen drawer and returned with a pair of barber's scissors, which he used to slice through the layers of tape and paper. Then he and Melissa tore off the bubble wrap to reveal her portrait.

"Oh!" she cried, and covered her mouth with both hands.

Nina shifted from foot to foot, nervously watching her. She knew she'd done a good job with the painting, but you could never be sure about people. Sometimes they had a very different picture of themselves than the artist envisioned.

"It's beautiful." Joe spoke first. He grinned at Nina. "You're a genius."

"It's perfect." Melissa turned to Nina, her eyes shiny with tears. "Even better than I imagined. Thank you so much."

"I'll hang it as soon as I can find a hammer," Joe said. He looked around the disordered apartment.

"We'll buy a new hammer if we have to," Melissa said. She took both Nina's hands in hers. "It's wonderful. Amazing."

"You were a wonderful subject to paint," Nina said. Melissa was so colorful and creative herself, Nina had felt free to exercise her creativity.

"I'll get your check," Joe said, and disappeared into what Nina assumed was the bedroom.

"Your timing was perfect," Melissa said. "Joe just got in from Amsterdam last night. And next week the two of us are headed to Trinidad for a few weeks."

Melissa was a dancer who worked part time as a chorus girl or a dance teacher. The schedule left her free to travel with Joe several times a year. "What are you doing in Trinidad?" Nina asked.

"Melissa and I are working on a jazz musical together." Joe returned from the bedroom and handed Nina a check.

"He's doing the music, I'm choreographing the dances, and we're writing the book together," Melissa said. "Our friends have offered the use of their place in Trinidad as long as we like."

"I'm jealous," Nina said. This was the kind of life she wished for herself and Danny—not long weeks apart and no time to work on projects together.

With more thanks and praise of her genius, Nina was ushered out the door. She drove home in a cloud of happiness. What artist didn't like to be praised—as well as paid—for her work?

Back at the apartment, Danny was in the kitchen, shopping bags crowding the countertops. "How did it go?" he asked, kissing her hello.

"They loved it."

"Of course."

"Joe and his band just got back from a tour of Amsterdam. And he and Melissa are leaving next weekend to go to Trinidad. They're writing a musical together."

"Now that I'd like to see." He turned back to the sink, where he was washing a pile of colorful peppers. "The receipt for the groceries is on the table. Your half comes to forty-three dollars and eighty cents. Oh, and two dollars and sixty-three cents for the bananas."

"Two sixty-three for the bananas?" He'd actually bothered to figure them separately?

"You know I don't eat bananas, so you should pay for them." His expression remained pleasant. Logical.

She stared at him, anger rising. "They're just bananas," she said.

"I never liked bananas." He turned and went back to washing peppers.

She stared at the back of his head, debating whether or not to strike him with a pot. But she doubted that would knock some sense into him. Danny just didn't get it. He thought he was being logical and fair to divide expenses the way he did. He didn't see how he was sapping every bit of romance out of the relationship. Her mom had been right; he was treating her like a roommate. One he welcomed into his bed, but not into his bank account.

She fled the kitchen, not wanting to start an argument right before their guests arrived. She told herself that with a little time she'd calm down. After all, this time she really did have plenty of money to pay him, and he knew it. So it wasn't as if he was placing a burden on her. But she couldn't shake her annoyance at what she saw as his stinginess.

By the time their guests arrived, she was jittery with nerves, grateful for the distraction of company. Thad and Erin, tan and glowing from their honeymoon, arrived first; followed closely by Randy and Morgan, who were still an item months after the dinner party where the others had first met her. Tawny and Lawrence came in last, wind-blown and laughing, having ridden over on Lawrence's motorcycle. "Look!" Tawny said as soon as they'd caught their breath and accepted drinks. She rolled up her sleeve to reveal a string of Chinese symbols tattooed on her bicep. "It's Lawrence's name. He's got mine, too."

Lawrence displayed his own bicep, and a similar string of letters.

"That's so romantic," Erin exclaimed.

Nina didn't know about romantic, but it was certainly permanent, and a bigger commitment than she would have expected from Tawny about any man.

"How do you know it's really your name?" Danny asked. "Maybe it says Stupid White Man."

The others laughed, but Tawny frowned. "We picked the letters out of a book. I'm sure it's right." She gave Lawrence a worried look.

He shrugged and patted her back. "Hey, we know what it means to us. That's all that matters."

"How was the honeymoon?" Randy asked.

"It was amazing!" Erin smiled dreamily. "Fiji was so beautiful. And I wish you could have seen Thad bargaining in the market for some beads I wanted."

"I was terrible at it," Thad admitted. "Erin had to step in and negotiate for me. She talked the woman into cutting her price by two-thirds."

"They don't respect you if you don't bargain," Erin said.

"She's a born negotiator." Thad put his arm around his wife. "I knew it as soon as I saw the deal she cut for our house."

"In this market they were asking too much," she said. "If there's one thing I know, it's real estate prices, especially in this neighborhood."

"You're staying in Brooklyn?" Nina asked. "I thought you were moving to Manhattan."

"We were, but then we decided we'd be more comfortable in Brooklyn."

"All Erin's friends are here, and I can live anywhere," Thad said.

"You'll have a longer commute," Danny said.

"It won't be too bad. Besides, there are a lot of opportunities in Brooklyn real estate right now."

"I'm thinking of starting my own business, buying and selling properties," Erin said. "I'm going to start studying for my real estate license right away."

"Morgan and I are thinking of starting a business, too," Randy said. "Party services. We'll handle the music and bartending, of course, but also catering and decorations—everything."

"We figure we can do weddings and bar mitzvahs and anniversary celebrations and things like that," Morgan said.

"Congratulations," Nina said, the word almost sticking in her throat. All of their friends were embarking on exciting new ventures—together—while work only drove her and Danny apart.

"How's your job going?" Randy asked. "I was back in Pittsburgh visiting my folks a couple weeks ago and saw an Hombre store there."

"We're set to add twenty-five more stores by the end of the year," Danny said. "Business is booming."

"That's incredible," Thad said. "Sounds like you and your cousin have really found your market niche."

"We've got some great new clothing designs," Danny said. "People really like the concept."

Some of the original designs had been Danny's, Nina knew. But when was the last time he'd been able to devote time to the creative side of the business? He was too busy shopping for real estate, hiring store managers, and dealing with local regulations. He claimed to enjoy the work, but was it really what he wanted to do?

"Nina just finished a portrait," Danny said. "A commission. The woman loved it."

"Congratulations," Erin said, and the others around the table echoed the sentiment.

"Your paintings are so beautiful," Erin said. "They should be in a gallery. Someplace really prestigious."

"You should enter one of those juried shows," Morgan said. "Winning one of those might get you some real attention."

"Good idea," Nina said. "Though the entry fees are sometimes expensive." More than her budget would bear.

"Everything in New York is expensive," Tawny said. "Lawrence and I have seriously thought about moving. Almost anyplace else in the United States we'd be living the good life on the money we make, instead of scraping by."

"Prices here really are ridiculous," Morgan said. "But the city has so much to offer that you can't find anywhere else."

"That doesn't matter if you can't afford to go out and do anything," Tawny said.

Nina silently agreed. For the last few years she'd thought the struggle was worth it, sure success was just around the corner. But New York was the kind of place where even modest achievement in art wasn't enough to make a living. She could see the day coming, not too far in the future, when to pay her bills she might have to give up on her dreams and take a job clerking in a store or waiting tables. The thought made her shudder.

"Let's not talk about money, please," Morgan said. "It's too depressing. I want to hear more about Fiji. What was the weather like? And the food—what did you eat?"

Erin obligingly launched into a description of the luxury hotel where they'd stayed and the feast they'd attended, which included a whole roast pig and Polynesian dancers who'd persuaded Thad to join them. Soon they were all laughing at Thad's antics and toasting the newlyweds.

The guests left very late, and Danny sat on the sofa, empty drink glasses scattered on tables, pillows on the floor. "That was fun," he said. "We should do that more often."

Nina picked up a pillow and sat at the opposite end of the sofa from him, the pillow hugged to her chest. "I don't think so." All evening her thoughts had churned, until she'd finally reached a conclusion. She didn't like the decision she'd reached, but the inevitability of it weighed on her.

"What do you mean? Didn't you have a good time?"

"I enjoyed seeing all our friends, but I just don't think I can do this anymore."

"Can't do what?"

"I can't afford to live in New York. Tawny's right. Everything is too expensive. I make money from my art—enough to live on in other cities, but not here."

A deep V formed in Danny's brow, and he leaned toward her. "You've been doing really well. That portrait of Melissa was only a start. If you advertise more, get in some shows . . ."

"It wouldn't matter. I'd still always be struggling, always worried about paying the bills." She looked into his eyes, silently pleading. Here was his opportunity to offer some solution, some way she could stay here and they could be together.

Instead, he sat back, his expression stunned. "Where would you go?"

She swallowed a knot of tears. "Back to Boulder. At least for a little while."

He nodded. "We can still see each other. We'll talk on the phone and I'll come visit."

So calm and logical. Damn him.

"What about the cats?" he asked.

"You'll have to keep them. My mother won't allow them."

"All right."

She had the surreal feeling of being in a play. She and Danny weren't really talking; they were reciting lines. As if it didn't really matter that she was leaving. She looked away, not wanting him to see how much this hurt her. She had thought he would care so much more.

"I don't want you to go." His voice was husky. Strained.

She shook her head. "I can't stay. I can't even afford the damn bananas." Then she dissolved into tears.

He moved over and put his arms around her, holding her close, not speaking. If only he would *say* something—that he'd do anything to make her stay. That she was more important to him than the price of bananas. "I love you," he said instead.

"I love you too," she said. "But right now, that isn't enough."

"I guess not," he said.

Wrong answer. Not the one she needed to hear. She began to cry harder, mourning the loss of all they'd had together—but also the loss of her dreams of what they could have been.

Thirteen

You are missed right now,
More than you think, and you are loved
More than you know.

TWO DAYS LATER, DANNY WOKE with a pounding headache and the feeling he was suffocating. He knew before he opened his eyes that the bed beside him was empty. Nina had driven away yesterday morning, her car packed with her clothes and art supplies, headed for Boulder, Colorado, where her mother had assured her that her old room was waiting. Danny had spent the rest of the day trying to numb the pain with alcohol.

He opened his eyes, wincing at the light pouring through the window. "Meow!" A whiskered face confronted him. Another furry face appeared beside the first. Both cats stared at him accusingly. They were both sitting on his chest; that explained the smothering feeling. He struggled into a sitting position, shoving the cats aside, and peered at the clock beside the bed. It was after ten. Well past the time the cats were used to being fed.

"Meow! Meow!" Their complaints followed him to the bathroom, where he turned on the shower full blast. While he waited for the water to get hot, he stared at his face in the mirror. He looked twenty years older—bags under bloodshot eyes, a stubbly beard darkening his jaw and cheeks. Nina used to fuss that he didn't shave often enough; she had never been one to find the scruffy look sexy.

Nina. He squeezed shut his eyes, fighting back tears. He couldn't believe she was gone. She had been the one woman he was sure he'd stay with forever. They had been so right for each other, like two halves of a whole. How could she have left him?

He stepped into the shower and let the scalding water pour over him. After the shower he shaved and dressed, then went to the kitchen and fed the cats and made coffee. When he opened the cabinet to get a cup he stared at a mug Nina had left behind. She'd bought it on their trip to Canada; it had a decal of a Canadian maple leaf on the side.

He knew this was how it was going to be—everywhere he turned he would see something that reminded him of Nina. He shoved the mug farther back into the cabinet and took out a plain black one, then turned toward the cabinet where they stored the bagels. But before he could open it he was confronted with the fruit basket with three freckled bananas on top. Nina's bananas.

He snatched up the bananas to toss them in the trash, but couldn't bring himself to let them go. He stood over the trash can, staring at them. What was it about those bananas that had upset her so much? Was it because he'd asked her to pay for them? But they'd agreed to share expenses. They'd wanted to be partners. Equals.

But there'd been nothing equal about their finances. That was part of the problem. Nina was a broke artist. And she'd been right—New York really was too expensive for her. Maybe they should have divided the bills by percentages. . . . He shook his head, still feeling foggy. No, that wasn't right. But who could understand women?

After two cups of coffee and a bagel he felt a little better, but now that he was fully awake the pain of Nina's absence was even more intense. He needed to get out of the apartment. Walking around the city would help him think. He needed to figure out where he'd gone wrong. How he could fix things. He solved problems for a living—surely he could solve the biggest problem he'd ever faced in his life.

Nina had moved into the apartment on a warm summer day when the trees made islands of shade along the sidewalk. Danny remembered how happy he'd been that day. Now November winds had stripped the trees of their leaves, and the sky was as gray as Danny's mood. His walk took him past the dollar store where he'd run into Nina his first day in the neighborhood. He paced off the steps to her old apartment building and stared up at the window that had been hers. They'd made love just once in that little room, when he'd gone over to help her with some boxes she was moving into his place. She'd kissed him when he came in the door and as the kisses turned more passionate they'd forgotten all about the boxes around them and ended up sprawled across her bed, unable to get enough of the feel of each other's bodies.

It had always been that way with him and Nina—the need for each other that ran deeper than mere lust. Making love with her had really fit the description of coming together to create something bigger than themselves. Something that nourished and energized them both. How would he live without that now?

He turned back toward his apartment, but walked past it to the café where he used to work. A woman he didn't know was behind the counter. Danny ordered coffee, then walked over and studied the little gallery of Nina's photographs by the door. One of the photos she'd taken at Coney Island was there—the Ferris wheel outlined in a blur of lights. The night he'd gone there with her he knew he was in love. He'd felt connected to Nina in a way he'd never been to any other person. She had an open, almost childlike way of looking at the world, and he'd been able to see things through her eyes. She saw beauty and humor in things other people merely passed by.

When she looked at him, he felt taller, and smarter, and better than he probably had a right to feel. He felt *special*. With Nina he could be a better man than he was without her. And now he'd screwed up and let her get away.

"Danny!"

He turned and saw Rob crossing the room toward him. "I haven't seen you in a long time," Rob said. "How are you doing?"

My whole life is falling apart. But all he said was "I'm fine. How are you?"

"I'm doing good. You remember that woman I was dating—the photographer?" He pointed to another set of photographs opposite Nina's. "Sandra."

"Sure." Though Danny had only a vague recollection of the woman.

"We're engaged."

Danny blinked. Was the whole world getting married? "Congratulations," he said. "That's great."

"Thanks. Say, how's Nina? You two still together?"

"No. Nina's moved back to Boulder."

"That's too bad. She was a sweet girl."

"Yeah."

"It was good seeing you, man. See you around."

He went back to his office and Danny left the café. He felt the need to keep moving. If he let himself stop, if he gave himself a chance to think too much, he might never get going again.

He turned into the first subway station he saw and descended to the platform, where he took a train heading south. He rode to the end of the line—Coney Island. He told himself that in broad daylight on a November weekday the place would look too different, but as soon as he stepped out of the subway station the aromas of popcorn and hot dogs drifting from the boardwalk, and the salt air of the sea took him back to that night on the boardwalk with Nina. He half expected her to peer at him from around a post, straw hat at a rakish angle on her head, a pink plastic water pistol aimed at his heart.

He doubted any real gunshot could hurt worse than the pain he felt now. He pulled his cell phone from his pocket and punched in Nina's number. She answered on the third ring. "Hello?"

"I'm calling to see how you're doing," he said. "How is the drive so far?"

"Oh. Fine. I spent the night in some little town in Ohio and got an early start this morning."

He wondered if she'd had trouble sleeping—or if she was anxious to put that much more distance between them. "Where are you now?" he asked.

"Somewhere in Indiana."

"I miss you," he said.

"I miss you, too."

And then there didn't seem to be anything else to say. He could tell her he loved her, but she knew that. Knowing it hadn't changed her determination to leave. "Call me when you get to your mom's," he said. "I want to know you're all right."

"I will."

And then they hung up. He stared at his phone for a long while, at the picture he used as his screen saver—Nina waving at him from the window of the apartment they'd shared, her hair a soft-brown cloud around her face, her eyes shining with such happiness and love he'd thought would be his forever.

How could he have been so wrong? How could he have failed to make things work with her? He'd spent his whole life being successful at everything he tried, but he'd managed to screw up the one thing that mattered most.

"Ninochka, darling. I'm so glad you're finally here." Natasha enveloped Nina in a strong hug, then stood back to survey her daughter. As tall as Nina, Natasha wore her shoulder-length hair in a layered cut, the brown artfully streaked with blond. Dressed in pale blue yoga pants and a light- and dark-blue sleeveless top, she looked more like Nina's older sister than her mother. "You look exhausted," she said.

"It's a long drive, Mom." Nina walked past her into the living room and dropped her purse and a duffle bag on the floor. "I have a lot of stuff in the car to unload."

"We can get all that in a little while. For now, sit down and rest. I'll make some tea." Natasha steered Nina to an armchair, then hurried off to the kitchen.

Nina closed her eyes and leaned her head back against the chair. The trip had been a nightmare of endless miles of highway stretching before her. Normally she enjoyed traveling, but she'd ignored the passing scenery, driven by a compulsion to reach home, to the safe haven where she could try to put her life back together again. When she was forced to stop for the night, she tossed and turned in a cold, lumpy hotel bed, missing Danny more than she'd thought it possible to miss someone, crying herself to sleep and waking at first light with sandpapery eyes and the heavy feeling of loss.

"This needs to steep a bit, but it will help you feel better." Natasha returned with two steaming mugs.

"What is it?" Nina asked, sniffing the fragrant steam.

"Chamomile to calm your nerves, passionflower for stress, and some lemon balm—for grief."

Nina almost lost it then. But she'd cried so much already she hadn't the energy for more tears. "Thanks," she said, and sipped at the hot liquid, which was weak but still pleasant tasting.

Natasha patted her knee. "Breakups are always hard," she said. "It hurts so much at first, but you'll get over him. Probably sooner than you expect."

"I really loved him, Mom. I still love him."

"There's love and there's love," she said, with the attitude of a sage. Nina could imagine her leading a yoga class, imparting her wisdom. But Nina wasn't one of her eager students.

"I love Danny," she said again. "We just couldn't make things work."

"I'm not saying he doesn't care for you, but if he really loved you he would have tried harder to make you stay." She sipped her tea. "I may be twice divorced, but when I was with a man, I was really with him. Both of my husbands would have fought to the death for me. Love isn't worth the trouble without that kind of passion."

Nina stared at her mother. She couldn't imagine either her father or her stepfather so much as insulting a waiter on behalf of anyone, but her mother seemed to view them both as gladiators. Maybe that was what was missing from her and Danny's relationship—that kind of delusional thinking.

"Thanks for letting me stay here for awhile," she said.

"You can stay as long as you like. Today we will get you settled into your room, and tomorrow you can come with me to my first class of the day."

"Mom, I don't know about the class." Natasha taught tantric yoga to both couples and singles.

"Don't be silly. It's just a beginning hatha yoga class. I took it on as a favor because the regular teacher had to go out of town to take care of her sick father. It will be good for you, help you rid your body of some of those toxic emotions. And I thought tomorrow afternoon you could help me with the labyrinth I'm building in the back yard."

"The what?"

"Labyrinth. It's an ancient meditative practice—walking the labyrinth. I'm certified to teach the technique now and want to offer a labyrinth here for my students."

"Of course." Nina had no doubt her mother would have willing students lined up at her door, eager to pay for lessons in walking the labyrinth. After all, this was Boulder, where there was an alternative remedy for anything that ailed you. Nina was skeptical about most of her mother's practices, but she welcomed the distraction. In some ways, life here with her mother in Boulder was like an alternate reality. That was exactly what she needed if she was going to figure out a way to live life without Danny.

Tuesday morning, Danny showed up at the door of John's brownstone, a cat carrier in each hand. Chickadee and Snuffleupagus loudly protested as Danny rang the bell and waited for John to answer.

The door flew open and John, wearing only a pair of sweatpants and a scowl, glared at him. "You had better have a damn good reason for waking me at six-thirty in the morning!"

"I'm on my way to the airport—the Vegas store, remember?"

He set the cat carriers in the hallway, one on either side of his cousin. "I need you to look after Chick and Snufflegoose while I'm gone."

"What?" John stepped back from the carriers as if afraid one of the cats might suddenly break free and attack. "Why do I have to look after the cats?"

"Because I can't leave them alone in the apartment all week while I'm gone. I've got their litter box and food in the car. Just set them up in your guest room and they'll be fine. Chickadee is the black and white and yellow one. Snuffleupagus is the yellow tabby."

"What kind of bizarre names are those?"

"Nina named them." She'd been so thrilled the day they adopted the kittens; he'd felt like a hero for letting her talk him into it. The memory was another glass shard to his heart.

"Then why doesn't Nina take care of them?"

Here it was then—the moment he'd dreaded. The moment when he'd have to admit out loud that she was gone. "Nina's gone back to Boulder to live," he said.

"I'm sorry to say it, but I had a feeling it wouldn't last. Those artist types are so flighty."

"Shut up."

The menace in Danny's voice silenced his cousin. John studied Danny's face, real concern in his eyes. "I'm sorry," he said. "It doesn't matter what I think. You shouldn't have to go through this. Do you want to come in for coffee? Talk about it?"

"I have to get to the airport." The last thing he wanted was to hear John put Nina down. He understood the reason for his cousin's cynicism; John's ex had put him through the wringer. But Nina wasn't like that. There wasn't a mean or vindictive bone in her body. And he couldn't shake the feeling that she was gone because *he* was to blame—because he hadn't done something he should have.

"Don't worry about the cats while you're gone," John said. "And call me if you need to talk."

"Thanks." He fetched the cat supplies from the car, then set out for the airport. On the plane he tried to sleep, but all he could think of was all the trips he and Nina had talked about taking—to visit her home in Russia, to Italy and France and Iceland and Turkey, and a hundred other destinations near and far. He wanted to discover the world through her eyes, to sit for hours talking over coffee in foreign cafés, then lie beside her and watch her sleep for a lifetime of sunrises. Because he loved her so much—more than he'd ever loved any woman—he'd assumed that would all happen. They were meant to be together, so what more did they need?

But Nina apparently needed more. More money if she was going to live in New York, yes, but more from him, too. She'd never said as much, but he'd sensed it. If only he could figure it out.

In the meantime, he had to go through the motions of living. He had to work, and take care of the cats, and pretend that everything was normal, all while he was dying inside.

Within a week of moving back into her old room at her mother's, Nina landed a part-time job teaching art to children in an after-school program. It was only a six-week program, and not what she wanted to do with her life, but it would give her a chance to get on her feet financially. And she loved the children. She thought of Tomas and the afternoon he'd spent at the apartment, shaping animals out of clay. If she'd stayed with Danny, would they have had a little boy or girl that she'd one day teach to hold a paint brush and sculpt with Play-Doh?

But that kind of thinking was too dangerous. So she threw herself into work and keeping busy, and trying not to think of Danny—an effort made more difficult by the fact that they still talked on the phone several times a week. He told her about work or funny stories about the cats that made her smile through tears she was glad he couldn't see.

"You should make a clean break with him," Natasha told her one afternoon as she and Nina were moving a pile of rock slabs Natasha had selected as the raw materials for her labyrinth. A chilly wind blew dried leaves around their feet, but the intense sun kept them warm as they worked in jeans and light jackets. "Tell him you don't want to talk to him anymore."

"I can't tell him that." Nina positioned a slab of slate where Natasha indicated. "I want to talk to him. He's still my friend."

"You can't go from lovers to friends," Natasha said. "It never works."

"You and Dad are still friends," Nina said, referring to her stepfather.

"We are not *close* friends," Natasha said. "There's a difference. Now bring that shovel over here and dig out around this rock so that it sits level."

"Danny's my best friend," Nina said. "That's even tougher to find than a lover. I can't just abandon that."

"I thought Erin was your best friend. Pick up the other end of this rock."

Nina hoisted the end of the rock, and she and her mom crab-walked it to its designated spot in the labyrinth. "Erin is my best girlfriend. But Danny is the person I can talk to about anything, anytime. He gets me."

Natasha looked up from the drawing she was consulting. "You're romanticizing, Ninochka. Never a good thing. If he understood you so well, he would have understood that you needed him to contribute more to making sure you could stay with him. From what you've told me, his bank account was more important to him than your presence."

"I don't think it was all about money." Nina sat down on a boulder. "Danny isn't selfish."

"Then he is clueless, which isn't any better. Now get up. We still have a lot of work to do."

"Why don't you hire some workmen to help you with this?" Nina said, as she strained to move yet another rock.

"Because I have you here. And because you could use the exercise."

Nina bit her lip. Natasha was probably right, but that didn't lessen Nina's urge to protest that she didn't need her mother telling her what to do.

"By the way, I ran into Alex Lessing yesterday." The overly studied casualness of Natasha's tone had Nina on instant alert. "I told him you were back in town and he seemed very interested," Natasha continued.

"Mom! I'm really not interested in Mr. Bugger-Eater."

"Don't say that until you've seen him. He's turned out very nice looking. One thing you can say about bicycle racers—they're very fit."

"Really, Mom. I think it's too soon for me to date again." The very idea made her heart hurt.

"You don't have to date him. But it wouldn't hurt to get together for coffee." Natasha tossed a shovel full of dirt, just missing Nina's feet. "He could introduce you to other people your age in the area. You need to get out more instead of spending all your time cooped up with me."

"I don't mind staying home with you," she said. She and Natasha got along surprisingly well—when they weren't arguing about Danny or Nina's future.

"I don't mean to be blunt, dear, but you're cramping my style. It's rather awkward to invite a man over when you're just in the next room."

Nina felt her face heat. "Anytime you want to entertain, just tell me. I'll go to the movies or something."

Natasha leaned on the shovel. "I suppose we could arrange some sort of signal, like a lowered window shade or a candle in the window."

Or maybe Nina should find her own place—soon.

An hour later Nina came into the house, muscles aching. Thankfully, her mother had stopped nagging her about Danny and had made no further mention of Alex. She was on her way to the shower when her cell phone rang. She lunged for it, thinking maybe she should confront Danny—ask him straight out why he hadn't begged her to stay or offered any solution other than her leaving.

But the call was from Erin. "I have the most exciting news!" she said, as soon as Nina answered.

"What is it?" Knowing Erin, she might have just found a new dress on sale—or learned how to cook roast duck. In addition to her real-estate courses, Erin had signed up for gourmet-cooking classes.

"Thad has a chance to get transferred to Denver. You and I could be practically neighbors again."

"That is wonderful news," Nina said. The best news she'd heard in awhile. She'd missed seeing all her New York friends, especially Erin.

"It's so amazing how it happened," Erin said. "Apparently, Thad's boss mentioned the possibility to him weeks ago, but the silly goose was afraid to tell me. Can you believe it? He thought I'd be upset because I've got all these plans for my real estate business but, honestly, I can sell real estate anywhere. I mean, I'm sure Denver has houses and office buildings like anywhere else."

"I think it's sweet that he was worried about your feelings," Nina said.

"Sweet, but silly. Of course, it's not a done deal yet. The big boss of their Denver office wants Thad to interview, but once they meet him, I know they'll love him."

"And he's okay with moving so far from his family?" Nina asked.

"Are you kidding? That's part of the attraction. Not, mind you, that his family isn't perfectly nice, but there's a lot of pressure on him to live up to their standards. They think he should buy a house near them, join their country club, and enroll our future children in the private day school Thad and his sisters attended. They just don't get that we might want to do things differently. Living farther away would be a good thing for us."

"Then I hope Thad gets the job. Let me know when you're ready to go house hunting."

"Absolutely. I'm counting on you to go looking with me. But okay, enough about me. How are you doing?"

"I'm okay. The job's good, and I'm thinking I'll take my camera up to the mountains soon and get some photographs in the snow." Her art supplies had sat mostly unused since the move, and she hadn't taken the camera out once.

"I ran into Danny the other day. I stopped by that café where he used to work and he was in there getting dinner. He didn't look very good. I think he's lost weight, and he said he hasn't been sleeping well."

Nina felt as if a fist squeezed her heart. *What did he do?* she wondered. *What did he say? Did he mention me?* "He's probably working too hard," was all she said.

"I think he misses you."

The fist squeezed tighter. "I miss him, too," she said, fighting tears.

"Maybe . . ." Erin hesitated. "Maybe you could give him another chance."

"I can't move back to New York. Not if things are going to be the same as they were before. Besides, he hasn't said anything about wanting me back."

"You've talked to him?"

"We talk all the time. We're still good friends."

"You still love each other."

"He doesn't love me enough to make any effort to get back together."

"So what are you going to do?"

"Nothing, I guess."

"It doesn't sound good," Erin said. "Stuck on a guy you can't have. Maybe you should go out, try to meet some new people there."

"Now you sound like my mother."

"Ouch! But you know, mothers sometimes do know best."

Nina sighed. "I guess I really ought to try to make some friends here. I can't sit home with my mother all the time."

"When I'm there I'll make sure you get out and meet people. I've got to go now. I'm meeting Thad downtown for dinner."

Nina tossed the phone aside and went into the shower. Erin was right—she was in danger of getting stuck, wanting Danny but not having the power to change him into the man she needed him to be. She had to get on with her life, to start looking for a

place to live and making new friends and getting back to her artwork. She'd already lost part of her heart to Danny. She couldn't
lose the rest of herself, too.

Fourteen

Between love and loss
Lies a point of convergence
Where the circle breaks.

"YOU LOOK AWFUL. Do you need to see a doctor or did you just party too much over the weekend?"

"Shut up." Danny shoved aside a stack of catalogs and slumped onto the sofa in his cousin's office. Last week they'd both made the trek to Miami to spend Christmas and the New Year with their parents—a subdued celebration lightened only by the arrival of Tomas on Christmas afternoon. Home again, the cousins hadn't seen each other for the first week of the New Year, each preferring to nurse his depression alone.

John, of all people, ought to know Danny's current condition had nothing to do with partying. No weekend bender would account for the weight he'd lost or the permanent dark bruises under his eyes. He had the aches and pains of a man twice his age, and every bite he put in his mouth tasted like sawdust. But no doctor was going to be able to help him.

"I'm worried about you," John persisted. "If you don't see a doctor, maybe you should see a counselor or something."

"I don't want to talk about it." He especially didn't want to talk about his feelings with some shrink. He knew he was taking this breakup with Nina badly, but he loved Nina too much to simply go on with his life as if she hadn't meant something special. And in a way all his suffering seemed right—what he deserved. Every time he talked to her on the phone it was like digging a knife into a wound, drawing out the pain, seeing if he could take it.

Last night had been the worst. Unable to sleep, he'd phoned Nina, wanting to hear her voice. When he asked what she was up to, she'd hesitated, then told him she'd just come in from dinner with an "old friend from school." A male friend. The knowledge had made Danny feel physically ill, as if he might throw up right then and there. The rest of the conversation had been obscured by a red haze in his mind—a blinding jealousy he hadn't known was in him. He'd wrestled with the emotion all night, sleeping fitfully to dream of Nina on a raft in the ocean, drifting ever farther away from him.

"You haven't heard a word I've said for the last five minutes, have you?"

He looked up to find John frowning at him. "Sorry," Danny muttered. He sat up straighter and tried to focus. "What was it you needed?"

"I was talking about the Pittsburgh store. Sales are lagging there and I suspect it has something to do with management. I need you to go down there, and see if you can figure out what's going on and straighten them out."

Pittsburgh. Danny had a vague memory of a disgruntled manager who'd been annoyed at taking direction from Danny, who was at least ten years younger. "You should go," Danny said. "He'll respond better to you."

"All right. But then I'll need you to visit the Baltimore store to talk about their expansion into a new space."

Danny mentally ticked off a list of all that trip would entail: meetings with real estate agents, builders, city inspectors, store management . . . crunching numbers and massaging egos, and doing all the things that were almost second nature to him now. There was nothing creative or challenging or interesting in that work. It paid well and it helped his cousin, but was it really worth all he'd given up to do it? He no longer had time for music and film and art and all the things he loved. Half a dozen ideas for businesses of his own sat gathering dust while he crisscrossed the country on planes. And maybe the work had contributed to him losing Nina. He'd left her alone so much of the time, the gap between their incomes ever widening. . . .

"Danny, are you going to answer me, or are you just going to stare off into space all morning?"

Danny looked at his cousin. John was thirty-two. Good-looking. Smart. He could afford to hire the best managers in the business. He didn't need Danny to help him. And Danny didn't need his cousin to watch over him, no matter how well-intentioned John was. "No," he said.

"No?" The furrows on John's brow deepened. "No what?"

"No, I can't go to Baltimore. Or Pittsburgh. Or anywhere else. I quit."

"What do you mean you quit?"

"I can't do this job anymore. It's stifling me. I don't have time for a life. For the things I really love."

"I thought you liked working with me. We were building the business together."

Danny cringed at the hurt in his cousin's voice, but refused to weaken. "It was a great opportunity, and I appreciate it. But I need something more creative. More flexible."

John pinched his lips together, and sat back in his chair,

continuing to study Danny. "Are you sure this doesn't have something to do with your breakup with Nina?"

"My being gone all the time didn't do anything to help our relationship, I'm sure. But you know I've always wanted to work for myself. To do something creative. I have all these ideas, but no time to pursue them."

John hesitated, then sagged back in his chair. "You're right. I think you're crazy and making a big mistake, but you're right. You've always done what you wanted, even if it wasn't what I would do. What are you going to do now?"

Danny took a deep breath. He felt as if he'd just shrugged out of a very heavy coat. "I think the first thing I have to do is go to Boulder."

"To see Nina."

"Yes. She may throw me out, but I have to at least try to get her back."

John looked away, his expression unreadable. Danny steeled himself for an argument. John had never hidden his feelings about Nina, and his own breakup had made him cynical about women in general. But family loyalty apparently won over all his objections. "Go," he said. "I'll keep the cats."

Danny stood and grabbed his cousin's hand. "I'll drop them by tonight."

"Call me and let me know how it goes." John grabbed his hand, holding on. "And good luck."

"You really mean that, don't you?" Danny asked, surprised.

"I never saw you happier than you were with her. If you can have that again. . . ." He shrugged. "I hope everything works out for you."

"Thanks." Danny squeezed John's hand, hard, then turned away, his emotions too close to the surface. He had too much to do to break down now. He had to make a plane reservation and reserve a rental car and pack and get a haircut. By this time tomorrow, he planned to be with Nina, one way or another.

Danny's flight arrived in Denver in midmorning. A cold wind sliced through him as he made his way toward his rental car, and shiny Christmas garland still decorated the exit signs in the garage, out of place in the cold January sunshine. He navigated the airport maze to find the freeway and head toward Boulder. He'd never been to Colorado before, though John had talked about opening a store in Denver. Danny stared out the car windshield at the brown, flat landscape. Where were the mountains?

As he drove north and west toward Boulder, snow-capped peaks began to appear in the distance, rising up against an impossibly blue sky. Approaching Boulder itself was like driving through a postcard, but he was too focused on finding Nina's mother's address to pay more than passing notice to the sweep of red rock peaks and rolling green spaces. He located the house, down a sun-washed side street, snow piled neatly along the curb. He didn't see Nina's car out front, but it might be in the garage.

As jittery as if he'd drunk six cups of coffee, he hurried up the front walk and rang the bell. After a moment, a tall woman with brown hair streaked with blond answered the door. Her eyes were not as blue as Nina's, but the resemblance was clearly there. She surveyed him critically, as if she didn't approve of what she saw. "Yes?" she asked, her Russian accent more pronounced than Nina's.

"I'm Danny de Zayas. I'm here to see Nina."

Her expression remained cool. "Nina is not here."

"Oh." He fought the urge to fidget, like a child standing before a disapproving teacher. "Where is she?" Had she taken her own apartment and failed to mention it to Danny?

"She is out."

"Will she be back soon?"

"I don't know."

This game of twenty questions wasn't getting him anywhere. "Thank you," he said, and turned back toward his car.

"Where are you going?" Natasha demanded.

"I'll call Nina and see when would be a good time for us to meet." Maybe he should have called to begin with, but he'd wanted to surprise her. He wanted to watch her expression when she'd had no warning of his coming, to read the emotions there and see if she still cared for him as much as he hoped.

"You don't need to do that. Come in and wait with me."

He couldn't think of a polite way to refuse her invitation, which was delivered more like a command, so he followed her into the house. The first thing he saw was a tote bag he recognized as Nina's, a bundle of brushes and tubes of paint sticking out of the top. Some of the tension went out of his shoulders. Nina had been here; she would be back.

"Sit here." Natasha gestured toward a low sofa that faced a trio of windows. "I will make some tea and we can get to know each other better." She left the room, her bare feet making no sound on the thickly carpeted floor.

Danny sank onto the sofa. The windows offered a view of a snow-covered field, and in the distance the flatirons, their red rock glowing in the blinding sunlight. Beautiful as the scenery was, he focused instead on the inside of the room, searching for some other sign of Nina's presence here, for clues to what she'd been up to.

The glass coffee table in front of him contained an art book that appeared to be photographs of people in various yoga poses. Beside it was a sculpture of a nude man and woman embracing. Books filled shelves by the window: *Working With Your Chakras, Ecstasy Through Tantra,* and similar titles.

Natasha returned with two mugs of tea. She handed one to Danny, then sat beside him on the sofa, close enough that she was almost touching him, both legs folded gracefully in a lotus pose. She stared at him, her gaze intense. He thought uncomfortably of a cat hypnotizing its prey.

He looked away and sipped the tea. It tasted like stewed ditch weeds—muddy and slightly bitter.

"What's the matter?" she asked. "You don't like my tea?"

"I prefer coffee," he said, and set the mug on the table.

"The tea contains pine for guilt, skullcap, and lemon balm."

Was she trying to poison him, or was this her idea of a home remedy? She set aside her own cup. "Why are you here, Danny?"

"I came to see Nina."

"Did you come to try to win her back?"

What would she say if he told her *yes*? "I think I'd rather discuss that with Nina."

She sat back on the sofa, knees tucked under her now. "Tell me something. If Nina was murdered, would you avenge her death?"

"Murdered?" He stared at her, alarmed. "What are you talking about?"

"It is a simple question. If someone murdered Nina, would you avenge her death? Would you want to kill that person also, to make him pay for what he had done?"

"Is Nina in some kind of danger?

"No, but what if this happened? What would you do?"

"I don't know. I suppose I'd let the police handle it."

She shook her head, frowning. "That is not the right answer."

Danny's emotions warred between anger and bewilderment. Clearly, Natasha didn't approve of him, and part of him felt she had no business interrogating him this way. But if he left now, he would have to wait that much longer to see Nina. So he settled back on the sofa, quelling his annoyance, determined to wait out whatever further torture Natasha devised for him.

Nina assumed the unfamiliar car in the driveway belonged to one of her mother's students. In addition to teaching at the yoga studio, Natasha held private classes in her home. At least her mom's home studio was at the back of the house; Nina didn't risk walking in on some tantric exercise she'd just as soon not see. Not that her mother—on more than one occasion—hadn't offered to teach her some techniques she guaranteed would improve Nina's sex life. But since the only man she was interested in having sex with lived a thousand miles away, Nina had declined the offer.

Juggling half a dozen plastic shopping bags, she fumbled with the key in the lock and pushed open the door.

"Hello, Nina."

She froze, her hand still on the doorknob. So this is what it had come to—from lovelorn fantasies and daydreams to hallucinating the sound of Danny's voice.

But if she was hallucinating his voice, she was imagining the rest of the man as well, standing in her living room, his face mirroring the mixture of elation and fear running through her. She felt as if every part of her, including her tongue, had turned to rubber, none of her body parts capable of moving or speaking or anything but standing there feeling wobbly and awkward.

"Danny and I have had a nice time getting to know each other." Natasha's voice penetrated Nina's trance. She stared at her mother, who sat on the sofa, a cat-eating-cream expression on her face. Oh no. Not a good sign. Natasha looked entirely too self-satisfied, as if the conversation had only confirmed her previous assessment of Danny as a man with no staying power.

"Here, let me help you." Danny came forward and took half the shopping bags from her. He glanced in one, at a head of lettuce and three lemons. "Should we take these into the kitchen?"

"The kitchen? Yes!" Nina took his arm and hurried him toward the kitchen. She sent a look over her shoulder at her mother—a look that very clearly said *leave us alone!*

As soon as the door of the kitchen closed behind them, Danny set his bags on the counter and pulled her into his arms. "I missed you so much," he said, and kissed her.

Though a kiss hardly seemed the word to describe the swoon-worthy meeting of their lips. If the first kiss they'd shared on the Fourth of July had been their own fireworks display, then this embrace was a long-banked fire blazing to life once more. Danny slanted his lips across hers, hard, and pressed her up against the counter, letting her feel how much he wanted her. Nina had lain awake nights remembering what it felt like to be with Danny, but reality was so much better than those dreams. How could she have forgotten how wonderful it felt to be in his arms . . . how good he smelled . . . how good he *tasted*.

A pounding on the door pulled her from this fog of pleasure. "Enough, children," Natasha said from the other side of the door. "You cannot lock me out of my own kitchen."

Nina would have moved out of Danny's arms, but he held her tight as they moved over to let Natasha in. Natasha frowned at Nina. "So just like that, you kiss and make up?" she asked.

Nina touched her lips, which still tingled from the kiss. "Danny and I aren't angry with each other," she said. Though, for all the passion in that kiss, things were still unsettled between them. But he was here. He had come all the way to Denver to see her. That had to mean something—right?

On the heels of this hope came a thought to dash it. "Are you opening an Hombre store in Denver?" she asked.

His arm tightened around her. "No. I came to see you."

Aware of her mother glowering at them, Nina carefully unwound his arms from around her. "Let's go for a drive," she said. "So we can talk."

"Remember what I said," Natasha said. "You want a man who is really with you."

In the living room, Nina collected her purse and followed Danny out to his rental car. "Where should we go?" he asked.

"Just drive. I'll show you." She directed him to Baseline Road, west and away from the city. "We'll head up Flagstaff Mountain," she said. "There are some good views of the city from there."

They were silent as Danny focused on guiding the car up and around the steep switchbacks. Fortunately the roads were clear, and this time of day the traffic was light. Nina took advantage of the opportunity to study him. She loved the intent way he focused on the road, his shoulders slightly hunched, his thick eyebrows drawn together as he concentrated.

"Pull in on the right up here," she said, directing him to a designated scenic overlook.

He parked the car and they got out. An icy wind hit them and Nina huddled farther into her coat. Danny put his arm around her as they stared out at the city spread before them. "What did your mom mean, when she said you wanted a man who was really with you."

"My mom has some odd ideas about romance . . . especially for a woman who's been divorced twice." She glanced at him, at the dimple in his chin, and the beard stubble along his jaw. "What did she say to you, before I came home?"

He grimaced. "She asked me if I'd avenge your death if someone murdered you."

The preposterousness of the question surprised a laugh from Nina. "What did you say?"

"I told her I'd let the police handle things. She let me know that was the wrong answer."

"It's the right answer for me. I wouldn't want you ending up in jail or dead yourself, going after some murderer."

"I don't even like to think about anything happening to you." He drew her close and kissed her again, enveloping her in warmth that made the winter chill recede around them.

When they broke apart at last, breathless, she stared into his eyes. "You've lost weight," she said, tracing her forefinger along his right cheekbone.

"I've been miserable without you." He rested his forehead against hers. "I've been a real prick," he said. "There you were, struggling so hard to make ends meet, and I was dividing the bills up to the penny and making you pay for your own damned bananas, instead of doing everything I could to make sure we could be together."

She felt weak in the knees with relief. This was what she'd longed to hear him say. "That's all I ever wanted," she said. "For us to be together."

"*Ya tebya lyublyu*, Nina. Please give me another chance."

"We won't divide the bills?"

"You'll pay whatever you can pay. All the money in the world doesn't matter to me if I can't have you to share it with."

"Oh, Danny." They kissed again, and she tasted the tears sliding down her cheeks.

"Don't cry," he said, and wiped the tears away with his thumbs.

"I'm crying only because I'm so happy," she said.

"Come on, let's get back in the car," he said. "It's cold up here."

They returned to the car, and sat looking at the panorama of the city. "It's beautiful," Danny said. "I've always wanted to see the Rocky Mountains."

"How long can you stay?" she asked. "I could show you around."

"I can stay as long as I want," he said. "I quit my job."

"Danny! Did you and John have some kind of argument?"

"No. He was sorry to see me go, but he understood."

She turned toward him. "I don't understand. What happened?"

"The job was taking me away from everything I love. You— but also music and writing and creating things for myself." He took her hand. "I want time to develop some of the business ideas I have. And I want us to work on projects together, the way we used to talk about doing."

"That's wonderful." Excitement bubbled up in her at the memory of the times they had talked into the night about projects they'd like to collaborate on and places and ideas they wanted to explore. She laughed. "But now you won't be able to afford to live in New York, either."

"Not for long. I've been thinking about that, and I have some ideas. But I have savings, too, so we don't have to make a decision right away."

"I still have some money saved as well."

"Then you'll come back with me?"

"Yes!" She crawled across the seat into his lap. Danny obligingly slid the seat back to make more room.

"What are you doing?" he asked, even as he slid his hands beneath her sweater.

"Didn't I tell you? This is a very famous make out spot in Boulder." She feathered kisses along his neck.

"And you know this how?" He reached around and unsnapped her bra. "Did you come up here with boys when you were in high school?"

"I'll never tell." She wiggled closer, enjoying the slightly glazed expression that flooded over his face as she did so.

A car pulled up alongside them. Doors slammed and Nina looked up to see a small boy peering in at them. She jerked back from Danny. "I'm guessing this is more of a make-out spot at night," he said.

"Yes." She blushed. In her excitement at seeing Danny again, she'd overlooked that little detail. "Where are you staying?" she asked.

"I don't know. I came straight from the airport."

He had been so anxious to see her he hadn't even made plans. Her stomach fluttered with the knowledge. "I would ask you to stay at my mother's, but she would never give us any privacy."

"I'll get a hotel."

"I'll come with you."

Danny didn't know what the hotel clerk thought about the two of them arriving in the middle of the afternoon and demanding a room, but the clerk handed over two keys with practiced indifference. At least Danny had luggage. He refused the services of the bellman, and he and Nina sedately made their way to the elevator; but as soon as the doors closed behind them, they were in each other's arms once more.

When the doors slid open one floor up, Danny reached behind him and blindly hit the door closed button, catching only a glimpse of a startled woman before the doors slid shut once more. Nina sighed and snuggled closer to him, and he lost track of the floors passing as they kissed. He managed to fit the card key in the slot on the door of the room while Nina was still wrapped around him. They left a trail of clothing behind them on the way to the bed and fell naked onto the mattress.

He and Nina had made love so many times before, yet this time he felt he was learning to know her all over again. They'd taken a step forward in their relationship, pledging to be there for each other in an uncertain future. Her mother had talked about Nina needing a man who would really be with her. That was what he wanted—to not be pulled in ten different directions by other people's demands, but to be led by his own desires and imaginations, and by Nina's as well. He was sure that together they would make discoveries he wasn't capable of on his own.

Though right now all he wanted was to discover if the hollow at the base of her throat tasted the same and if the inside of her thigh was as soft as he remembered. She made a soft sound like a kitten as he slid into her, and he delighted in one more affirmation that all was right in his world again. He was with Nina, and he would stay with Nina—in New York or Boulder or wherever life took them.

They both came quickly, desire fueled by deprivation. Afterwards, Nina wrapped her legs around his waist, holding him in her. "I won't let you go again," she said.

"I won't go, I promise." He kissed her. "You're stuck with me now, for better or worse." A shiver ran through him as he said the words he'd heard countless times in marriage vows. He would probably marry Nina one day, though he saw no need to rush. Let them get their lives on a more even keel first. They had plenty of time before they needed to worry about that final commitment.

Fifteen

Fear is a restraint,
A harshness that prevents us
From living fully.

NINA'S MOTHER WASN'T HAPPY ABOUT Nina's decision to return to New York with Danny. "You know, there is a saying about a person who keeps doing the same thing, expecting different results," she said as she watched Nina pack. "That person is a fool."

"It *is* going to be different this time," Nina said. She folded a sweater into the suitcase and added a stack of T-shirts. "Danny quit his job and we're going to work together. We're not going to worry about dividing everything exactly down the middle and keeping score."

"You say that, but a man can't change his character," Natasha said. "I know these business types—it's all about their ambition and making things happen. They do not understand that with art, you have to step back and allow things to happen. They can't bear to give up that much control."

Nina shut the suitcase and forced the zipper closed. "I like that Danny is ambitious," she said. "I like that he thinks about the future. He helps motivate me and pushes me to do better."

"You see him with stars in your eyes. You won't feel the same when you are stuck in New York with no money. Think how much better off you would be to stay here in Colorado. And what about Alex Lessing? You were just getting to know each other again."

"We went out for dinner one time. As friends." They'd spent the two hours they were together discussing school friends and Alex's business. He'd offered to introduce Nina to some people, but when she told him she wasn't interested in seriously dating anyone he hadn't pressed. She'd liked him for that, and if she'd stayed in Boulder they probably would have been friends, but nothing more.

"Can't you be happy that I'm happy?" she asked.

Natasha's expression softened. "Of course I want you to be happy. That is the whole reason for my concern."

"Danny makes me happy. I love him and he loves me."

"Then I hope your love will last," Natasha said. "For as long as is meant to be."

How like her mother not to wish for a love to last forever. Was it because her own experience had led her to believe such a thing was impossible? Or because such an answer guaranteed she'd be right, no matter the outcome?

Danny arrived that afternoon to help Nina finish loading her car. The plan was for Nina to follow him to the airport to return his rental, then they would spend the night at Natasha's and set out the next morning for New York.

"At least he is good-looking," Natasha conceded, as she watched Danny carry a stack of boxes to Nina's car. "And tall enough to look you in the eye."

Nina interpreted these remarks as a verbal peace offering from her mother and gave her a quick hug. "Thanks, Mom," she said, then went to help Danny pack the car.

That evening, before he returned his rental car, Danny insisted on taking Nina and her mother to dinner. Nina assumed Danny intended the meal as an opportunity for him to charm Natasha into giving her approval of the relationship. Nina's mother, however, saw it as a chance to continue her interrogation.

"If you are leaving your job with your cousin, what will you do for a living?" she asked, before the salads had even arrived.

"I have a couple of online projects I want to pursue, and I can go back to being a DJ in clubs," he said.

Natasha sniffed. "That won't be enough to support you in New York."

"I was thinking Nina and I might open some kind of business together."

"What kind of business?" Nina asked, intrigued.

"Something creative, involving art and maybe writing."

"I've thought about handmade wedding favors," Nina said. "When I was helping Erin with her wedding, I was shocked by how much those things cost."

"Wedding items would be good," Natasha said. "You could get ideas to use in your own wedding."

Nina wished she'd been watching Danny's face when her mother said this. But by the time she glanced over at him he was calmly cutting into his salad, as if he hadn't heard Natasha at all.

When he noticed both women looking at him, he smiled, an engaging curve of his mouth that made Nina's heart turn over in her chest. "We were talking about weddings," Natasha said.

"There's a lot of money to be made with weddings," he said. "Our friends Randy and Morgan are doing pretty well providing music and bar service for receptions."

"I could do handmade favors or invitations," Nina said.

"Or wedding photos," Danny said. "Those pictures you took for Erin and Thad's wedding were amazing. You could be a professional wedding photographer."

"You helped with those photos," Nina said.

"I could help at other weddings."

"New York is probably full of wedding photographers," Natasha said. "What do you two have to offer that's so special?"

Danny's eyes met Nina's and sparked with a fire that sent heat racing through her. "We have Nina's artistry and my style and our view of the world," he said. "We have us."

Nina smiled. She knew exactly what he meant; she'd known it that night at Coney Island, when they staged shots without either having to tell the other what they wanted. They hadn't needed words to communicate. Together, they could do something very special.

"When I was Nina's age, I was married and divorced again with a child to raise," Natasha said. "I had to get an education to work and to support us."

"That's very admirable," Danny said.

Nina wondered where her mom was going with this. But Natasha seemed not to have heard Danny. "I had to wait until Nina was grown before I felt free to explore, to learn what I really wanted," she said. "Maybe I made more mature choices because I'd already lived a more conventional life. But maybe I missed a lot, too, by not taking more risks when I was younger."

"Are you saying what we are doing is a good thing?" Nina asked.

Natasha nodded. "Yes. Go to New York and try to establish a business. If you fail . . ." She shrugged. "You are both young. You have plenty of time to try again."

"Things will work out for me and Nina, I'm sure," Danny said solemnly.

"They had better." Natasha fixed him with a fierce look. "You don't want to make a Russian woman angry."

Danny nodded, his expression still solemn. "No, I don't want that." His eyes met Nina's again. "I don't want that at all."

Nina did not always share Danny's optimism that "things would work out," but she had to admit she'd never known him to fail when he set out to do something. Her mother would likely have said the fates played their part when, a week after their return to New York, Morgan telephoned to ask if Nina could photograph her and Randy's wedding.

"You're getting married? I mean, congratulations," Nina stammered.

Morgan laughed. "I know. We've only been dating a few months. But Randy and I have known each other since college. We even dated for a while freshman year. I transferred schools and we didn't want to do the long-distance thing so we split up. But I could never forget him and this time, when we hooked up again, I knew he was the one."

Nina thought of her own futile efforts to forget her feelings for Danny while she was in Boulder. She hadn't been able to imagine herself with any other man despite their disagreements, which seemed petty now that she looked back on them. "That's sweet," she said.

"So anyway, I was blown away by the photos you did for Erin's wedding, and I wanted to know how much you'd charge for a similar photo package for my big day."

"Charge?" Nina opened her mouth to say of course, she'd take the photos as her wedding gift to the couple, then stopped. If she was going to make her living as a photographer, she needed to start soon. "Let me get back to you on the price," she said. "But I promise I'll give you my friends and family discount."

She hung up the phone and went into the living room, where Danny was working on his computer. "That was Morgan," she told him. "She and Randy are getting married."

"Really?" He looked up, frowning. "Randy's the last guy I thought would be marrying anytime soon. When's the ceremony?"

"I don't know." She sat beside him on the sofa. Chickadee crawled into her lap and she absently stroked the cat. "But she wants to hire me to take the wedding photos."

"That's perfect. Look at this." He clicked the mouse on his computer and angled the machine toward her, showing her web page filled with photos of happy couples, some from Erin and Thad's wedding and others Nina had taken of their friends. At the top of the page unfurled a banner that read *Nina Barry Photography*.

"You did this for me?"

"Do you like it?" His expression was so earnest, so eager for her to approve.

"I like it." She threw her arms around him. "I love it. I love you."

"I love you, too." They kissed, and she thought the kiss might lead to more, but he turned his attention to the computer once more. "Take a look at this."

He opened the website they'd built together. Haiku for You was a collaborative, interactive art project. People wrote into the website to share a story or anecdote or experience, and Danny and Nina wrote a haiku capturing the essence of that experience and illustrated it with a drawing or photograph. "We're up to ten thousand visitors."

"Oh my gosh—there's a comment from someone in New Zealand." Excitement swelled in Nina. This was all she'd dreamed of—the two of them working together to create something new and fun and meaningful.

"I've been thinking about something else," Danny said.

"Another blog? Or a business idea?" His mind never stopped coming up with new ideas; he amazed her.

"Neither, though it could tie into that. You know we can't really afford to stay in New York."

"Right. Have you thought of someplace we should move?"

"No. What I thought was that we should let others decide where we should go."

She frowned. "I don't understand. Let who decide?"

"Anyone. Everyone. We'd have a contest online. People could vote and whichever place gets the most votes, that's where we'd live for the next year."

"That's crazy." How could she put her fate in the hands of strangers? "What if they pick some tiny little place where we could never find work?"

"Hmmm. What if we started with a list of places for people to vote on, places we wouldn't mind living?"

"That might work. I've always thought Portland, Oregon, might be nice."

"Or Oakland, California."

"Or Savannah, Georgia." They looked at each other and burst out laughing. "It's a crazy idea," Nina said.

"It is," Danny agreed. "I think that's why I like it."

"It sounds exciting, too." She liked the idea of the two of them taking such a risk. It would prove that wherever they ended up, she and Danny could make it together.

Besides, how many people would even know about their contest? Most likely their friends or Danny's family would end up sending them to Florida or keeping them here in New York. "Let's do it," she said.

"All right. Let's draw up a list." He opened a new file on the computer and she snuggled in close.

"Where would you live if you could live anywhere?" she asked.

"Anywhere in the United States," Danny said. "Emigrating to another country would be trickier."

"All right. Anywhere in the United States." She pictured herself on the beach in California, or sipping mint juleps in a picture hat somewhere in the Deep South, or maybe walking through corn fields in the Midwest. And always Danny would be by her side—the only man she knew who was crazy enough to take such an adventure.

"Okay, let me turn on the camera." Danny leaned forward and switched on the video camera he'd positioned on a tripod in front of the sofa.

"I can't believe we're doing this," Nina said. "A YouTube video?"

"It'll be a great way to get people to the website to vote."

"Do you really think we'll get a million votes for any one city?" When Danny had proposed the number, it had seemed impossible. It still did, but he was sure it would work.

"A million is the kind of number that will capture people's attention," he said. "Are you ready? I'm going to turn it on."

"Your nose is going to look huge right up against the lens that way."

He tried to stifle laughter as he said, "Danny and Nina. Take one," and sat beside her, still choking back giggles. How could he not love a woman who could always make him laugh?

"Hello," Nina said for the camera.

He managed to control his mirth enough to speak. "Hi, I'm Danny and this is my girlfriend Nina."

"We're looking for a place to move," Nina said.

They ran through the little script they'd prepared, introducing themselves and their contest. Danny held up a piece of paper with the website address and Nina urged everyone to vote. "If you don't vote, something scary is going to happen," Danny said.

"And it involves alligators," Nina said.

He switched off the camera and they both dissolved into laughter again. "Alligators?" he asked.

"Alligators are scary," she said.

"I guess they are." He unscrewed the camera from the tripod.

"What happens now?" she asked.

"I post the video on YouTube and our website, and I send out a bunch of press releases and we wait."

He pulled up their website: *Danny and Nina. Our Lives Are In Your Hands.* "So ominous sounding," she said.

"I'm hoping it will get attention."

"What if no one votes?" He heard the doubt in Nina's voice— a doubt he fought as well.

"People will vote," he said. "Once they hear about it, they'll vote. Who could resist the chance to decide someone else's fate?"

"My mother believes everyone is guided by outside forces, that nothing is truly random."

"Then she ought to love this. Have you told her what we're doing?"

"Yes. She thinks it's crazy, but then, I think a lot of what she does is crazy, too, so you could say in that respect we are a lot alike."

Danny made a face. "Are you going to take up labyrinth walking or yoga?"

"I might. What would you think of that?"

"I think I'd probably end up building a labyrinth and learning how to twist myself into all kinds of crazy yoga poses."

"Ah. You would do that for me?"

All that and more. Those weeks apart had taught him he didn't want to live without Nina. It frightened him a little, giving another person so much control over him. He could talk about putting their lives in the hands of strangers with this contest, but the truth was, they could back out of that anytime. A relationship was something more; you couldn't walk away from that without doing a lot of damage. Not that he wanted to walk away from Nina.

"You could probably get me to do all kinds of crazy things," he said. "But don't tell anyone. It'll be our secret."

She threw her arms around him and hugged him close. "I won't reveal my secret powers over you. And I promise to use them only for good."

"Of course." He didn't believe Nina had an evil bone in her body. But without even trying, she could hurt him deeply, if she ever left again. He wondered if she realized that. He hoped she would never find out.

"What time is it?" Nina asked.

"Almost one. Why?"

"We have to take pictures for Randy and Morgan's engagement announcement. We're meeting them in Prospect Park, remember?"

"I still can't believe those two are getting married."

"Believe it. I saw her dress and it's gorgeous." She stood and retrieved her camera bag from the table by the door. "I have to remember to take some of my cards. Morgan promised to hand them out to the wedding planners she and Randy are working with."

"You're doing great," Danny said. Nina wasn't always so eager to promote herself in a businesslike manner, and he had to push her. But she was learning.

"I'm worried I'll get established here and have to start over somewhere else," she said.

"You'll have a good portfolio to show off and plenty of references. Starting over won't be hard."

"For you, maybe." She stood before the mirror by the dining table and arranged a scarf around her neck. "Sometimes I think I'm not as flexible as you."

He put his hand on her shoulder. "I'll be there to support you. You don't have anything to worry about."

She smiled, a look that set up a warm glow in his chest. "Believe me, I wouldn't do something so crazy with a man I didn't love," she said.

"So love has made you crazy."

"Crazy and reckless. I highly recommend it." She slung the camera bag over her shoulder. "Now come on, we have to go."

"Crazy and reckless and bossy."

"You need someone to boss you around."

I need you, he thought. But he didn't say it. He merely shut down the computer and prepared to follow her—to Prospect Park to Charleston to wherever this crazy of idea of theirs led them.

Danny met John for lunch two weeks later at a bistro near John's office. "You're looking good," John said after they greeted each other. "I guess being your own boss agrees with you."

"It does," Danny agreed. He loved waking up every day, his mind filled with projects he wanted to complete and ideas he wanted to explore. Despite the unpredictable outcome of their contest to decide where he and Nina would live, he felt energized and more in charge of his own destiny than he had in awhile. Where they ended up didn't matter to him; when they got there, they'd be responsible for their own happiness and building the life they wanted.

"You could at least pretend to miss me a little," John said with mock hurt.

"I still see you. How's the guy who took my place working out?"

"All right. He doesn't talk back to me as much as you did." They followed the hostess to a table near the front window. "So what's up with this contest you and Nina are having? Are you really going to let a bunch of strangers decide where you live?"

"We are." Danny glanced at the menu. "We've gotten some great publicity so far and the votes are starting to come in." So far they'd done interviews with newspaper reporters in six states, Germany, and Great Britain; and other blogs all over the web had linked to theirs. Every morning when he logged on to their site the vote tally had multiplied. "Apparently some booster club in Portland, Oregon, is urging people to vote for their city, so that's in the lead right now."

"Is that what this is about?" John asked. "Being some kind of internet celebrity?"

"No! It's more of a . . . I don't know. A social experiment. A chance to be creative and try something new."

"What are you going to do if you end up in someplace like Plano, Texas?"

"It'll only be for a year. We'll figure out something. Nina can make anything fun."

"Life is about more than fun," John said.

"But it doesn't all have to be a grind, either."

The waitress arrived to take their order. When she departed, Danny looked across at his cousin. John looked so much older than Danny felt. He was scarcely past thirty, yet already his hair was graying at the temples, and the lines around his eyes seemed deeper. "How is Tomas?" he asked.

"I talked to him yesterday. He likes it down in Florida. He's making friends."

"Have you thought of moving down there?" Danny asked.

"Just because you're moving doesn't mean I want to."

"You could operate the business anywhere, and in Florida you'd be closer to Tomas."

"And closer to Caridad."

"Come on, you don't hate her that much, do you?"

John squeezed a wedge of lemon into his tea. "At one time I did, but now seeing her just makes me tired."

"So don't see her. Look after your son and forget about her."

"Spoken like a man who's never been divorced."

A man who never will be, Danny thought. Seeing John's struggles had made him more determined than ever not to make the same mistakes. "You don't have to give up your place in Queens if you don't want to," Danny said. "You could lease an apartment in Miami and stay there part of the time."

"I'll think about it. It's not a bad idea." He sat back and studied Danny. "How are you doing, really? You'd tell me if you needed money, right?"

"I don't need money. The websites bring in a little money, and I've started designing sites for other people. And Nina's photography business is picking up. It's not enough for us to live on in New York, but I'm encouraged."

"She's photographing weddings?"

Danny nodded. "That's the bulk of her business right now. And of course, she still paints."

"All those weddings are going to give her ideas."

"What do you mean?"

"She'll want to get married. I'm surprised she hasn't already brought it up . . . or has she?"

"She hasn't said anything about it." He shifted in his chair. Nina never said a word about wanting to marry, but sometimes he caught her looking at him, a wistful longing in her expression. Those looks make him feel that he'd disappointed her somehow, but he was reluctant to ask for an explanation. Things were good between them right now. He didn't want to disrupt that harmony. "Nina knows I love her," he said. "And that we're going to stay together. We don't need to be married."

"What about children? "

Danny blinked. "What about them?"

"You want them, don't you? I don't care what the fashion is among celebrities, you ought to marry the mother of your children. If nothing else, it makes the legal entanglements more straightforward."

"Nina isn't pregnant," Danny said. Even saying the words made him feel a little faint. Of course she wasn't pregnant. She would have said something. . . .

"Maybe not now, but she'll want to be one day. So you won't be able to put off those wedding vows forever. Not if you want to keep her."

"What is it with you and these worst-case scenarios?" Danny asked. "Have you always been this gloomy?"

"My gloom offsets your insufferable optimism." John pulled his chair closer to the table as the waitress set a plate in front of him.

"Well, keep your gloom to yourself." Danny added pepper to his pastrami. "Nina and I are happy."

"And I hope you stay that way. I truly do." John took a bite of his sandwich and chewed thoughtfully. "Do you think you'll be happy in East Podunk?"

"That's part of the point of the project—to find out," he said. "Our happiness shouldn't depend on where we live."

"Maybe you're on to something there," John said. "So many people tie the knot, then it all comes undone when something happens to really test the relationship. You're testing yourselves first—building a business, moving to a new location—all the things that can put a strain on a relationship."

"Exactly," Danny said. "I'm not saying Nina and I won't marry. We probably will. But why not wait until we're absolutely sure?"

"Except, when is anyone absolutely sure?"

"I'll know when the time is right," Danny said.

"Let's hope Nina feels the same way."

"I'm pretty sure she does."

"But you're not brave enough to ask her."

"I'm not foolish enough to ask her." Why court trouble? At least let he and Nina get settled in their new home—wherever that turned out to be—before they worried about changing their situation any further.

Sixteen

Uncharted waters
Are choppy but can lead to
Wonderful places.

"WHO'S IN THE LEAD THIS MORNING?" Nina asked a month later as Danny logged into their website. She handed him a mug of coffee and curled up on the sofa beside him. They'd developed a morning ritual of having coffee and checking to see what votes had come in overnight, then reading comments and answering e-mails.

"Still Plano," he said.

Nina groaned. "I would have thought people would be tired of that by now."

"Maybe that German television show keeps stirring them up." Apparently, a German television show had learned about their contest and urged viewers to cast their vote to send Nina and Danny to the worst-sounding place they could think of: Plano, Texas.

"Plano's probably not that bad," Danny said. "It's near Dallas. The Germans just didn't like the name."

"I'm worried they know something we don't," Nina said. That was one thing about holding a contest like this—she and Danny had set themselves up as targets for every malcontent on the web. Along with all the positive comments and support had come some truly nasty e-mails and web postings. She'd made Danny stop reading them to her, and she did her best to ignore them.

"We have a new second place," Danny said.

"Oh?" She perked up. "What is it?"

"Denver."

"Colorado?"

He laughed. "Do you know another Denver on our list?"

She fought down dismay. "Is Fort Collins still high on the list?"

"Third place."

"So if we don't end up in Plano, we're likely to be in Colorado."

"I thought you liked Colorado," Danny said. "And Denver has a lot going for it—good climate, a great arts scene. Snowboarding in the winter."

"I love Colorado, but I'm not so sure I want to live so close to my mother."

"It'll be all right. Natasha's too busy with her own interests to meddle much. Besides, in Denver you'll be close to Erin and Thad."

"I almost forgot! I still think of her as being here in New York." Nina smiled. She watched as the website counter rolled over with another vote each for Plano and Denver. Both were in the high hundreds of thousands. "We're really going to make a million votes, aren't we?" she asked.

"We are."

She glanced at him. "I have a confession to make. I never thought we'd really do it."

"I was optimistic enough for both of us." He hugged her. "I knew we'd do it. We can do anything."

"Including moving to Denver, where my mother will recruit you to build labyrinths in her back yard."

"Or Plano, where I'll have to learn to wear a cowboy hat and boots."

"I don't know which is worse," Nina said.

"Definitely the boots." He affected a John Wayne drawl. "Howdy, partner. My name's Danny and this little filly here is Nina."

"Stop!" she pleaded. "I can't stand it. At least if we move to Denver I can teach you to snowboard."

"I'm not so sure about that," he said. "I really don't want to break my leg hurtling down a mountain on a skateboard without wheels."

"Don't be such a wimp."

"I'm a city guy—what can I say?"

The phone rang and Nina answered. "Hello."

"Nina, I was just on your website and I see Colorado is gaining the lead." As if summoned by thought, Natasha was on the other end of the line. "Are you really going to move here?"

"If Denver or Fort Collins gets the millionth vote, yes," Nina said.

"It will be good to have you close again." Natasha paused. "And it will be good for me to get to know Danny better as well."

"I know you'll love him once you get to know him better," Nina said.

"Maybe. At least you will be closer to home if things don't work out for the two of you."

"Why are you so negative about this?" Nina asked, mindful that Danny was listening.

"I'm not being negative. I was merely pointing out another good thing about you moving to Colorado. When will you know?"

"Whenever the millionth vote is cast," Nina said. "Soon."

"Give Natasha my love," Danny said, with a mischievous grin.

"Danny sends his love," Nina said.

"Tell him hello. And I hope Colorado wins. It's always good to have family close."

She hung up and Nina laid the phone on the table. "What did your mother have to say?" Danny asked.

"She hopes Colorado wins the voting."

"What was she being negative about?"

"She said if things don't work out for us, she's glad I'll be closer to home."

"Why is she so sure we won't stay together?" Danny's voice was light, but Nina didn't miss the troubled look in his eyes.

"She just doesn't know you well. She'll change her mind once we're there and she sees how you are."

"You're talking as if Colorado really is going to win."

She glanced at the computer screen, where another vote for Plano had tallied. "I can only hope it does win. I don't think the world is ready for you in cowboy boots."

A tense three weeks later, after five million votes had been cast for cities all across the United States, Denver emerged as the winner with one million votes. Nina and Danny toasted the victory, then started making phone calls and plans. "I can't believe you're coming to Denver!" Erin's voice bubbled with excitement over the phone when Nina finally got in touch with her friend. "I can't wait to see you." When will you get here?"

"The lease on our apartment is up at the end of next month. We're flying down next week to look for a place to live. The paper has already interviewed us, and I think there's a radio station that wants to talk to us while we are in town."

"You're celebrities," Erin said. "What does your mother say?"

"She's happy. She was skeptical about the contest at first, but now she's happy to have me close again."

"And Danny's okay with moving so close to her? They'll get along?"

"You know Danny—he's nice to everyone. And I can tell my mom is charmed. But she says she doesn't trust him, so she holds back."

"She doesn't trust Danny? Why not?"

"I think it's because he hasn't asked me to marry him. For all her crazy ideas, my mother is a little old-fashioned. She thinks if Danny isn't willing to commit that means he's bound to leave me eventually and she doesn't want to see me hurt."

"Marriage isn't a guarantee a man will stay."

"And she of all people should know that; she's been divorced twice. But I guess she wants to believe things can be different."

"You don't think Danny will leave, do you?"

Even the words made her feel a little sick. "No, of course not. But . . ."

"But?"

"I wonder *why* he hasn't asked me to marry him? He says he loves me. He talks about the future as if we'll be spending the rest of our lives together."

"Have you asked him?"

"I can't do that. I'm trying to be patient." What if Danny admitted marriage wasn't in his plans? What would she do then?

"Maybe he thinks you don't want to get married," Erin said.

"He can't think that. We photograph weddings all the time. I'm always saying things about how wonderful they are."

"What does he say?"

"He'll agree that the bride is beautiful, or he'll comment on the choice of music. But he doesn't say much else. How did you and Thad know it was time to get married?"

"He completely surprised me with his proposal. I was shocked, but I said yes right away. I guess I just knew."

"And you don't regret it?"

"No. I really don't. Thad and I belong together. And I think you and Danny belong together too. Maybe he's just waiting for the perfect moment to ask you. He's always struck me as the romantic type."

"Yes, Danny is romantic."

"Then give him a little more time. Make the move, get settled in, then see what happens."

"You're right. I'll do that. And it's not as if I need a ring on my finger to know he loves me."

"No one needs that ring," Erin said. "But it is a powerful symbol—the ultimate commitment. You can't leave a marriage as easily as you can a live-in arrangement. The ring makes things seem permanent, even if they aren't always these days."

Nina rubbed the bare third finger of her left hand. "One day I'll have that ring," she said.

"Of course you will. Meanwhile, maybe the mayor will give you the key to the city."

"Or we could offer him the key to our house," Nina said.

"I'd love to see his face if you handed him that. Okay, I've got to go now. I can't wait to see you. This move to Denver is going to be the best thing that ever happened to you."

Nina hoped Erin was right. After so many months of anticipation she was a mess of excitement and dread, optimism and fear. Starting over was fun and exciting and a little exhausting. She hoped they liked Denver and would decide to stay after their agreed-upon year. Maybe it was merely part of getting older, but she was ready to settle down.

For all his love of traveling and the excitement of the past months watching the votes come in for various locations where they might live, Danny was glad to arrive in Denver and take a break. Once that millionth vote had tallied, things had happened quickly—radio and print interviews, a whirlwind trip to Colorado where Erin had helped them find an apartment and introduced them to a bunch of other young people. Already, it felt as if he and Nina were surrounded by friends.

A number of those friends were young couples, some of whom were engaged to be married, or who knew other engaged couples, so Nina began to get more requests to photograph weddings. Through his music blog, Danny met some local bands and ended up photographing them and doing a few websites. Everything was coming together.

He stayed in touch with John and his friends in New York. Randy and Morgan still lived there, and he called from time to time. "Did you hear the latest?" Randy asked, one spring day when Danny and Nina had been in Denver almost three months.

"No, but I'm sure you're going to tell me."

"Tawny and Lawrence eloped."

"Eloped?"

"To Vegas. And not only that, but they decided to stay out there. They said the cost of living is cheap compared to New York. They got jobs in casinos and an apartment at some big complex with a pool. She sent me a picture of the two of them in front of this wedding chapel with a guy dressed like Elvis. She wore a white minidress with motorcycle boots to the ceremony. Lawrence was all in black leather."

Danny laughed. "It sounds perfect for them."

"You and Nina are the only ones of the old gang who haven't tied the knot yet," Randy said.

"No need to rush," Danny said.

"You're definitely not rushing. So how are things in Denver. You like it?"

"We like it a lot. We're already talking about staying here after our year is up."

"I check your blog all the time. Good stuff."

"Thanks. You and Morgan need to come for a visit."

"It'll have to be pretty soon. After the baby gets here I don't imagine we'll be going anywhere for awhile."

"Baby?"

Randy laughed. "Yeah. Can you believe it? I'm going to be a daddy. Around Christmas time, I guess."

"Congratulations. Tell Morgan congratulations, too."

"Thanks. I'm not sure I've wrapped my head around the idea yet, but it's pretty exciting."

The conversation after that failed to register; Danny was too preoccupied with the idea that his friend—a guy his age whom he'd known and worked with for years—was going to be a father. Fatherhood sounded so *settled*. So *mature*. Two things he didn't really feel himself to be.

When Nina came in from shopping Danny greeted her at the door. "Is something wrong?" she asked. "You look very pale."

He took the shopping bags from her hands. "Randy called and told me Tawny and Lawrence eloped to Las Vegas. Then they decided to stay there and got jobs in casinos."

"I can see the two of them in Vegas." She dropped her purse

onto the sofa and headed for the kitchen, both cats and Danny trailing after. "We'll have to go visit."

"That's not all. Randy said Morgan's pregnant. Their baby's due in December."

"That's wonderful!" Nina grinned. "Erin's going to be jealous. She and Thad have been trying for a couple of months now."

"They have?"

"She's hasn't announced it or anything, but of course she told me."

Weddings, then babies . . . Danny felt as if he was watching all his friends run past him in a race he hadn't even realized he'd entered. "I wish them luck."

"You know Erin. She's always impatient. I have a feeling it won't take her very long. And in the meantime, they can have fun trying." She took a bowl of grapes from the refrigerator and crunched down on one. "Did we get anything in the mail?"

"The deposit for the Wolinski wedding."

"They're such a cute couple," Nina said. "Did you know they were high-school sweethearts? Then they both married other people and got back together after he divorced and her husband died. She told me it was love at first sight."

"Do you believe in such a thing?" he asked.

"Not really, but . . ." She paused, a grape halfway to her mouth, and her eyes met his. "I hadn't known you very long before I knew I loved you. There wasn't any reason for the way I felt, I just . . . knew."

He'd known he loved Nina, too, though he'd resisted the idea for awhile. He'd told himself it was because he was involved with another woman, and because he didn't want to lose Nina's friendship if a love affair went bad. Later, when she'd left him, he'd had to rethink his definition of love and to be willing to give up

control of his finances and his schedule to something more powerful than his own desires and goals.

"I used to think love was all about how it made me feel," he
said. "Then I saw it was wanting to make someone else feel good,
too."

She set aside the grapes and put her arms around him. "You
always make me feel good, Danny," she said.

He held her tightly, thinking about how much she'd changed
him. For a long time he'd been afraid of giving up control—of his
money, his time, his life. Yet, since knowing Nina he'd let go of
all that. If the contest had been a test of his ability to let strangers
decide his fate, he'd come through that stronger. And though he
worked to be his own boss and develop his own ideas to make a
living, he did so with input from Nina. Over time they'd become
partners.

He realized he wasn't afraid any more.

"It feels so good to get out and do something that doesn't
involve work," Nina said, as Danny pulled the car into the parking lot of Garden of the Gods park near Colorado Springs, on a
bright summer day when they'd been in Colorado six months.
"It's a good thing I have you to pull me out of my workaholic ten-
dencies," Danny said. "That's the one downside of working for
yourself—there's always something to do."

"True. But this trip was your idea." She climbed out of the
passenger seat and walked around back to retrieve her camera
equipment.

"After all this time I thought it would be good to get out and
explore more of my new home state."

"I'm just glad you were able to tear yourself away from the

computer and *SportsCenter*." She nudged him and laughed.

Danny looked sheepish. "Most men wouldn't think I watch too much sports."

"And most women would agree with me that you do. Anyway, I'm glad you thought of this. I haven't been to Garden of the Gods since I was a little girl."

They made their way up the path from the parking lot to the entrance to the park. Red sandstone formations loomed over them, framed by the dark green of evergreens and the occasional burst of purple or red or yellow from patches of wildflowers. "Sometimes you can see mountain goats in the cliffs over there," Nina said, pointing across the way.

"Nice," Danny said. But he wasn't watching the cliffs; he was scanning the area around them, as if looking for something.

"Do you need to use the restroom?" Nina asked. "We'll have to drive to the visitor's center for that."

"No, I'm fine." He patted her shoulder. "Let's walk farther up this way." He indicated a deserted pathway that veered off to the side.

"Sure. Let me take a few pictures here, first. The colors in the layers of rock are amazing, like strawberry ice cream."

He fidgeted while she photographed. She smiled behind the camera. He really had been spending too much time in front of the television or computer if he couldn't even stand still while she took pictures. Usually he was right behind her, suggesting shots or posing for the lens.

At last she folded the tripod and they moved on. They passed a family climbing a low formation of smooth rock and a pair of buff young men scaling a steeper rock face, ropes dangling alongside them. "We should try rock climbing some time," Nina said.

"It does look like fun," Danny said. "Though maybe we'd better start in the gym."

They stood for a moment, watching the climbers, then Danny took her hand and tugged her on. "Let's go."

"Why are you in such a hurry?" Nina asked. "We have all afternoon."

"There's a lot to see," he said. "I don't want to miss anything."

He led her down the path, his gaze darting left and right. Nina was sure now he was searching for something, but she couldn't imagine what that might be.

At last, he turned off the path and led her into a secluded, shady area behind a large rock formation. "How nice," Nina said. "Too bad we didn't think to bring a picnic."

She raised her camera and snapped off a few shots of the large orange and red rock. The colors and textures were going to look fantastic when she enlarged the photos, like abstract paintings.

"We don't need a picnic," Danny said. His voice sounded different, as if it wasn't coming from the right location.

She lowered the camera and stared at him. He was on one knee in front of her. He took her hand and looked up at her. "Nina, I love you so much," he said. "I can't imagine life without you. I don't want to imagine it. Will you marry me?"

If Nina had drawn a cartoon of the moment, she would have shown her heart filling up until it was almost bursting from her chest like a balloon, then the balloon lifting her up off the ground. "Yes, yes, yes!" she squealed, pulling him to his feet and dancing around him. They hugged and kissed and happy tears slid down her cheeks. "Oh yes, yes, yes," she repeated.

From somewhere he produced a ring—a ring she'd admired on the Internet months before. Had he really been planning this proposal so long? She squealed again as she admired the ring, then kissed him again. "Oh, Danny, I love you," she said.

"And I love you. I'll always love you."

She shut her eyes and hugged him close, the ring heavy on her finger, the joy inside her almost too much to contain.

Danny picked up the camera and took her picture, then they found a passerby to photograph them together. This was a moment she wanted to capture forever; two people in love with each other and the world. She and Danny had come through so much—the financial struggles, the wild uncertainty of the contest, their own fears and doubts. In stories love always seemed so easy, as if all you had to do was find the right person and everything else would fall into place. But real love, love that would last, wasn't only about finding the right person. It was about letting that love transform you into the right person. Like a painting that took shape over time, love was its own work of art.

Epilogue

Serendipity
and unforeseen adventures
are the stuff of life.

DANNY PACED OUTSIDE the bathroom door—four strides in one direction, four strides back. His heart fluttered wildly and his stomach felt on the verge of heaving. He'd never been so nervous in his life—not the day he proposed to Nina, though that had been nerve-racking enough, having to pretend he wasn't about to ask the most important question of his life, searching for the perfect opportunity to make his proposal.

Not even at their wedding, which had really been more like a fabulous party, surrounded by friends and family on a gorgeous Friday afternoon. He and Nina had made so many good friends in Denver. When their agreed-upon year here was up, neither one of them had wanted to move.

He could laugh now about those days in New York when he'd thought his life was perfect, working for his cousin, living with Nina in their Brooklyn apartment. That happiness had been only a dim shadow of the joy he felt now.

Now they had a beautiful place in Denver with a view of the mountains and a circle of fabulous friends. They worked together every day, on the photography business, on websites, always thinking of new things to do and try. He and Nina were a team, and their sense of unity had only grown stronger since the wedding.

But now they were about to embark on the biggest challenge of their life. Maybe. He hoped.

If only Nina would come out of the bathroom.

He stopped and pounded on the door. "Let me in," he called.

"No."

"Nina, what's going on in there? Is everything all right?"

"Everything is fine."

"Why is it taking so long?"

"It's not taking so long. You are just too impatient."

He began to pace again. Snuffleupagus and Chickadee watched from their spot side by side on the sofa, whiskers and ears twitching as they followed him with their eyes. "This affects you, too," he told them. "You should be nervous, too."

Finally the bathroom door opened and Nina emerged, a little plastic stick the size and shape of a thermometer in her hand. Danny suddenly couldn't breathe. He was sure his heart stopped beating for a moment. "Well?" he asked. "What does it say?"

Nina's smile could have illuminated a dungeon. Tears glittered in her blue eyes, and her voice shook as she spoke. "I'm pregnant," she said. "We're going to have a baby."

"A baby." Nina was going to be a mother. He was going to be a father. He tried to swallow past the lump in his throat. Oh god, was he ready for this?

"Danny? Are you all right?"

He'd never been more all right. He held out his arms and gathered her close. "We're going to have a baby," he repeated.

"Yes." She laughed. "Isn't it wonderful?"

"It's wonderful." He kissed her. "You're wonderful." Then he slid his hand down to cover her still-flat stomach. "It's amazing. We made a baby."

"It will be our biggest project yet," she said.

"And the best." One created not from imagination and artistic talent, but from love—their love for each other and for the life they'd made together.

Submit Your Own True Romance Story

"The marriage of real-life stories with classic, fictional romance—an amazing concept."

—**Peggy Webb,** award-winning author
of sixty romance novels

Do you have the greatest love story never told? A sexy, steamy, bigger-than-life or just plain worthwhile love story to tell?

If so, then here's your chance to share it with us. Your true romance may possibly be selected as the basis for the next book in the TRUE VOWS series, the first-ever Reality-Based Romance™ series.

- Did you meet the love of your life under unusual circumstances that defy the laws of nature and/or have a relationship that flourished against all odds of making it to the altar?

- Did your parents tell you a story so remarkable about themselves that it makes you feel lucky to have ever been born?

- Are you a military wife who stood by her man while he was oceans away, held down the fort at home, then had to rediscover each other upon his return?

- Did you lose a great love and think you would never survive, only for fate to deliver an embarrassment of riches a second or even third time around?

Story submissions are reviewed by TRUE VOWS editors, who are always on the lookout for the next TRUE VOWS Romance.

Visit www.truevowsbooks.com to tell us your true romance.

TRUE VOWS. It's Life . . . Romanticized

Get Ready to Be Swept Away...
By More *True Vows*™
Reality-based Romances

Judith Arnold
MEET ME in MANHATTAN

Code 533x • $13.95

Alison Kent
THE ICING ON THE CAKE

Code 5356 • $13.95

Julie Leto
HARD TO HOLD

Code 5438 • $13.95

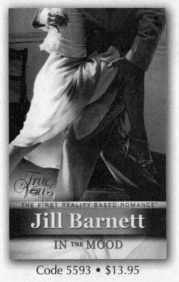